JIM ANTHONY SUPER-DETECTIVE

AIRSHIP 27 PRODUCTIONS

AN AIRSHIP 27 PRODUCTION

Jim Anthony: Super-Detective Volume Two
"The Hunters"
An Airship 27 Production
www.airship27.com

Airship 27 Productions
airship27.com
airship27hangar.com

Editor: Ron Fortier
Associate Editor: Charles Saunders
Production and design: Rob Davis.

ISBN-13: 978-0692341100 (Airship 27)
ISBN-10: 0692341102

Printed in the United States of America

10 9 8 7 6 5 4 3 2 1

Jim Anthony Super-Detective

Volume Two

CONTENTS

PART ONE
Death in Yellow
By Joshua Reynolds

Jim discovers murderous Yetis loose
in Manhattan. He tracks them down with the aid
Of the mysterious Russian Count Zaroff..4

PART TWO
On The Periphery of Legend
By Micah S. Harris

Jim travels with Count Zaroff to a lost South
Pacific island after the biggest game of all;
dinosaurs and a giant ape...79

ABOUT OUR CREATORS —
Meet Our Writers & Arists...172

AFTERWARD —
By Ron Fortier..175

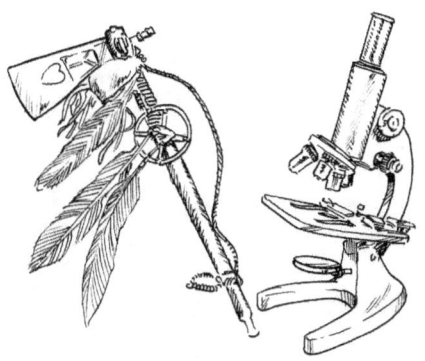

PART ONE
DEATH IN YELLOW
by Joshua Reynolds

1931.

New York at night looked like an ocean of stars from Edgar Phipps' penthouse balcony. Foam capped waves in the form of snow-encrusted roof tops rose from the sea of light, the crystals of ice glittering like a thousand jewels. But the heir to the Phipps Pharmaceuticals fortune had eyes only for night sky, and the actual stars glittering in its dark embrace.

Phipps was short and pleasantly round, plump rather than obese, and seemingly small for all his weight. Thinning, mussed hair decorated his avocado shaped head and his bubble-cheeks threatened to puff out even further as he smiled at his guest.

"Jimmy, champagne?" Phipps extended the bottle, cork long since popped, and shook it slightly, slopping clear liquid onto the balcony.

"And what exactly are we celebrating, Eddie?" Jim Anthony said, smiling, as he lounged in the doorway. His appearance was in stark contrast to that of his host. He was dark of mien, with thick hair and a broad shouldered, thin waisted build. A loose silk shirt covered his torso and muscular arms and rough-woven cloth trousers the color of pampas grass hid his long legs. His feet were bare, despite the chill of the evening. "They name a new star after you?"

"Even better," Phipps said, pouring himself a flute of champagne. He drained it and smacked his lips. "A comet."

"A comet? Well, that's quite an achievement." Jim stepped onto the balcony and hopped up onto the stone railing with the grace of a savage, sitting comfortably on the edge despite the snow crusted there, his legs dangling off and over the never-sleeping city. He accepted a glass from Phipps and took a sip. "Quality," he said, raising the glass in salute. Phipps nodded.

"Only the best. I can afford it. And, I needed to thank you."

"All I did was help you build the thing," Jim said, pointing at the telescope standing at one corner of the balcony. It was of unique design, with specially crafted lenses and a one-of-a-kind magnification system. Jim knew this because he had been the one to help Phipps design it, over crullers and a pot of rapidly cooling, bourbon laced coffee. "You came up with it in the first place."

"True, very true. But I have all of the practical application skills of a jellyfish." Phipps raised his own glass and threw it back, draining it in moments.

"You're not that bad."

"You weren't singing that tune when I soldered my cufflink to the housing."

Jim laughed and took another sip of the champagne. It was light and the bubbles popped pleasingly on his tongue. He held up the glass and then looked at Phipps. "So where'd you get this?"

"A speakeasy, where else?"

"The one on third?"

"Where else?"

"Good vintage."

"As long as it tickles my tongue, I'm happy."

"Yeah," Jim finished his glass and shook his head when Phipps shook the bottle. "Moderation, my friend. All things in moderation."

"Except fame and fortune," Phipps said.

"Ha," Jim said, noncommittally. He looked up, past the edge of the roof of the penthouse and into the sky. Snowflakes circled down in an endless dance and Jim felt a momentary flush of pleasant vertigo. His grandfather, the wily old Comanche, said that the stars were holes that the sun had burned into Moon's blanket to find Coyote.

Unconsciously, his eyes found the distant spire of his own penthouse at the top of the Waldorf-Anthony on Fifth Avenue and he wondered whether Mephito was sitting on the roof, as he often did, communing with the night sky. A chill flashed through him, and an image of Mephito's frowning face. He shifted on his perch.

"You were out west a while this time," Eddie said. "Come up with any new philosophical treatises on the psychology of the modern criminal?"

"Not this time," Jim said. "It was more like recovery. I just needed some time away." He thought of the Pueblo, his home away from home, far from the urban sprawl. A place where he could more fully be himself. A place where he could commune with his heritage. Both of them.

"Recovery? The great Jim Anthony, murderist extraordinaire, needed some relaxation?"

"Coming to the next meeting of the Gun Club, Eddie?" Jim asked, changing the subject.

"Hmmm? Oh, probably." Phipps, bottle still in hand, was bending down to peer through the telescope. He paused and looked at Jim. "Why do we call it the Baltimore Gun Club anyway? We're in New York, after all."

"Tradition," Jim said. He shielded his eyes. The wind was picking up, and the snow with it.

"Tradition should be geographically correct."

"I'm sure you could put forth a motion-"

"I'll stick to finding comets, thanks. One impossible thing a lifetime, I always say. I-" Phipps voice died in his throat, his words stuttering off into silence. Jim said,

"Eddie? What's wrong?"

"There's something-" Phipps stopped again, stepping back from the telescope, the bottle of champagne falling from his hand to shatter on the balcony.

Jim turned on his perch even as a shadow fell over him. Finely honed instincts pulsed to the surface of his mind and he reacted without thought, flipping up and off of the balcony rail to land in a crouch near the door. Something landed heavily on the space he had vacated, and a hot animal stink washed over him, carried by the rising wind. Claws scraped the brick as something white glared at them through mad eyes, jaws gaping, brutal fangs glistening.

Phipps screamed and the tableau was shattered. The white thing leapt from its perch with a grunt and shot long arms-impossibly long-towards Jim. Claws dug into his shirt, tearing the skin beneath as it hoisted him easily, swiftly.

Jim's mind whirled—it was fast, too fast—and he reacted with savage desperation, his legs shooting up, catching the thing in its taut belly. It gave a whuff of surprise and released him. Jim dropped to all fours and shot to his feet, one big fist popping out to catch the thing in its jaw.

"Eddie! Get out of here!"

The thing-the creature-howled and brought both of its own bludgeoning fists down, hammering Jim to his knees. Bleary-eyed, he looked up into its inhuman face even as it grabbed him and hauled him up over its peaked head like a sack of concrete.

"Oh hell," Jim said.

Then, with a growl, the white thing hurled him from the balcony!

* * *

Jim fell for what seemed like an eternity, plummeting into the spiraling whiteness of the New York night, his arms and legs flailing helplessly.

However, regardless of how long it seemed it was actually only a few, brief moments and Jim possessed enough lucidity to grab his belt.

It was composed of an almost infinitely stretchy fiber grown only in the Amazon and known only to a single tribe of natives. Well, and Jim Anthony of course.

With a burst of speed that had its origins in desperation, Jim whipped the belt from around his middle and cracked it with a single, superhuman snap of his wrist. The loop of the belt flapped out and snagged the head of a gargoyle as Jim passed it.

A yank and a wrench and Jim Anthony hung above the streets by one arm, his shoulder dislocated and his fingers threatening to loosen their grip. Muscles screaming in agony, Jim swung himself up, his uninjured arm slapping against the gargoyle. His tough fingers scrabbled at the porous stone even as his other hand spasmed and released the belt. Panting, Jim strained against gravity and his own weight, hauling himself onto the snow-encrusted gargoyle.

Eyes closed, Jim fought down the pain and marshaled his thoughts. His toes dug into the cracks in the gargoyle's hide and he was suddenly glad he had decided to forgo shoes, despite the snow.

Beneath him, New York moved, the streets interconnecting webs of light and sound, whistling, whispering siren fingers seeking to pull him down into their embrace. He closed his eyes, opened them, and took a moment to catch his breath.

Freeing his belt, he gingerly lashed his pain-inflamed arm as tightly to his body as he could, to counteract the potential balance problems, and stood in a half-crouch. Scanning the side of the building, he grinned, despite the agony seeping from his shoulder and into his chest.

There. A window.

Straightening slightly, he knew he would have only one chance. Sinking back down, his powerful legs bunched beneath him, he bent his arm, long fingers hooked and ready. Then, with a soft grunt, he leapt, a flurry of dislodged snow following him.

Hand outstretched, he reached for the ledge beneath the window. His fingers slapped the brickwork, slid, then found purchase. The soles of his feet smacked into the building and in one distinctly less than graceful movement, he scrambled up onto the narrow ledge and tapped against the window with his knuckles.

The window slid up and a concerned face peered out.

"Little late for washing windows, son," the old man said, his bald pate gleaming red. A walrus mustache twitched from side to side as he made a noise half-way between a harrumph and a huff. Jim's smile was strained.

"I agree completely. Mind if I come in?"

"I don't-"

"I really must insist."

"How did-"

"The sooner the better," Jim pressed.

"How can I refuse?" the old man popped the window wide and Jim slid gratefully off the ledge. The old man was broad and wrapped up in a dressing gown, slippers on his feet.

"Sir, I need you to call the police. Ask for Healy, in Homicide. Tell him Jim Anthony said there's been trouble at the Suydam Tower." Jim's voice was calm, but urgent, as he undid his belt and freed his arm to dangle grotesquely.

"J-Jim Anthony? THE Jim Anthony?"

"I'm the only one I know."

In front of the old man's wide, horrified eyes, Jim grabbed his arm and wrenched it back into its socket with a sickening pop. Looking at the old man, Jim said, "Now, please."

The old man moved haltingly, stumbling out of what Jim realized was his bedroom. The covers were turned down and he'd obviously been preparing for bed.

Rubbing his shoulder, Jim turned back to the window. A hateful demon face glared at him, clawed fingers clutching the edge of the window frame.

Blood smeared the white thing's muzzle and its black-blue lips peeled back from inch-long fangs, revealing pinkish stains on its yellowing teeth.

Jim acted without thought, snapping his belt out, the curved buckle smashing into the creature's almost nonexistent nose. With a screech fit to shatter glass, it reeled back, swinging away from the window, one spade-like paw brushing furiously at its snout.

As it swung back towards him, Jim tensed, ready to lash it again. Before he could move, however, the rumbling crash of a pistol filled the room.

The white thing shrieked and vanished. Jim turned, took in the whey-faced, shaking apartment owner and the smoking .45 in his hands, and then darted towards the window.

The creature was gone. Bloody prints marred the window sill and Jim felt a sickening lurch in his stomach.

Eddie.

He turned. "Did you call the police?"

"I-I-"

"I need you take a breath. Breathe." Jim's voice was soothing as he reached out and easily pried the gun from the old man's clutching fingers. "Did you call the police?"

"Th-they're on their way," the old man whispered. "What-what-"

"I don't know. But I'm going to find out," Jim said, his voice as hard as stone.

* * *

The door was locked. Jim grasped the knob and gave it a vicious twist, snapping the bolt in two with a prodigious display of strength.

He entered the apartment warily, his desert-trained senses straining to their limit. The pungent animal stink hung over everything. The living room was completely ruined. Blood was splashed carelessly on the walls and vicious claw-swipes decorated every surface.

Phipps was on the balcony.

Jim sank to his haunches beside the remains of his friend, his face a frozen mask. His hand hovered over the body, but did not touch it. Jim closed his eyes and pulled his hand back. Grief could wait.

"I'm sorry, Eddie."

Rising to his feet, he took stock of his surroundings, letting his eyes wander and his amazing brain calculate. The events occurring immediately after his fall were recreated in his head according to what he saw. Footsteps in the champagne. The balcony doors shattered. The couch overturned. The telescope loosed from its tripod, and broken in half. He looked down at Phipps.

There were white hairs clutched in his hand.

Jim frowned. Running a hand through his thick hair, he turned around. More hairs were scattered around. Caught in the glass and left behind in its bloodstained tracks. Jim had been a hunter since he could walk. Animals, then men. He plucked a strand of hair from the balcony door and examined it.

Was the creature shedding?

Before he could consider it any further, the front door to the apartment slammed open, propelled by a standard issue police shoe. Uniformed officers piled into the room, service weapons ready.

"Freeze!" one yelped, pistol flashing up in Anthony's direction. A nearly shapeless fedora flashed up and down, swatting the officer on the back of the head.

"Put your gun down, Lewis, before he feeds it to you!" Detective Turkish Healy barked, thin, sallow features coiled in exasperation. "Better yet, I'll do it."

"Hello, Detective Healy," Jim said, stepping into the apartment. Healy took in his ripped and blood-stained shirt and nodded, as if replying to some inner question.

"You look like three shades of shit," Healy said.

"I feel worse," Jim said. "You got here quickly."

"Fancy building. Rich folks. And you. All kinds of priority there," Healy sounded bored. He slapped his thigh with his fedora. "You want to give me your version?"

"We were attacked."

"By?"

"Something unpleasant," Jim said, holding up the strand of hair. Healy peered at it, bottom lip almost disappearing as he gnawed it.

"Animal hair?"

"It depends on what you mean by animal," Jim said. "I need to analyze this, to find out what it is-"

"Chief thinks it's a lion or a leopard got loose from the zoo."

Jim looked at Healy. "What?"

"Figured you wouldn't have heard, you being out west and all." Healy looked slightly smug. "Three other murders. Three fat cats, on their balconies, slaughtered. Like your pal there-"

"His name was Edgar Phipps," Jim said, quietly. Healy paused. He nodded.

"Same kind of hairs. I got tossed the case, on account of that thing last year with that Yogami fellow-"

"Yes. The so-called Werewolf of Red Hook," Jim said. He absently stroked a scar on his arm. "Did his body ever turn up?"

"Not so far. The sewers were dumping into the East River though, what with the flooding. He's probably at the bottom of the Atlantic." Healy waved a hand. "Actually, at first, I thought it was him come back, cause of the hairs. But they ain't nothing like the samples we got from Yogami's murders…"

"Wrong color for one," Jim said, thinking that the white thing bore little resemblance to Yogami, even at his most…unpleasant. He looked at the detective. "They think it's a leopard?"

"Or one of them white tigers. The Russian ones," Healy said. Jim looked back at Phipps' body, frowning.

"What were the names of the other victims?"

Healy shook his head. "Sorry, Anthony, but-"

"I've seen your killer, Healy. I was almost killed by it." Jim held the hair up to Healy's face. Healy sucked on a thumbnail.

"Yeah?"

"Yeah."

"I could get a court order"-

"Or you could just tell me. I helped you with the Yogami case, after all."

Healy hesitated, his face twisting. Then,

"Felton. Hammersmith. Wooster. Those were their names. You recognize them?"

"Yes, unfortunately. Russell Felton, Eugene Hammersmith and Guster Wooster?"

"Yeah. Yeah, how'd you-"

"They're all members of the Baltimore Gun Club. Just like Eddie." Jim clenched his fist, crushing the hair. "Just like me."

* * *

"So poor old Eddie Phipps is dead, hunh?" Tom Gentry said from the driver's seat of the car carrying Jim towards home. The street was nearly deserted, but not quite, despite the hour.

"Yes," Jim said, shortly.

"And you're taking it personal, aren't ya?"

"I can't exactly NOT take it personally, Tom," Jim said. Gentry snorted and squeezed the Ford's horn.

"Go back ta Jersey!" Tom snarled, then looked up at the rearview mirror. "I didn't mean it that way, Jimmy. I just meant-"

"I know what you meant, old friend." Jim held up his arm, examining the cuts that decorated it. "But he was murdered right under my nose, by something that I-" Jim stopped, eyes closed. Thinking.

What had it been? Anthropoid, certainly. A costume? No, no not a costume, or if it was, it was an exceptionally good one. Some form of ape then. If so, it had crawled right out of Poe.

"Dupin," Jim said, aloud.

"Hunh?"

"Murders in the Rue Morgue. Poe. A trained ape-"

"A trained what?" Tom sounded incredulous. He squeezed the horn again and stuck an arm out the window, shaking it. "I swear to the Blessed Virgin, I'm gonna-"

"It wasn't a conventional murderer. It was some form of primate. I'm sure that once I analyze these hairs, it'll yield the species of-" Jim began. But whatever else he'd been about to say was lost in the sudden shriek of tortured metal and shattering glass as a black car hurtled out of a side-street and slammed into the side of Anthony's own vehicle!

Horns bellowed as the two cars hurtled on, pressed tight together in an embrace of grinding steel. Tom cursed. "What in the-hang on Jimmy!"

Jim didn't answer, instead focusing his keen attention on the other car and its occupants. The windows were tinted, but even as he watched, horror coiling within him, they descended, revealing the muzzles of several Thompson sub-machine guns.

"Tom! Swerve!" Jim bellowed throwing himself flat in the back seat, his hands scrabbling beneath the cushion, fingers searching for a latch-THERE! The cushion lifted, revealing a unique-looking heavy caliber pistol with a curling, rams horn ammunition clip. Jim scooped it up even as Tom twisted the wheel with a Gaelic howl and sent their vehicle scraping into the other.

One of the Thompsons sputtered and Jim's keen ears heard rubber pop and thanked whatever muse of foresight had inspired him to install bulletproof panels in all of his automobiles.

"We've lost a wheel!" Tom said.

"We've still got three!" Jim said, rising back into a sitting position and taking aim. The gun in his hand bucked once, twice, a trio of thunderous booms and the passenger side window of the back of the other vehicle split like a spider-web caught by the errant finger of a child.

Though Jim's weapon was loaded only with mercy bullets, their effects were similar to the garden variety slug and one of the Thompsons vanished as its wielder was struck and sent sprawling across the seat.

The black car seemed to writhe across the space between the two vehicles and its front end sent them slewing around awkwardly. Jim cursed and fired again, but the lurching movement of the car threw his aim off.

"Tom, hold her steady!"

"Why?"

"I'm going to be a good neighbor and pay a visit," Jim said, sliding back and kicking his damaged door open. The black car swerved away as the door flew open and snapped off of its hinges, spiraling into the street. Cars honked and people screamed, but Jim ignored the cacophony and stepped out onto the running board.

"Jim! You can't!" Tom said, throwing panicked glances over his shoulder. "Are you crazy?"

Jim didn't reply. Instead, taking a breath, he leapt across the gap that separated both cars and lashed out with one bronzed arm, hooking it around the passenger window of the other vehicle. Even as his toes found the running board of the black car, he thrust his pistol through the open window and fired.

The car swerved wildly, and Jim lost his weapon. Swinging haphazardly, his shoulder screamed in remembered pain and Jim gritted his teeth and hung on grimly.

Jim reached out and grabbed the door handle and yanked it open, revealing the terrified countenance of a waxy skinned man, who swung a Tommy gun towards him. Jim grabbed the barrel of the Thompson and yanked it out of the gunsel's grip, hurling it away into their wake. Quick as lightning, his free hand shot forward again, grabbing a fistful of the man's shirt.

"Sorry friend, but this is where you get off!" Jim said, dragging the man out and tossing him one-handed into the street!

"You sonnuva- the driver roared, red beard bristling as he clawed for the roscoe holstered under his arm. Jim swung easily into the car and grabbed the wheel with one hand, even as his other curled into a battering ram fist and smashed across red-beard's jaw. As the big man slumped, Jim jammed his foot on the brake and guided the car up onto the sidewalk and to a complete stop.

Turning the key, Jim allowed himself to take a deep breath. Some crises were easier than others—

The sound of a pistol being cocked caused Jim to freeze. The cool steel of the barrel was pressed to the back of his head, and a rough voice said,

"Learn ta count, wild man."

* * *

"I did," Jim said, his voice calm. Carefully, he raised his hands.

"Yeah?"

"Quite. Hello, Tom."

"Hiya Jimmy," Tom said, aiming a Winchester through the window at the fourth gunman. "You. Put the peashooter down or I'll put a part in that greased back hair of yours."

"Maybe you should put yours down, hunh paddy?" The gun dug into Jim's skull a little harder. "Think you can cap me before I paint the window with his fancy brains?"

"Oh,I think so," Tom said softly. "I got it down to a science, me."

"And I got luck."

"Lucky for us all, I have both," Jim said. He turned with a beast's quickness, sweeping his arm across and down, trapping the pistol against the seat, and his fist snapped out like a piston, driving the gunman's head back and his lights out.

Tom let out a breath and raised the Winchester. "Hoo. Warn me next time, hunh?"

"I'll try," Jim said, smiling. He stepped out of the car, rubbing awkwardly at his shoulder. "I'm going to hurt in the morning."

"Welcome to the human race." Tom prodded the unconscious man with his rifle. "Who the heck do you think they are?"

"Well, that would be the first in a long series of questions I was planning on asking them." Jim deftly began removing weapons from the car, tossing them to Tom. "But first, let's remove temptation, shall we?"

"Sounds good-" Tom began, but was cut off as a machine gun rattled. Tom threw himself flat, his rifle spinning away. Jim jumped over the hood of the black car as bullets chased him, chewing through the body of the car and the unconscious gunmen. Tom scrambled to join him, bleeding from a graze on his cheek.

The last hood, the one Jim had tossed from the car, stumbled towards them, weaving through traffic, a battered Thompson cradled in his hands.

A car screeched to a halt and the driver pounded the horn, causing the gunsel to whirl and let a burst rip through the windshield, killing the hapless driver.

"No!" Jim roared, shooting to his feet. He vaulted over the hood of the car and pounded towards the gunman, arms spread, fingers hooked like claws. Meanwhile, Tom scrambled for his Winchester.

"You! You're dead!" the gunman snarled through a busted jaw. He turned, raising the Thompson as Jim charged towards him. Jim jumped, hurling himself forward like a bullet. Even as the Thompson spat, Jim was forcing the barrel upwards, his other hand clawing for the gunman's throat. A red rage suffused Jim's being as he grabbed the man's throat and tore the gun from his grasp. The muscles in his arm bulged as he forced the struggling gunman up into the air and slowly, slowly, throttled him.

"Jim," Tom said, softly, reaching out to put his hand on Jim's arm. "Jimmy, enough."

Jim glanced at his friend, his face twisted into an expression of rage that chilled Tom to his very marrow. Swallowing, the doughty Irishman said, "Jimmy, we need at least one of these guys alive."

Closing his eyes, Jim fought to control himself, control the animal hatred that flooded him. With a sound half-way between a groan and a sigh, he dropped the gunman.

Sirens sounded, not far away. The police were on their way. Jim looked down at the red-faced gunman, who lay still, either unconscious or doing an admirable job at pretending.

Traffic had come to a dead stop on the street. People were milling about, looking around. Not many, but enough night owls and early birds to cause a scene. Jim, leaving Tom to look after the unconscious gunman, strode back towards the car. Two of the other gunmen were dead, killed by their own fellow. But the red-bearded driver still lived, miraculously having avoided being hit by a stray bullet. As Jim approached, he stirred.

Bleary-eyed, he groped for his pistol. But, finding it missing, gave a sigh and laid his head across the steering wheel. Jim approached cautiously, and leaned down.

"Who are you? Why did you try to kill me?"

"Because you have to die. Why else?" red-beard grunted. He looked at Jim. "He said-said-" He clutched his chest, coughing. "I-" With a bone-breaking shudder, red-beard jerked back in his seat, clawing at his chest and throat. Jim took a step back as a yellowish vapor exploded from the man's nostrils and lips, followed by a nicotine-colored spittle.

Mouth covered, Jim backed away. Poison. It had to be. Whoever had hired them, hadn't planned on paying them. Jim spun, reaching out towards Tom.

"Tom, get away from him!"

"What?" Tom turned, even as the man on the ground began to jerk and strangle slowly. The same yellow vapor boiled out of his open mouth. Tom jumped back with a curse. "What in the name of-"

"Poison. Don't touch him. Don't get close. Officers," Jim shouted, even as several police cars screeched to a halt and several officers got out. "Keep these people back." He gestured at the growing crowd of rubberneckers. While several of the cops looked to want to argue, one or two recognized Anthony and leaped to obey his orders as if they had been given by their own sergeants.

Jim tore a strip from his shirt and wrapped it around his face as he squatted beside the body on the ground. The gunman had expired seconds earlier, as had red-beard. Cautiously, Jim tilted the dead man's head one way, then the other, observing the discharge that was rapidly drying on the man's nose and lips.

"First the monkey, now this?" Tom said. "What is this?"

"Connected," Jim said, simply. "It has to be." He stood. "There are only a few poisons that leave a discharge like this."

"Yeah, and I bet you know all of 'em," Detective Healy said, walking towards them, slapping his hip with his hat. He looked at Tom. "Gentry."

"Healy."

"I do have a working knowledge of poisons, yes. And I have a few guesses, but-" Jim turned to Healy. "But, I'd need a sample. Offhand I'd guess it's the distillation of the Mariphasa Lupinum-"

"The wha-hunh?"

"Tibetan Moon Blossom. Extremely toxic to humans," Jim said. "As I said though, I'd need a sample-"

"And you expect me to just turn it over to you?" Healy said, his tone implying that he knew Jim meant exactly that. "What next, you want a squad car?"

"That would help. Our car, as you can see-" Jim indicated their car, languishing where Tom had parked it. It sat at an angle, two of its tires destroyed. "Has seen better days."

"Anthony, you-" Healy began, then shook his head. He snapped his fingers, catching the attention of a young officer. "Billings, get 'em home, would you?"

Jim tore a strip from his shirt and wrapped it around his face as he squatted beside the body on the ground.

"Actually, we have somewhere else to go," Jim said.

"Really. Where?" Healy said unhappily. Jim crossed his arms.

"The Gun Club. Four dead men, all of them members."

"We've already investigated-" Healy protested. Jim nodded.

"So you have. And I presume you questioned everyone?"

"Yeah!"

"Well then, I have some new questions for them, due to new evidence that has come to light." Jim gestured at the bodies. Healy opened his mouth. Closed it. He smashed his hat on his head and waved a hand.

"Go on then."

"Thank you, Detective. I knew you'd see it my way."

* * *

The club-house of the Baltimore Gun Club was a nondescript brownstone, lost among others, differentiated only by the gold plaque on its front door. The plaque was engraved with the outline of an immense cannon and when one rang the bell, it played the 1812 Overture.

The sun was beginning to crest the tops of the buildings as Jim and Tom walked up the steps towards the door, leaving the young policeman cooling his heels in the squad car. Tom had left his Winchester with the police as evidence, but had a .45 holstered beneath the battered flight-jacket he wore. Jim, for his part, had traded his ripped shirt for a more intact one. Silk and deep black, it hugged his form beneath the pale sports-coat he'd had Tom bring him. Despite the snow on the ground and the chill in the air, he still didn't bother with shoes.

"Anybody even gonna be in this early?"

"There's always someone in the club," Jim said. "I think half of the gentlemen who are members actually sleep here." He pressed the bell with a knuckle and frowned. "Come to think of it, I've spent the night here."

As the 1812 Overture sounded, Jim looked at Tom. "Healy is a good detective, but I have a feeling that he didn't ask the right questions."

"Place probably made him as nervous as it does me," Tom grunted, blowing into his hands to warm them up. He looked down at Jim's feet. "Can't believe you haven't lost a toe yet."

"Temperature is a state of mind," Jim said. Tom snorted.

"So's psychosis."

"Are you implying something?"

"Yer nuts."

"I would describe my mental state as steady, actually. Considering the kind of night that I've been having so far."

Before Tom could reply, the door swung open, revealing the squat, bullet-headed form of the Club's attendant, Apples. Apples was long armed and bandy-legged, with a coarse, heavy-browed face. He grinned widely as he saw them.

"Mr. Anthony. Mr. Gentry. Do come in." He swept a long arm out, indicating that they should enter.

"Is anyone in the common room, Apples?"

"Messer's DeLancy and Zaroff, Mr. Anthony."

"Zaroff is back?" Jim said, eyebrow raised. "I thought he had retired to that island of his-"

"I did." The voice was harsh, and the accent was thick. "But I found that I had pressing business here, Anthony."

The man was big and his hair the color of the snow outside. Dressed in a dark suit of European cut, he extended a wide hand towards Jim. Jim took it, examining the pinkish scar that ran up the side of the man's bearded face.

He'd heard rumors that Zaroff had died on that island of his. A castaway had spilled an incredible story to a Portuguese paper a few years previous after being picked up by a merchantman and taken to a continental port. It had been picked up by several other papers, then had faded as the public's interest waned.

Apparently the castaway—a raving lunatic named Rainsford—had been wrong. Count Zaroff, formerly of Russia, last of the true Cossacks, lived.

"A new scar for your collection, I see."

"You as well," Zaroff said, turning Jim's arm slightly. "I heard about that dreadful Yogami business. If I had been here, I would have liked to have been in on that hunt."

"I'm sure you would have," Jim said. "I daresay you would have done better than I did."

"Men are harder to track than beasts," Zaroff said dismissively. "Trust me." He traced the scar on his face with one long finger. "But for now, I am back. And eager to learn more about these killings—you've heard, I assume?"

"I have," Jim said. "In fact, that's why I came to the club. Eddie Phipps is dead."

"Phipps?" Zaroff looked interested, but not overly dismayed. "That makes four."

"Eddie? Eddie is dead?"

Jim and Zaroff turned. A man stood in the doorway, visibly trembling. He was a scarecrow wrapped in a pinstripe suit, his slicked back hair arrowing off into weird divergences. He seemed about to faint, his pale fingers clutching the doorframe tightly. "What did it? Did you see it? What was—"

"Go sit back down, Otto," Zaroff snapped. "Have another brandy."

"DeLancy, wait," Jim said. "Do you know something about this?"

"He does. And he came to me for help," Zaroff said, stroking his beard. "If you wish to aid me in my hunt, Anthony—"

"Hunt?" Jim said. "This is no animal, Zaroff."

"Oh? You have proof of that?"

In reply, Jim held up the hairs he'd taken from Phipps' body. Zaroff's eyes widened slightly.

"Where did you—"

"It's something far more than an animal, Zaroff," Jim said. "I've seen it. Felt its strength. If it is a beast, it's like none I've ever seen."

"More things in heaven and earth," Zaroff murmured, examining the hairs closely. He looked at Jim. "You said you saw it?"

"It's big. And strong. And not an escaped leopard."

"Hh." The sound wasn't quite a hiss. Zaroff stroked his beard and suddenly smiled. "Excellent. Simply excellent."

"What? Zaroff—" DeLancy squawked. Zaroff waved him into silence.

"Excellent." He held out his hand. "May I?"

"Be my guest," Jim said, dropping one of the hairs into Zaroff's palm. "I'll need the other for my own analysis."

"Of course," Zaroff purred. Jim eyed the Count for a moment, then turned away. DeLancy trembled as Jim's gaze fell on him like a ton of bricks.

"Otto."

"J-Jim, is Eddie really–"

"Yes," Jim said. He put a hand on DeLancy's shoulder and guided him away from Zaroff, who was busying himself with a magnifying glass and the hair Jim had relinquished. When they were standing near the large picture window that looked out on the street, Jim turned DeLancy to face him.

"Zaroff," Jim said, quietly. DeLancy swallowed and nodded weakly.

"I had to, Jim. You don't know what it's been like—the fear—the others—"

"What do you know, Otto?"

"I–" DeLancy shook his head. "It's insane. Impossible!"

"After what I've seen tonight, my mind is quite open, I assure you, Otto. Now tell me."

"It's Bertie Freis." The words spilled from DeLancy's lips in a rush. "He's come back. And he wants all of us dead!"

* * *

Jim was speechless for a moment. Then, "Freis? I was wrong, Otto. That is impossible."

"Only it's not." DeLancy was shuddering slightly as he stared out the window at the snow-covered street. He turned, looking at Jim. "Were you here when he left, Jim?"

"No. I was in Paris, helping the police on a case," Jim said absently. "A band of thieves, Les Vampires-"

"He asked for money," DeLancy continued. "Needed it for his expedition-"

"And you gave it to him?"

"No! That's just it! Phipps, Wooster, none of us gave him anything! We refused!"

"Why?" Jim asked quietly. He remembered hearing about Bertie's proposed expedition. It had been the talk of the Club for months.

"Why? Why? It was idiocy, Jim! The sheerest fancy!" DeLancy said, flapping his hands. "A lost city in the Himalayas? Preposterous!"

"It rather depends on your definition of 'city', I should think," Jim murmured, rubbing his chin thoughtfully. His thoughts flitted briefly to the cave cities of the Anasazi, or the ancient pyramids of the Aztecs. Neither would fit the classical, western idea of a city. Not really. DeLancy grunted.

"Regardless, it was madness."

"His airship went down somewhere among the peaks in Tibet, didn't it?" Jim said, thinking back. Trying to recall all of it. He had been knee-deep in unpleasant elixirs in the Parisian catacombs at the time, hunting a mad thing that called itself Fantomas. Weeks spent tracking the murderous fiend from one hidden lair to the next, his every sense, every ability tested to superhuman limits by the faceless monster. In the end, Fantomas had eluded him. It still rankled. Jim pushed the brief spurt of anger aside and concentrated on what DeLancy was saying.

"Yes. Nothing left but a burning hulk. Not surprising, considering the substandard materials he used-"

"That was why he needed the money," Jim said. DeLancy nodded.

"Undoubtedly. We all offered to help, you know. All of us. Not with money, but with expertise. But Bertie wouldn't have it. He knew best," DeLancy said, with some bitterness. "Or at least he thought he did."

Jim said nothing. His memories of Bertie were dim at best. A thin man, blonde and almost not there. A long New England face on top of a skinny neck.

Truth be told, despite the implied social element of the Gun Club, the members—Jim included—were a solitary bunch. Not much given to association outside of the Club itself. A few, like Phipps, or Ironcastle, were social animals, but the rest—well, there was a reason for the Silent Lounge and the sound-proof rooms.

"Why Zaroff?" Jim said, after a moment. DeLancy quivered, wringing his hands.

"Protection. When that detective-"

"Healy."

"Yes. Foul man," DeLancy said. "When he came by the club, questioned us, he let a few things slip. Asking us about exotic pets and such." He looked at Jim, eyes wide. "I was frightened. I saw the connection, you see. The pattern in the murders. Zaroff arrived a few days ago. I asked him for his help. The man is the world's greatest hunter-"

"Actually, the world's greatest hunter is a tiny man in Africa. He is only three feet tall and he hunts elephants," Zaroff said.

Jim turned to find the Russian smiling at him. The Count held up the hairs. "You're right, it's not an ape. At least not any I've encountered."

"I know," Jim said. Zaroff frowned. Jim took the hairs from him. "I faced it, as you recall."

"So you say," Zaroff said. It was Jim's turn to frown.

"I do."

"And nobody here will gainsay you, of course," Zaroff said. He waved a hand. "But I do wonder how you managed to survive, Anthony…"

Jim didn't reply. Instead, he turned back to DeLancy. "How many others did Bertie try and cadge money out of?"

"There were six of us, including me and-and-" DeLancy hesitated. Then, more softly, he said, "And Pike."

"Franklin Pike?" Jim said. Memories of a tall man, rugged in looks, who had an enthusiasm for the more unique brands of rifle, flooded his mind. DeLancy nodded. Something about the name set off a chain-reaction in Jim's head. A kaleidoscope of events, parties, faces leading to-

"He married Bertie's sister, didn't he?" Jim said. "Just before I left for Paris."

"Yes. Social event of the season. For us, at least." DeLancy smiled weakly. "Bertie wasn't happy. But then, he and his sister were always a bit close."

"Ha!" Zaroff snorted. "Close is too polite-"

"Jim!" Tom hissed, from the lounge's doorway. Jim turned. Gentry motioned towards the window and mouthed 'outside'. Jim blinked, then, as if it were the most natural thing in the world he shifted, looking out the window without actually appearing as if he were doing so.

Outside, everything was white. The snow was falling heavily now, heavier than Jim ever remembered seeing. Thus, the black car, nearly identical to the one from earlier, that was parked across the street was clearly visible. As was the tall figure standing in front of it, face hidden by a bright yellow scarf fluttering in the wind and dark goggle-like glasses. A long coat of oriental cut obscured the form, save for the implication of a skeletal thinness.

What concerned Jim, however, were the three men stalking towards the parked police car, hands hidden in their coats. Even as the young officer stepped out of his car and raised his hand to stop the men, one lunged forward, something flashing in his hand. The policeman staggered, clutching at his throat as the snow was dappled red. The three men kept moving, not even stopping.

Jim turned and shoved DeLancy towards Zaroff. "Both of you, get down and stay low."

"Anthony, you-" Zaroff began, but Jim was already moving for the window. He tossed one last glance at Tom.

"The door!" he said, then, with a sudden rush, Jim flung himself through the window!

* * *

Jim landed in a crouch, glass raining down around him. Even as one of the three men turned, eyes wide in surprise, Jim was up and moving for the tall man still standing near the car!

As quick as a cat, Jim surged forward, teeth bared. Mysteries were fine, but it was always helpful to go directly to the source, and Jim had a feeling that if the thin man was anything, he was that.

The sound of pounding feet behind him alerted him that the three killers had turned away from the Club's doors and were-

A sudden sharp prickling on his nape sent Jim spinning to the side as the snow where he'd been seconds before was chewed into sludge by the sting of a Thompson! He hit the ground and rolled to his feet, hoping that Tom had understood his message.

The crack of a .45 renewed his faith in his childhood friend. Jim rose even as the gunman carrying the Thompson toppled, his finger tightening on the trigger. The machine gun savaged the ground, forcing the other two gunmen to stumble aside. Jim bounded over the falling man, arms extended. Steel fingers wrapped themselves in the lapels of the closest gunman, the one who'd killed the police officer, as Jim yanked him from his feet and swung him aside, hurling him into the side of the patrol car.

He turned to see Tom struggling with the last man. Even as Jim started forward, Tom jerked the would-be killer towards himself and gave him a vicious head butt, dropping him like a stone. He looked at Jim.

"Who the heck are these loons, Jimmy? They're comin' out of the woodwork!"

"No clue, chum, but I think he can tell us," Jim said, turning back to face the thin man, who was still standing by the black car, apparently unconcerned.

"Who are you?" Jim said, his voice almost swallowed by the snow.

In reply, the thin man swung his hand up, revealing the chunky shape of a Mauser. Jim froze.

"Vengeance," the thin man said. It was a dead sound. Emotionless. Empty. Jim was about to reply, when-

"Jimmy! Look out!" Tom screamed. Jim turned and something flashed towards him-a cutthroat razor-and then there was the sharp report of a rifle and the killer fell, his blade slicing into Jim's coat rather than his throat.

Zaroff saluted Jim from the shattered window, a smoking rifle cradled in his arms. Jim waved a hand and turned back to the thin man, only to find the black car barreling towards him! Jim threw himself to the side as the car skidded over the curb and away.

Jim pushed himself up out of the snow and restrained a virulent curse.

"Jimmy, just what in the hell is going on?" Tom asked. Jim shook his head, but didn't reply. Instead, he squatted beside the man Tom had knocked out and rolled him over. Jim sucked in a breath. Yellow foam dripped from his lips and he was quite dead.

"Chinese?" Tom said.

"Tibetan," Jim said, fishing a circular amulet out from under the dead man's yellow scarf.

"Tcho-Tcho, to be exact," Zaroff said, his rifle over one shoulder. He grimaced. "Detestable people. A degenerate race."

"You've had contact with them?" Jim said, rising to his feet.

"If you can call it that," Zaroff prodded the body with his rifle. "They tried to kill me, while I was in Tibet, hunting for the elusive Mi-go-"

"The whosits?" Tom said.

"The Yeti," Jim said. "The so-called 'abominable' snow-man."

"It exists," Zaroff said, with a sniff. He looked at Jim, a sly light in his eyes. "Does it not, Mr. Anthony?"

"The creature-" Jim said, thoughts clicking into place.

"While I was not successful in finding the creature, someone else obviously was."

"And they brought it here to-what? Commit murder?"

"It's just like I said, isn't it?" DeLancy said, from the stairs of the club. Apples stood protectively nearby, big fists clenched. "It's Freis! He's come back to kill us all!"

"Jimmy, what do you think?" Tom said, quietly. Jim stood, the amulet clutched in his hand. Tightening his fingers around it, he looked to where the body of the young police officer lay stiff and ghastly in the snow.

"I think we need to inform Healy that his officer has been murdered. And then, I think we need to pay a visit to Franklin Pike and Bertie Freis' sister," Jim said.

"And I will begin my hunt for the Yeti anew," Zaroff said, flicking snow off of his rifle. He smiled at Jim. "You have yet to say thank you, by the by, Anthony."

"Thank you for saving my life, Count. And I'll thank you to save your hunt for another time."

"And why would I do that?"

"To do otherwise means interfering in an ongoing investigation," Jim said. Zaroff laughed.

"The laws of men mean little to me, Anthony." Zaroff leaned forward, nearly nose-to-nose with Jim. "It is only the law of the jungle that I respect. You would do well to remember that."

Zaroff spun on his heel and stalked back towards the club, not sparing Jim another glance. Jim frowned and looked down at the amulet in his hand. He looked up at Tom.

"Let's go."

* * *

Tom yawned as he wove the police car through the growing morning traffic.

"Late night, Jimmy," Tom said without taking his eyes off the street.

"Morning, actually," Jim said, sitting beside him. Unlike his friend, Jim showed little fatigue from the events of the previous night. His dark eyes seemed to glow faintly as they followed the arc of the rising sun and for a moment, his hawk-nosed outline was illuminated by a hazy aura. Jim broke the aura as he ran a hand through his hair and gave a soft snort.

He held up the amulet and watched it spin. It depicted a Byzantine maze of lines that seemed to go nowhere and everywhere. Jim felt a brief tug at the corners of his memory, as if he'd seen it somewhere before. He flicked his wrist and scooped the amulet into his hand.

"Healy seemed surprised," Tom ventured. Jim snorted.

"Furious, rather. And I don't blame him. Can't blame him." His fingers rat-tap-tapped on the window as his mind worked. "If the…creature was the weapon of choice, why not use it at the Club?" he said, suddenly. Tom shrugged.

"Maybe you hurt it," he said. "You said that old coot shot it-"

"I doubt he hit it, even at that range. No, there's something else going on…" Jim trailed off. He rolled the medallion around in his palm. "Something I'm not seeing."

"Like what?"

"Bertie Freis died in one of the most inhospitable climes known to man. It is, however, not beyond the bounds of reason to theorize that he survived. But why go to the trouble of capturing an unknown anthropoid to use as a murder weapon? Why bother committing murder in the first place?"

"Maybe he's just crazy," Tom said. "C'mon Jimmy, you know how the crazies can affect a guy-"

"Still, to hire gunmen? And be organized enough to send those self-same gunmen to bump us off a mere hour after Healy shows up at Suydam Towers? He had to have had people in place, watching-" Jim stopped. His eyes narrowed. "That's why they came to the Club *sans la bete*," he said softly, smacking a fist into his open palm. "An attack of opportunity!"

"What?"

"He was watching," Jim said, looking at Tom. "He watches the beast kill. Perhaps to ensure it accomplishes its task, perhaps simply to enjoy the result, but he watches nonetheless!"

"Jesus, Mary and Joseph." Tom shook his head. "That's-that's-"

"Inhuman," Jim said grimly. "Only a mind twisted by the most extreme psychopathological conditioning could conceive of it."

"So you think DeLancy was giving it to us straight? That it's Freis?"

"It can't be," Jim said. "But I'm growing convinced it is." He settled back in his seat, his eyes closing. "Which is why we need to see his sister immediately."

"To warn her?"

"To see if she's involved," Jim said, softly. He cracked one eye. "Blood is thicker than water, Tom."

"Yeah. Yeah," Tom said. He kept his attention on the street as Jim fell into a micro-sleep. A burst catnap of only a few minutes that he would awaken from fully refreshed and re-energized. Tom smiled sourly. He rarely felt envy, but a good nap was high on his list of priorities at the moment.

"Sleep tight, Jimmy." Tom smiled. "Because you're driving back."

If Jim heard his friend on any level, he gave no sign. Instead, his magnificent brain slowly began to re-boot itself, section by section.

Memories swam to the surface, floating in the enforced darkness of his mind. A snarling face, bloated with blood, black, wiry hair covering it jowl to nape. Yogami. A swami, a conman, but also a—Jim's mind shied away from the word the papers had used. Despite the spiritual nature of his early education, Jim looked to science for the ultimate explanation.

Yet the dream-smell of raw sewage, mingled with Yogami's abattoir breath, exploded in his sinuses nonetheless. A storm. The sewers had been flooding swiftly. The feel of Yogami's hands—no, his claws—around his throat—something glinting amongst the hair—

Leng.

Jim's eyes popped open and he looked at the medallion in his hand. What did it mean?

"Ah," Jim said.

Tom looked at him. "What?"

"Nothing. Or something. I'm not entirely sure."

"Well, you'd better figure it out, Jimmy, because we're here," Tom said, pointing a finger at something outside Jim's window.

The 'Silk Stocking' District of Fifth Avenue wore its affluence well. Families with names like Rockefeller, Kennedy and Whitney resided in homes that would have put the old money of any major European city to shame. The family home of the last heir of the Pike Diamond Concern was no different.

The house was not so much big, or even imposing, as it was solid. Real. Power lurked here, inscribed in every brick and tile. Jim stepped out of the car and closed the door behind him. He had put on shoes, out of consideration for where they were, and his feet felt confined and uncomfortable. Jim frowned.

"What is it?" Tom said, leaning across the roof of the car. "Them Comanche senses of yours picking something up?"

"Comanche senses? As opposed to my other, Irish senses?"

"I calls 'em likes I sees 'em."

"To answer your question, nothing overt. There's just a sense here. Something-" Jim shook his head. "It's nothing." What he wanted to say was that he felt they were being watched. But to alert Tom would be to alert whoever was doing the watching. And Jim wanted to see how things played out.

The direct approach had failed. Thus, it was time to try something more oblique.

* * *

A sallow faced butler showed them in. The man looked unhappy about something, though whether it was due to Jim's lack of proper attire or Tom's insistence on tracking muddy snow into the foyer, Jim couldn't say. Nor, in truth, did he care.

"Jimmy!" Franklin Pike boomed, arms wide, broad face beaming. Jim allowed himself to be enfolded into a brief hug by the larger man.

Franklin Pike was a Brooklyn behemoth, with a giant's face and a baby's grin. He was impulsive, loud and filthy rich, with an inordinate fondness for experimental firearms. He set Jim down and launched a wide hand at Tom. "And Tommy too! How are ya, paddy?"

"Breathin'," Tom said, taking Pike's hand. "Heard you got married."

"Ball, chain and all," Pike said, laughing. "Sad you fellows missed it. How was Paris?"

"Wet," Jim said. "How is married life treating you, Pike?"

"Oh fine, fine. Hard to settle down, you know, once you've been the places I been," Pike said, crossing his arms. He smiled and shook his head. "You remember Maple-White Land, Jimmy?"

"I remember your gun jamming at an inopportune moment, if that's what you mean."

"Aw, Ki-Gor was there-" Pike waved a hand. "And you wasn't no slouch yourself. When that monster-"

"Ha," Jim said, waving the thought away. "Speaking of monsters, have you heard about the others?"

Pike's face grew solemn. "You mean Wooster and them?"

"Yes."

"I heard the police thought it was a big circus cat-"

"You should know better than that, Pike." Jim looked around. "Is your wife at home, by chance?"

"Jimmy-"

"How did she take it when her brother died, Pike?" Jim pressed. Pike's face grew red, and he opened his mouth to reply, but, before he could someone else did it for him.

"Half-brother, Mr. Anthony. You are Jim Anthony, yes?"

Jim turned as a slender woman swept down the staircase towards the landing, dressed in a hiking outfit reminiscent of that worn by a member of the British gentry.

"And you are Bertie Freis' sister," Jim said.

"Half-sister, as I said." She had the barest trace of an accent, French perhaps. "I saw you in London once. That horrid incident with the Steel Claw that was in all the papers."

"Yes," Jim said. "It was unpleasant, Mrs. Pike. But you are anything but, I must say." He stepped past Franklin and took the woman's proffered hand, lightly sweeping his lips across her knuckles.

"Please, call me Fleur," she said, deftly removing her hand from Jim's. "What was that you were saying about poor Bertie?"

"Listen doll, this ain't the kind of thing you need to be–" Pike began, but a look from Fleur silenced him. Jim's silent estimation of her rose a few notches.

"My half-brother," she said again, fixing her eyes on Jim. They were luminous and green, those eyes. A deep green that spiraled into blue and then black in spots, pulling you into its embrace the way the sirens of old were said to pull sailors into the sea. Jim felt a sympathy for those sailors in that moment, as he drowned in her gaze. Whatever he had been planning to say dried up in his throat, replaced by a blunt statement, issued flatly.

"Is he dead?"

She blinked, and the spell was broken. "The last I'd heard, yes."

"Jesus, Jimmy!" Pike said. "You can't just push up in here and ask that kind of-"

"I'm sorry, Pike. But it's quite necessary, I assure you." Jim looked at Pike, then back at Fleur. "Is he?"

"And you are Bertie Freis' sister."

"Oh, I am quite certain of that, Mr. Anthony...Jim," Fleur said. "I had his body brought back from Tibet, after all."

"Fleur!" Pike said, sounding strangled. Jim glanced at him. His face was pale. Fleur's, in contrast, was perfectly composed.

"Did you really expect me to simply let him rest in some grubby little Tibetan graveyard, Mr. Anthony?" she said, without looking at him. "Of course I brought him home. He and all his effects. Every scrap of bone, every twist of scorched hair. I brought it all home."

Jim was silent for a moment. Then, "I'm sorry. But there was some question-"

"And are you investigating, then? Looking into those awful deaths for the police?" Her eyes batted coyly. It was an obvious ploy, and Jim knew that she knew it was. Changing the subject. For Pike's benefit, or hers?

"I am. There was a theory that-"

"My brother orchestrated the murders, perhaps?" Fleur laughed, a throaty purring sound. "My brother could not plot his way out of a wet paper bag, Mr. Anthony. And that was before his pitiful remains were languishing in the family mausoleum."

"Fleur, honey-" Franklin said, shoving past Jim and taking her arm. "You ain't got to-"

"Oh, but I do, Franklin. You killed him. Your damned Club, you all killed him. And now you want to muddy his name? No. No, I think not," she said, her voice dropping to a hiss. Jim stepped back, momentarily nonplussed. She had gone from composed to vicious in a matter of seconds.

"No one is trying to say nothing about Bertie, baby," Pike said, interposing himself between his wife and Jim. "Look, just let me get them into the drawing room, tell Jimmy what he wants ta know, and then they'll be gone, right?" He took her shoulders in his hands. "It'll be okay, baby. Don't you worry none."

Fleur twisted in his grip and he released her. She glowered at the three men for a moment more, then continued down the stairs and around, out of sight without another word. Pike watched her go, then whirled on Jim, one fingers jabbing the air under Jim's nose.

"You cheap so and so! Why you gotta come in here with that cockamamie-"

Jim grabbed Pike's finger and pushed it down. "Four of our friends are dead, Pike. Four men who were at your wedding. Including Eddie."

"Eddie?" Pike said. He stepped back, shaggy head shaking. "That's-" He looked up. "When?"

"Last night."

"Damn." Pike sat down on the stairs, his great shoulders sagging. "Damn."

Jim looked down at him. "DeLancy is in hiding. He says Eddie and the others refused to loan Bertie any money. He says you did, too."

"DeLancy?" Pike looked up, eyes narrowing. "Hunh."

"Well?" Jim pressed. Pike sighed.

"Yeah. It was a dumb idea. You remember Bertie, Jimmy...no common sense. Too much money. Well, he ran out of money, but not foolishness. Damn near bankrupted the Freis fortune putting together that expedition."

"DeLancy said that he was trying to find a city?"

"Yeah. Some swami in New Orleans gave him a map to Leng. Or so he claimed."

The hairs on the back of Jim's neck bristled and the sense of déjà vu swept over him again, as it had in the car. "Leng?"

"Yeah. The Plateau-City of Leng. The Doorway to the Lost Valley of Carcosa." Pike rubbed his face with both hands. "All he found was high velocity winds and sharp rocks, though."

"Are you sure?" Jim said. He retrieved the medallion from inside his coat and dangled it in front of Pike. "Do you recognize this?"

"It's-hunh." Pike took the medallion gingerly and turned it around and around. "Follow me," Pike said, standing. Jim and Tom followed Pike through the house and into what Jim took to be the drawing room Pike had spoken of before.

Guns of all shapes and sizes adorned the walls. Some in glass-faced cases, others mounted on brackets. All freshly oiled, all lethal.

Several leather chairs were arranged in a rough circle in the center of the room, on top of the skin of an Allosaur Pike had shot in Maple-White Land. The creature's skull and most of its spine was mounted on a stand in the corner of the room, jaws agape, scythe-like teeth polished to a fine, pale glow.

Pike dropped heavily into one of the chairs after fixing himself a drink at the small bar set opposite the dinosaur skull. Ice clinked as he knocked back the bourbon. "Drink, boys?"

"Don't mind if I do," Tom said. He glanced at Jim, who waved a hand. Tom shook his head and set about preparing his own drink. Jim lowered himself smoothly into the chair opposite Pike.

"What did you want to show us, Pike?"

Without a word, Pike pointed upwards. Jim looked up. His eyes widened. "Is that-"

"Yeah." Pike looked up, frowning. He took another drink. "Exactly what it looks like."

On the ceiling, stretched out from one end of the room to the other was the white furred hide of some strange beast. Jim had an inkling that he knew exactly which beast it was, too. It had been attached so that the tanned side looked down on the floor. And on that tanned, stretched surface was a tattoo.

Jim looked at the medallion in his hand, then up at the tattoo.

"Good God."

* * *

"It's something, ain't it?" Pike said, emptying his glass.

"What is it?" Jim said.

"Something Bertie and Fleur's daddy brought back from Tibet. It's a map. A map of the inner city of Leng, in point of fact." Pike smiled. "Bertie was obsessed it, but I don't have to tell you that, do I, Jimmy?"

"What is it the skin of?" Jim asked, thinking of the white hairs in his pocket and the claw marks on his skin. Pike shrugged.

"Some animal."

"Pike," Jim said. Pike looked at him.

"Jimmy, I'm showing you this because I want you to understand exactly how Bertie and his sister were raised. Old Man Freis left Tibet in 1910, with that skin and Bertie. No one knew much about how he got either of them. He settled down in Paris, married an heiress named Dumas. Used her money to try and put together expeditions to Leng. He got a fever-some bug he'd picked up in Nepal-about two years later, kicked it, and Dumas, Bertie and baby Fleur came to New York." He stood to make himself another drink. "Bertie, he couldn't let it go. Became withdrawn. More like his father."

"Let what go?" Jim said, though he knew. Pike gestured up at the map.

"What do you think?"

"And?"

"Then their mother died. Accident. She and Bertie had a knockdown drag-out row over the money he was spending and she had a coronary. Boom! Dead."

"Fleur must have been beside herself."

"Yeah…" Pike trailed off. "We met around then. Bertie was spending money like water. Out of grief, she figured."

"Fleur told you all this?"

"Some of it I saw for myself. I helped Bertie track down a few pieces of the puzzle here and there. Individuals who-ah-might know how to reach Leng."

"And then New Orleans," Jim said.

"Yeah. Chanda-something. Queer fellow, always wore gloves," Pike said, sipping his drink. "Anyway, he traded a map that supposedly showed the way to Leng to Bertie for some sorta key Bertie bought in Massachusetts. Strange stuff, right?"

"With a map to the city, and a map of the city, Bertie decided it was time to see the city itself." Jim leaned back in his chair. "But-" He waved a hand at Pike. Pike nodded.

"Yeah. Bertie blew through most of the family funds doing his research."

"But you didn't give him any money," Jim said. "Why?"

"Fleur," Pike said, simply. "She and Bertie never got along too well. Amicable, but not much else, you know? After her mom's death—well–"

"She doesn't—didn't—share her half-brother's obsession?"

"You kidding?" Pike said. "Only reason I still got this thing—" he said, gesturing upwards. "Is because I stuck it up there where she doesn't notice."

"Why didn't you get rid of it?"

"You know me, Jimmy. Can't bear to throw anything away," Pike said, smiling slightly. He tapped the dinosaur skin rug with his foot.

The scream came so suddenly, so loudly, none of the three men at first registered what it was. Jim reacted first, leaping over the back of his seat and sprinting for the stairs.

As he ran, he kicked off his shoes and slithered out of his coat. He grabbed the rail of the stairs and vaulted over. Jim pounded up the stairs, cursing himself as he ran. He had been hoping something would happen, but not this.

At the top of the stairs, Fleur suddenly appeared, stumbling back, arms raised, mouth open, her face twisted in an expression of terror. And following after her came the familiar, hulking shape of the white thing!

"Mrs. Pike, move!" Jim roared as he leapt from his position and landed between the beast and its prey. The Yeti reared back, snarling. Jim wasted no time, launching himself at the creature, his hands seizing its iron wrists, forcing it back through sheer momentum. The Yeti snapped at him, its putrid breath rolling over him. Jim kicked at its knee and the creature staggered.

Muscles screaming, Jim spun the off balance beast towards the stairs.

It wrenched a hand loose from his grip and its claws raked across his chest, opening a four shallow crimson wounds.

Jim pulled the creature towards him and smashed his free fist across its sloping skull. It reeled back and swatted him from his feet with a flailing blow. Jim skidded across the landing and struck the wall.

"Jimmy!" Tom called. The pilot was on the stairs, his pistol clutched in both hands. Back pressed to the railing, he fired three shots. The creature squalled and leapt towards the Tom.

Tom flung himself over the railing as the Yeti crashed into the spot where he'd been standing, its claws gouging great chunks out of the wood.

The Yeti turned, grunting shallowly, its eyes searching. Fleur screamed again, and the creature's eyes fixed on her. It growled and sprang for the landing railing, bypassing the stairs entirely. It hauled itself up and over, reaching for the woman.

A thunderous crash sounded and part of the railing exploded into splinters. The beast turned, screeching. Down below, Pike ejected the spent round from the long, bulky rifle he carried and hurriedly reloaded. The creature's eyes narrowed, as if contemplating this new attacker.

Jim had regained his feet and charged towards the Yeti before it could act. He regretted not bringing a weapon, but part of him relished the physical challenge the creature poised. It spoke to a part of him. A wild and fierce section of his soul, that gloried in the hunt and the chase.

Jim hit the creature, his shoulder smashing into its taut belly, his weight sending it toppling from the railing and, indeed, bringing part of the railing with them. They fell, tangled together, in a cloud of splinters!

* * *

The next few moments were a blur as man and monster hung suspended for the barest moment and then came crashing down to the floor below! The creature took the brunt of the impact, but seemed none the worse for wear. It surged up, blood mingling with the froth in its jaws and thrust Jim away, slamming him into the staircase with primitive fury. Jim grabbed its long arms, locking his feet around its shoulder joint and stretched his body. Something popped and the creature squealed.

"That's for earlier, chum!" Jim said. The creature snarled in reply.

Jim was thrown aside as the creature whirled, one arm hanging much as Jim's had done the evening before. Tom smashed it across the back with a piece of railing, but the creature displayed little notice, berserk as it was.

"Jimmy, get out of the way!" Pike bellowed, bringing his rifle to bear. Jim scrambled to his feet, but the creature was already moving, good arm looping towards Pike. A claw slammed down, sending the rifle spinning. It discharged loudly. The Yeti swatted Pike aside and scrambled back up the wall, seemingly intent on returning to its original prey.

However, instead of attacking the cowering Fleur, it hurled itself at the large windows at the top of the stairs and crashed through!

Jim followed, shimmying up the wall, using the holes the creature had gouged as handholds. At the landing, he spared a brief glance for Fleur, who appeared to rapidly be regaining her composure, and leapt up onto the windowsill.

The Yeti hissed at Jim from the edge of the roof of the building opposite. Then, eyes blazing, it whirled and scaled the roof on its three working limbs.

"Jimmy, what's-" Tom began, making as if to follow him. Jim waved him back.

"Help Pike see to Fleur. I'll see if I can corral our furry friend."

"But-"

"Tom," Jim said. "You'll only slow me down."

Tom made as if to argue, but gave up and shook his head. He tossed Jim his pistol. "Real bullets, not those play bullets you like. The mercy ones didn't even make the monkey blink, so I reloaded."

"Thanks, Tom." Jim stuffed the gun into his trousers and gave a wave. Then, taking a breath, he jumped from the window, reaching for the edge of the roof opposite.

The brick scraped his already bloody chest, but Jim made no sound. Swiftly, he hauled himself up onto the peaked roof, just in time to see the white thing vanish down the other side. Bare feet slapping the roof, Jim followed.

Even as he ran, his gray cells were stirring, firing down complex avenues. Had the creature's attack been one of opportunity? Or had the intended target been Fleur and not her husband? The latter made little sense on the face of things...why attack the wife when the husband was the intended victim?

Jim reached the peak of the roof and slid sideways as a white claw swung up, narrowly missing his head. The beast rose up over him, eyes rolling in its sockets. It blinked and lashed out again. Jim slid backwards, desperately fighting to keep his footing on the snowy peak.

His balance lost, Jim flung out a hand desperately. His fingers hooked into something hard, invisible in the swirl of the creature's mane. His weight caused whatever it was to snap free and he fell back, sliding towards the edge of the roof. The creature followed him, jaws wide.

Jim hit the gutters on the edge of the roof and stopped. He clawed the pistol from his trousers and took aim as the creature's shadow fell over him.

Before he could fire, however, a shot echoed across the rooftop, and the creature reared back, screaming! It toppled over Jim, falling into the gap between buildings, crashing into the alley below.

"Feel free to thank me anytime, Anthony," Count Zaroff said, standing on the peak of the roof, a smoking rifle cradled in his arms. "Or are you paralyzed by fear?"

"Zaroff," Jim said, rising slowly to his feet. "Convenient." He turned and looked over the edge. His eyes narrowed as he peered through the falling snow, trying to find the beast's shape. A blotch of red caught his eye, and he sank to his haunches.

"Convenient? Hardly. Lucky is the word I'd use. I've been stalking the beast across the rooftops for the past hour. I picked up its spoor at DeLancy's apartment-"

"DeLancy?" Jim turned. Zaroff smirked.

"He's fine," he said. "I took him back to the club as soon as I realized the beast had been there. Naturally, I assumed that-"

"That Pike would be next, yes," Jim said. He held up his hand, finally looking at the thing he'd pulled from the beast's neck. It was a thick black collar, studded with tiny boxes. Jim pried one of the boxes loose and examined it. "Hunh."

"What is that?" Zaroff said.

"An electric collar," Jim said. Zaroff grunted.

"Intriguing. I've never heard of-"

"I have," Jim said. "Now, let's go check on your kill." Readying himself for a moment, Jim bounded from the roof, rolling through the air. His feet slapped the wall of the Pike house, and he ricocheted back towards the other wall. Jim bounced back and forth between the two buildings until he reached the ground, landing in a crouch, the collar clutched between his teeth, the pistol back in his waistband.

However, of the beast, there was no sign, save a thin drizzle of blood that led towards the street. Jim stepped through the slush and snow, his feet tingling.

The street was a blur of white. Cars were little more than hillocks of snow and buildings like mountains. Jim followed the prints of the Yeti out into the street and into another alleyway. His fingers traced claw marks in the wall, and his head tilted, following the traces of the beast's flight.

"It's going to ground."

Jim turned as Zaroff approached, rifle ready. The Count looked every inch the Cossack hunter, fur coat flapping around his legs, plump hat perched on his lupine head.

"Perhaps," Jim said. Zaroff snorted. Before he could reply, a shout from across the street caught their attention. Tom was hurrying towards them, carrying one of Pike's rifles.

"Jimmy, you okay?" Tom called. Jim waved a hand.

"I'm fine, Tom. Mrs. Pike?"

"Frankie's with her. She's shook up some, but that's one tough dame," Tom said admiringly. "Where did it go?"

"Up," Jim said, pointing. Zaroff slung his rifle and started for the alleyway.

"Then that is where I am bound for."

"No," Jim said, grabbing the Cossack's shoulder. Zaroff whirled, a snarl on his face not unlike that of the Yeti.

"You dare-"

"Yes. Even if the creature is hurt, that does not mean that it won't make another attempt on DeLancy's life. Someone is controlling it, and that someone saw everything that has occurred." Jim held up the collar. "I don't doubt that they are already moving to regain control of the beast."

"All the more reason to finish it off!" Zaroff thundered. Jim met Zaroff's glare and held it.

"There is more going on here than the depredations of a wild beast, Zaroff. I know you see that," Jim said. Zaroff frowned. "A mind is behind this. A twisted, hateful mind, but a mind nonetheless. A human mind. And it is watching our every move!"

"I have been hunted before, Anthony," Zaroff said. "That beast's hide, however, is mine."

"If you do as I ask, I'll help you mount it," Jim said. "Just get back to DeLancy and get him to my penthouse."

"Your penthouse?"

"We need a safe house. Can you think of anywhere better?" Jim said.

Zaroff started to speak, then closed his mouth, smiling slightly.

"You are more cunning than I gave you credit for, Anthony. And your ruthlessness is second only to my own." Zaroff clicked his heels and ducked his head, then started back towards the street and one of the cars parked there. Tom watched him disappear into the swirling snow, then turned back to Jim.

"What the heck did he mean by that?"

"Zaroff is a hunter. And he recognized my request for what it was—bait for a trap."

* * *

Jim turned and started back towards Pike's home. "Get the car ready. I'm going to call Dawkins, and have him prepare for guests."

"You sure about this, Jimmy?" Tom said. "I mean, we still don't know for sure what's going on."

"Do we ever?" Jim said, smiling slightly. Tom shook his head as Jim loped towards the house.

Inside, Pike sat comforting his wife. A shotgun rested near his leg, and he had twin shoulder holsters containing a matched set of .45s hanging beneath each arm. They looked up as Jim entered. "Well?" Fleur said. Jim stopped.

"It's gone to ground. Zaroff-"

"Zaroff!" Pike said, looking up. "I thought that crazy Russian was dead!"

"Apparently not. He managed to wound it. But the creature isn't the real danger here." Jim squatted in front of them. "Do you recognize this, Pike?" He held out the collar he'd ripped off the creature's neck. Fleur's eyes widened, and Pike cursed.

"You bet I do. That's one of my Tesla-collars!" Pike said, standing abruptly. He snatched it from Jim's hand and flipped it over, fingers tracing a tiny embossed plate on the inside of the collar. He looked at Jim. "I designed these for the Maple-White expedition. I had a few leftover and gave them to...to Bertie. For his trip..." Pike's voice went soft. His eyes widened. "Oh God."

"What does this mean?" Fleur said, looking at Jim. She clutched Pike's arm. "What's going on? What was that thing?"

"Nothing less than a weapon. A weapon in a campaign of revenge," Jim said, rising to his feet. He touched the shallow wounds on his chest.

Thanks to his amazing physiology, the wounds were already scabbing over. But they still stung.

"Tom is going to take you both to the Waldorf-Anthony. You'll be safe there, if anywhere, until I can figure out what, exactly, is going on."

"What about you? Where will you be?" Fleur asked, as her husband helped her up.

"The Freis family cemetery."

"What?" Fleur's eyes widened. "Why-"

"To satisfy a nagging voice in my head that says another piece of this unpleasant puzzle lies there. I'll see you at the penthouse when I'm done."

"Jimmy, are you planning on doing what I think you're planning on doing?" Pike said. Jim looked at him and frowned.

"I'm afraid I must, Pike. I'm sorry."

"What is it? What is he going to do?" Fleur said. She turned to Jim, her face contorting. "What are you going to do?"

"An autopsy. Of a sort. I'll need to borrow your phone, Pike," Jim said. Pike nodded, but Fleur grabbed Jim's arm.

"What kind of autopsy? Why?"

"To see if the remains you brought back are, in fact, your brother's." Jim gently removed her hand.

"Jimmy, car's ready," Tom said, standing in the doorway. Jim pushed Fleur towards Pike.

"Get to the penthouse. Wait there. I'll be back as soon as possible," Jim said. Pike extended his hand and Jim took it.

"You sure you're going to be okay, partner?"

"They're not after me, Pike," Jim said, with a smile. "At least not yet. Now, where's the phone?"

"In the-"

"You can't do this! I will not allow you to disturb my brother's resting place!" Fleur said, pulling away from her husband. She pointed at Jim. "Haven't you done enough?"

"Frankly, no." Jim looked back at Pike. "Phone?"

"Study. In the alligator."

Pike took Fleur by the arm and pulled the protesting woman gently but firmly towards the door. Jim watched them go, then headed back into the study.

True to Pike's word, the telephone was inside the skull of a mounted alligator. Jim plucked it free and dialed his penthouse. Dawkins, true to form, answered on the first ring.

Jim swiftly outlined recent events for his manservant, grateful for the Englishman's phlegmatic calm. Then, he requested certain tools from his laboratory be delivered to the Freis family burying ground at New York's Wildwood Cemetery. As Jim hung up, his mind raced through possibilities and potentialities.

Jim was well aware that most criminal schemes only made sense in retrospect. There was more going on than he could discern from surface events alone. However, he did have his suspicions.

He moved swiftly through the streets of New York, clad once more in coat and shoes, as well as Tom's pistol, properly holstered now, beneath his left arm, and a Nepalese kukri dagger borrowed from Pike's collection sheathed at his waist.

The snow was falling harder now, and Jim could smell the beginnings of a blizzard on the wind that curled between the buildings that stretched around and over him.

Part of Jim luxuriated in the feel of the cold wind coiling around him. It was the same part that gloried in physical confrontation, in the act of hunting. Some would ascribe it to his Comanche heritage, as if the blood of his mother were infected with an inherent savagery. But Jim knew that it was something else, something unexplained. There was a part of himself that was either less or perhaps more than the shape he wore.

It was this same part that alerted him to the fact that he was being followed. He had predicted as much, but the rapidity of his opponent's responses was slightly alarming. But Jim kept on his course, wondering if and when those shadowing him would make their move.

As he walked, his mind worked, trying to link events together. Four men killed by a Tibetan myth-made-flesh. Men who had refused Bertie Freis money. Freis had disappeared in Tibet. His sister was sure he was dead. Others were not. On the surface, the solution was obvious. Freis was not dead. His sister was covering for him, which explained her demands that Jim not investigate the cemetery.

But why were there two disparate versions of the siblings' relationship? DeLancy and Zaroff had seemed to think they were unusually close, but Pike and Fleur herself implied that the opposite was true. Was it simply an assumption on the part of those outside the family? Or was there something else at work?

Jim relied less on questions and more on observation in his techniques, and what he was observing was that all was not what it seemed.

With that thought in mind, he stopped and looked up. The iron gates of the Wildwood Cemetery loomed over him, its named spelled out in wrought letters. The gate was locked, but Jim had little time for niceties. He took the chain in both hands and with a single wrench, snapped it. Then, he pushed the gates open.

But before he could step through, something prodded him in the back. Jim whirled in surprise. His jaw dropped.

"You?"

* * *

"Yes," the wizened skeleton of a man said. Clad in a thick, colorful blanket, his ice colored hair held out of his hatchet face by a snakeskin band, he was as dark as baked clay and as thin as straw, though his wiry limbs possessed an evident strength. He prodded Jim again with the barrel of the Winchester he carried. "Surprised you, eh?"

"Well, I did know someone was following me-"

"Excuses," Mephito said, dark eyes boring into Jim's pitilessly for a few moments before he looked down. "Brought you your medicine bag." He handed Jim a satchel case, after giving it a good shake.

"My forensic kit is hardly magic. They are simply tools," Jim said. Mephito grunted.

"More excuses."

"Science," Jim countered.

"Science excuses," Mephito said, waving the rifle. "Magic is magic."

"I bow to your wisdom, grandfather," Jim said. Mephito swatted him on the back of the head.

"Comanches do not bow."

"Neither do Irishmen, according to my father," Jim said, entering the cemetery. Mephito followed, the Winchester over one skinny shoulder.

"Thank you for coming out here, grandfather," Jim said. "I know the cold disagrees with you-"

"Winter disagrees with everyone," Mephito said, trudging through the snow among the headstones. Like his grandson, the old Comanche gave little sign that the weather affected him one way or another.

Jim fell silent. Despite the affection he had for the old man, Mephito could be hard to talk to. As if to disagree, the Winchester's barrel thumped against Jim's shoulder. He turned and saw Mephito pointing.

"There."

Jim did not bother to ask how the old man knew exactly what they were looking for, knowing Mephito wouldn't answer.

"Surprised you, eh?"

The Freis mausoleum rose up out of a tangle of snow-covered shrubs, a flat looking edifice, with 'FREIS' carved into the stones over the door.

Locked, of course. Jim considered the door for a moment, then gestured for Mephito's rifle. The old Comanche tossed the Winchester to his grandson without hesitation. Jim raised the rifle and struck the lock with the butt, breaking it off on the second blow.

Tossing the weapon back to Mephito, Jim picked up his bag and entered the tomb. He looked back at his grandfather.

"Coming?"

"I don't bother the dead. They don't bother me," Mephito said, settling himself cross-legged on the snow, his blanket pooling around him. He smiled, slightly. "Go work your magic, grandson."

"It's not-" Jim began, then stopped. He shook his head and moved into the tomb.

Finding Bertie's drawer was easy. It was the only one not covered in the dust and detritus of age. Bertie and Fleur's father had been buried in France. No one other than Bertie had been interred here in years.

And that had evidently been a private affair, judging by Pike's reaction when Fleur made mention of it. Jim swiftly took a specially coated syringe filled with acid and traced the contour of the drawer. The gentle hiss of the acid at work was in marked contrast to the deathly silence of the tomb.

When the acid had done its work, Jim slipped a pair of gloves onto his hands and swiftly pried the front of the drawer free and placed it aside. Then he reached in and removed what was inside.

The remains were a pitiful sight. As Fleur had said, nothing but scraps. Jim stirred the remains with a finger. He didn't believe for a moment that the body was really that of Freis, despite his earlier dismissal of DeLancy's theories. He'd seen death faked too many times, and knew that in the out of the way corners of the world, it was easy to replace one body with another, living or dead.

The syringe replaced in the bag, he withdrew a stoppered vial containing a chemical solution of his own design for the detection of man-made fuel sources. With a steady hand, he drizzled several drops on the remains. The liquid glowed softly for a moment in the darkness and Jim grunted. The remains checked positive for machine oil. Unexpected, but not unexplainable. The airship had exploded, after all, and it had had a crew aboard.

The skull was mostly intact and Jim held it up, his keen eyes making use of what little light there was. Removing a glove, he traced the contours of the skull to see whether or not it matched up to his memory of Bertie's face. In his mind's eye, muscle and flesh overlaid the blackened chunk of calcium in his hand, forming a dream-shape of the face it would have had.

Jim sucked in a breath. It wasn't possible-shouldn't be-couldn't be-but was, regardless. Setting the skull down, he rifled through his bag, bringing out a tin of clay and set of bone pins. Dexterously, he stabbed the pins into the skull at the points where the flesh was thicker. Then he began to swab clay onto it, recreating the facial structure as gently as he could. Even so, the skull cracked and crumbled in places.

When he finished, he stepped back and frowned.

"Damn," he said.

The skull was indeed that of Bertie Freis.

Someone entered the tomb. Jim turned.

"I thought you were planning on-" he began, but stopped dead as he caught sight of the Mauser aimed at his head.

* * *

"Please. Outside," the gunman said, his voice soft and carrying the slightest lisp. Jim raised his hands and stepped past him.

"You are a Tcho-Tcho, aren't you," Jim said. The gunman started slightly, but did not otherwise react.

"No concern of yours," he said, motioning towards the doorway. "Outside, please."

Jim stepped out into the cemetery, the snow crunching beneath his shoes. The sky was growing dark and was full of coiling serpents of white.

Two more men waited, their features betraying their shared heritage with the gunman. Stone-faced, they both carried curved knives sheathed at their waists. There was no sign of Mephito.

"Why are you here? In New York?" Jim said calmly.

"Always been here," one of the men in front of him said, his accent straight out of Brooklyn. Unlike the other two, he could have passed for any one of a dozen races, if he were not in the presence of his fellows. "Some of us, anyway."

"No matter," the gunman said. "It is of no matter to you."

"Oh but it is," Jim said. "It matters very much to me."

"But not to us."

"What is the connection? Who brought you here, if not Freis? His sister?"

"Goodbye," the gunman said, raising the Mauser. Jim tensed.

A Winchester snarled. The gunman gasped, spun, fell. Jim lunged forward, hands clamping down on the shoulders of one of the men in front of him, driving him to his knees. Jim's own knee rose to meet him and the man fell backwards. Something in his mouth crunched and he clawed at his throat as a cancer-yellow fluid sprayed from his lips. He was dead before he hit the ground. The third man, the one with the Brooklyn bite to his words, drew his dagger and swiped viciously at Jim.

Jim leapt back and brought both fists down on the man's hand, knocking the blade from his grip with ease. Grabbing the man by his collar, Jim hauled him into the air and threw him towards the tomb, knocking the air out of him.

Mephito appeared at his elbow, eyes sparkling. "Good?" he grunted. Jim nodded.

"I'm fine." He smiled. "Could have warned me though."

"Could have. Didn't."

Jim laughed and sank to his haunches beside the man he'd thrown against the Freis tomb. The man was trying to get to his feet, but Jim held him flat easily, one hand pressed against his chest.

"Be still. If I wanted, I could crush your collar bone from this position. Grandfather, would you mind getting my bag?"

"I-you-" the man gasped as Jim gently increased the pressure on his sternum.

"Your name?"

"M-Max."

"You're a Tcho-Tcho."

"I-" Max began to tremble and cough in a familiar manner. Jim frowned. Mephito appeared at his elbow, bag in hand. Jim took it and swiftly dug through it, pulling out a cloth wrapped bundle. Unrolling it with a flick of his wrist, he revealed a line of stoppered vials held in place by cloth pockets sewn into the lining. He glanced at his grandfather.

"This-" he said, indicating the vials."-is my medicine bundle."

Mephito smiled. Jim turned back, and plucked one vial in particular from the roll. As Max began to twitch, Jim popped the stopper loose and poured the contents down Max's throat.

"Extract of Mariphasa Lupinum-the Moon Blossom of Tibet," Jim said.

He held Max's jaw closed and rubbed the struggling man's throat. "A deadly poison, and one our foe has used before on his hirelings. But not this time. Not when I have the antidote so close at hand."

Abruptly, Jim wrenched Max's jaw open and, snatching up the man's discarded knife, stabbed the blade into his open mouth. Mephito grunted in surprise.

"False tooth," Jim said. Something popped and Jim carefully withdrew the blade. Balanced perfectly on its tip was a single tooth. "Evidence vial, please, grandfather."

Mephito pulled one of the dozen empty vials Jim kept in his bag out and held it so Jim could tip the tooth in. Mephito held the vial up and shook it, letting the tooth rattle around.

"Huhm."

"Yes," Jim said. "Fanaticism is unpleasant."

"Not-not fanatics," Max slurred, struggling weakly against Jim. "R-royal g-guard."

"What?"

"Royal guard. Of the King in Y-Yellow," Max said, blood dribbling down onto his chin. Jim sat back.

"The King in-" He stopped. "Ah."

"Grandson?" Mephito put a hand on his shoulder. "What is it?"

"The King in Yellow was the ceremonial title of the rulers of Leng. It's been at the back of my mind all day. The medallion, the map, the fact that everywhere I go, someone shows up to stop me from…what?" Jim took Max's jaw in one hand. "Who are you working for?"

"I told you-"

"His name."

"No name. Only the King in Yellow! IA!" Max surged up, despite the pressure on his chest. Jim fell back onto his rear as Max clawed at him.

"We were content to live here! To work here! Huddled masses, yearning to be free!"

Mephito swung the Winchester around, but Jim forced the barrel away. He shoved Max back and pinned him to the side of the tomb.

"What are you saying?"

"We tried to stop him! Stop them all! Keep them from Leng! That's why we spread to the great cities of the world, why we blended in with you-" Max struggled against Jim's grip. "But all for nothing. We killed ourselves for nothing." He slumped, abruptly. "He came back. Roused the Mi-Go in their caverns, demanded we honor the old oaths. We tried-we tried-"

"Tried what? What did you-oh." Jim drew back, allowing the other man to slump to the ground. "You tried to kill him. But it didn't work, did it?"

"You cannot kill that which cannot die," Max whispered. "You cannot put down that which you call up."

"You might not be able to. But I'm a different story altogether," Jim said. He looked down at the slumped figure. "Leave. Go home. Go away."

"Yes," Max said. Then, with surprising speed, he snatched up the dagger Jim had tossed aside and raised it. "It calls for the blood of six," he said, almost apologetically. "Five by hate, one by love. And then the last gate to Carcosa will open and the King in Yellow will once more sit upon his throne."

Then, having said his piece, the man drove the dagger into his own chest. He toppled forward, and lay still in the crimson snow.

* * *

Jim and Mephito rode the private penthouse elevator in silence. The old man seemed unconcerned by what he had just witnessed, but for Jim, it rankled.

A useless waste of human life, in service to a tainted belief system. That was what all the pieces were adding up to. What was truly frustrating was that he knew, with an iron certainty, that he was only grasping the edges of the thing. The incidentals, as opposed to the whole of the picture.

Four men dead. Murdered by a monster. A monster evidently under the control of the mysterious King in Yellow. But why? Simple revenge? Apparently not. The revenge was a by-product. Two birds with one stone. Or maybe not. Maybe he was reading it wrong, and there was no revenge angle. Maybe it only looked that way. Coincidence.

Jim hated coincidence. It mucked up perfectly good crimes, making them nigh impossible to solve.

His fingers tapped out a sullen beat on the wall of the elevator as he thought.

It couldn't be coincidence. The effort put into the murders seemed to say it was anything but. To unleash a wild beast on a man, to kill him in the most terrible, hateful-

Wait.

Jim blinked. What had the man in the cemetery said? 'Five by hate'. Jim rubbed his chin. He made a noise. Mephito looked at him.

"Two out of six remain. Both in one spot. If I'm right, we'll see the end of this confusing affair tonight."

Mephito grunted, though whether in agreement or not, Jim couldn't say. He didn't ask as the elevator doors slid open, revealing his penthouse.

"Master Anthony," Dawkins, his butler, said, his cockney accent betraying his place of origin. "Find what you needed, sir?"

"More pieces to the puzzle, Dawkins. But that'll have to be enough. Is everyone here?"

"All accounted for, last I checked."

"Good man. Grandfather-" Jim turned, but Mephito was already heading for the windows that led out onto the balcony. "Never mind."

Jim and Dawkins entered the sitting area and Jim saw that everyone was gathered there. Zaroff, standing near the windows, smiled as Jim entered the room.

"The bait is laid out, eh Anthony?"

"Bait? What is he talking about?" DeLancy said. He was holding a cup of tea in both hands. He was visibly trembling. "Jim?"

"You'll be safe here, Otto," Jim said. Arms crossed, he looked at them. "You'll all be safe."

"Says you," Pike said, though not unkindly. He had a drink in hand, and looked three sheets to the wind, but looks could be deceiving, Jim knew.

"I do," Jim said, his gaze settling on Fleur. She sat away from her husband, at the other end of the leather couch they had occupied as their own. Legs tucked beneath her, she looked like the epitome of calm.

"Did you find what you were looking for, Mr. Anthony?" she said. Jim nodded.

"More than I expected."

Fleur frowned. "I assume you took care not to damage anything?"

"Gentle as a lamb," Jim said. He looked at Tom and crooked a finger. Tom hurried over.

"Yeah?" he said, quietly.

"You're armed?"

"Always."

"Mercy bullets?"

"Aw, Jimmy-"

"Mercy bullets, Tom. No more bloodshed if we can help it. Try and stun them. Keep them from killing themselves."

"What about him?" Tom said, hiking a thumb at Zaroff. The Count had doffed his coat and hat, and stood near the windows, hands on the pistols belted at his waist, a black hussars coat with gold trim hiding a third holstered beneath his arm. He was smoking a thin cigarillo, and Jim's nose wrinkled.

"I'll talk to him."

"Good luck." Tom looked at the others. "DeLancy seems kind of edgy. I think he might make a break for it."

"Keep an eye on him. On Pike, too. Try and keep them from doing anything too unwise."

"You really think something is going to happen?"

"You really think something won't?" Jim countered. He caught Dawkins' eye as the latter moved through the room with a tray of warm drinks balanced delicately on his palm.

"Sir?"

"Are you armed, Dawkins?"

"Quite, sir," Dawkins said with a sniff. Jim waited. Dawkins' face was a study in blankness. Jim sighed.

"Should I bother asking?"

"I was in India, sir," was all the explanation Dawkins gave. Jim waved him away and wandered towards Zaroff.

"Ah, Anthony. I must compliment you on the view. Simply magnificent," Zaroff said, smoke rolling from his nostrils.

"You said you'd met the Tcho-Tcho before," Jim said. Zaroff frowned, then nodded.

"Yes, briefly. I gather I got too close to one of their sacred spots or some such. They warned me off with a knife in my thigh."

"Be honest with me," Jim said. "Were you searching for Leng?"

"No," Zaroff flipped a hand. "I wanted a Yeti pelt for my wall. That the legends of the Yeti and Leng intersect is not my concern."

"But afterward?" Jim pressed.

"Anthony, what are you digging for?" Zaroff said, turning his cold gaze on Jim.

"Information. It's my favored prey."

"Ha!" Zaroff patted his pistols. "Mine is altogether more lively."

"Tell me about the Tcho-Tcho."

"I do not know much," Zaroff admitted. "Legends, mostly. They are a people who cultivate mystery like others cultivate wheat."

"Tell me what you know," Jim pressed. Zaroff looked at him, frowned, then spoke.

"They lived in a city above the clouds, on the high, vicious slopes of the mountains—no one is sure where, exactly—where they worshipped demons and made sacrifices of men from the lowlands." Zaroff's gaze became unfocused, and he stared out at the night. "They served a King.

The King in Yellow. A sort of priest-king, I expect. Religion is important to these Eastern types. Hereditary title. Passed down through one family. Mad as hatters after a while. One day, one went even madder. He unleashed the demons of the hills on his own people-"

"The Yeti," Jim said. Zaroff nodded.

"I suspect so, yes. Though how he controlled the beasts, who can say? Regardless, he died. Or was killed. Or was struck down by the gods. Who knows? And rather than raise a new man onto the throne, to suffer underneath the same madness, they left Leng, god-cursed as it was."

"They scattered to the four corners," Jim said. It wasn't a question. Zaroff smiled.

"So the legends say. Some stayed, obviously. Ostensibly, to make sure no one got too close to Leng."

"But?"

"Crop failure? Cataclysm? Plague? Who knows what the real reason was," Zaroff said. "Some left. Some stayed."

"It was more than that though, wasn't it?" Jim said. "They made an effort to disappear. To vanish-"

"It happens. I gather they were ever only a small number. Less than a few thousand by the time they began leaving." Zaroff shrugged. "It happened to the Aztecs. To the Auxumites. Even to my own people, to some degree."

"Huhm," Jim said. He looked at Zaroff's weapons." Try not to kill anyone," Jim said. Zaroff grinned.

"The beast is mine."

"If it shows up."

"It will. We have its prey, after all."

"Yes." Jim left Zaroff standing there and sauntered towards the couch where Pike sat, nursing his drink.

"Pike, I need to speak to you. In my laboratory."

"Franklin–" Fleur began. Pike patted her knee awkwardly.

"Don't worry baby. You'll be safe."

He followed Jim out of the room and into Jim's lab—a spartan room devoted to scientific research of all types. Dawkins had placed Jim's forensic bag on one of the long tables that lined the walls. He took out the false tooth, as well as several other items he had collected from the cemetery. When he placed Bertie's skull on the table, Pike cursed

"Jimmy! You–"

"Quiet please, Pike." Jim turned and leaned against the table, arms spread, legs crossed. "Just listen. How close was your wife to her broth-er?"

"I told you, they wasn't–"

"Pike." Jim met his friend's eyes and held them. Pike matched him with a glare, but eventually he looked away.

"Close. Closer than was decent, sometimes. Like twins, only they weren't." Pike emptied his glass and stared at it mournfully. "He wasn't happy, when she met me. You remember him, don't you Jimmy?"

"Only vaguely."

"Yeah. Vague. That's what everyone says. Bertie was the original man who wasn't there. Unless it concerned Tibet. Or Leng. Or his sister."

"Half-sister," Jim said. Pike twitched.

"That was Bertie's favorite phrase," he said harshly. "Why she's started using it, I don't know. She acted half scared of him sometimes. Sometimes I think that's why she married me…to get away from him."

"And now?"

"We got engaged, it seemed to drive him nuts. He started planning that blasted expedition, and well, you know."

"Tell me anyway."

"When he died, she was—I don't know how to describe it—overjoyed? Relieved? Then she went to reclaim his—uh—his body."

"Without you?" Jim said. Pike looked away.

"I told her we should leave Bertie in Tibet, since he'd been so all-fired eager to go. We fought."

"And when she came back?"

Pike frowned. Jim nodded. "She was cold," he said. "Distant. Different."

"Yeah," Pike said, softly. "I figured she was still mad at me."

"But now?"

"I think she saw something that scared her." Pike looked up and licked his lips. "Is that him?" he said, pointing at the skull. "Is it?"

"As near as I can tell without further examination," Jim said. "What exactly did she bring back with her?"

"Nothing but the-ah-the remains," Pike said. "Nothing else."

"I should rephrase…did she bring anyone back with her?"

"No! Why would you-"

"Bertie's mother. What did you know about her?"

"Nothing. She died in Tibet."

"Of course she did." Jim rubbed his chin. He pinched the bridge of his nose, as if struck by a sudden pain. "Of course."

"What is it?"

"Five by hate," Jim said. "How much do you know about the Tcho-Tcho legends?"

"Not much," Pike said, looking at him strangely.

"How much does your wife know?"

"Only what Bertie told her, presumably."

"How dare you!"

Both men turned to see Fleur standing in the doorway, her eyes locked on Bertie's skull. She looked at Jim. "You!"

"Fleur-honey-" Pike stepped towards her, but her glare stopped him in his tracks.

"And you...you knew about this?"

"I-"

"You always hated him. I'm not surprised," she spat. "But this?"

"Pike knew nothing about this, Fleur," Jim said, making as if to step between them. "I had to be sure-"

"Sure? Sure of what?" Fleur said. "My brother suffered enough humiliation in life, must you make him suffer it in death as well?" Her eyes glistened as she threw herself at Jim, fists battering against his broad chest. "You bastard! Bastard!"

Jim put his hands on her shuddering shoulders gently. "It wasn't intended that way. I needed to be sure it was your brother in that tomb. In order to dismiss him as a suspect," he said. "But in a horrible way, it only proved that he still was."

Fleur looked up, face shifting rapidly with emotion. Jim pushed her away. "The human mind is a fluid thing. It shifts and coils in ways that do not conform to logic or theory." He looked at Pike. "You had a whirlwind romance. A flurry of affection." He looked back down at Fleur. "And you had a protector."

She went pale and drew back. Jim's grip on her shoulders tightened. Pike made a noise.

"Jimmy—what—"

"You hated your brother. But he loved you." Jim's voice was flat. Business-like. "It was a twisted love. Strange and demented. You didn't recognize it at first. Perhaps you were frightened. Repulsed, maybe. It's only natural to feel that way when a loved one tries to force-"

"No!" Fleur screamed. Her hand flashed out and cracked across Jim's face. He dropped her arms and stumbled, surprised. Fleur turned and ran from the lab.

Jim rubbed his face. "In the end, it always boils down to one of two things. Either love or hate."

"Jimmy, are you saying-"

"I-"

The sound of a Winchester barking, interrupted them. Then Fleur screamed. Both men ran out of the lab and into a scene of purest chaos. White shapes loomed on the balcony. Mephito and Zaroff stood in front of the windows, rifles cracking, Dawkins just behind them. Fleur was struggling with DeLancy, near the elevator. Tom lay stunned, a bottle of whiskey nearby—the same bottle that had cracked across his skull.

All of this flashed through Jim's mind in the briefest of seconds. Choice made, Jim charged towards the elevator. But too late. DeLancy and Fleur fell into the open elevator and the doors thumped shut even as Jim smashed his fists into them.

"Damn it!"

"Sir!" Dawkins bellowed in best parade ground voice. Jim whirled, even as the blood-stink of the Yeti rolled over him. Reacting on instinct, Jim spun, fingers stripping the belt from his waist. He twisted aside even as the gangly beast slammed into the elevator and then, in one fluid motion, he was upon its back, his belt looping around its throat.

More than one. He hadn't even considered it. One Yeti was fantastic enough, but four? As the creature flung him side to side, he caught kaleidoscopic images of what was going on in the penthouse.

Pike had drawn his .45s and was blazing away at one of the beasts. As before, bullets seemed to have little effect. Mephito and Zaroff were doing much the same, as two more of the beasts came through the windows. A claw snared him and Jim grunted, his attention brought firmly back to the task at hand.

Legs wrapped around its barrel chest, Jim twisted his belt tight. The creature scrabbled for him, but Jim held on grimly. Something crunched and the beast sank to its knees, and then collapsed. Jim stepped off of it, his chest heaving, arms burning with strain.

Mephito's rifle snarled again and again, the old Comanche's hands flashing as he cocked and fired. The creature looming over him screeched with ape-like fury, arms raised. Crimson marred its white fur, but it didn't appear to be weakened. Jim snatched the kukri knife from his belt and threw it with deadly accuracy. It chopped into the side of the Yeti's elongated skull with a sound like an axe hitting wood. The beast spun and fell, twitching.

Zaroff's rifle was slapped from his hand as the third Yeti lunged for him. The wily Cossack leapt back, drawing his pistols, two thick-bodied Webley Bulldogs, and pulled the triggers. The Yeti fell to its knees, but surged back up, as unstoppable as an avalanche. Zaroff cursed in Russian and fired again, backing away steadily.

Dawkins approached the wounded beast from the side, a yellow length of cord clutched in his hands. Jim recognized it as a Thugee strangling cord even as his faithful man servant looped it around the Yeti's throat with a skilled toss and a pulled it tight!

The Yeti reared, and Dawkins clung on grimly. Zaroff took advantage of the creature's position, to toss aside his pistols and snatch Jim's knife from the skull of the other brute and drive it into the last creature's chest with brutal force.

The Yeti's dying scream echoed through the room and then, there was silence. Franklin Pike broke it, his voice rough with shock.

"It happened so quick. So damn quick," Pike said. He looked at Jim. "Where's my wife?"

* * *

"She hit me on the head with a bottle! That's no way to treat a whiskey!" Tom said as they charged down the stairs.

"I don't understand, why would Fleur hit him?" Pike said. Jim didn't answer. As they hit the floor just beneath the penthouse, Jim slammed through the door and out towards the public elevators. His private one was stuck at the bottom. He had a sickening feeling he knew why. He smashed the side of his fist into the buttons and the elevator sang open. Jim stepped in even as Pike, Tom, Mephito and Zaroff hurried after him. Dawkins had stayed behind, intent on cleaning up.

"Tom, when we hit bottom, get one of the cars ready. The Ford. Grandfather, go with him, please," Jim said. "Pike, you come with me. Zaroff—"

"I am going after the beast." Zaroff checked the cylinders of his pistols. "None of the ones upstairs bore the mark of my rifle. It is still on the loose."

"Of course you are. I only wanted to wish you good hunting," Jim said. He looked at the Cossack. "It lost its control collar in our last engagement. The others were driven to berserk frenzy, the better to kill their prey. It will not be so heedless, or so mindless."

The wily Cossack leapt back, drawing his pistols, and pulled the triggers.

"Good," Zaroff said, snapping the pistols closed. "Truly, the most dangerous game."

"You're not even worried about DeLancy are you, you crazy Russian?" Tom said. Zaroff laughed.

"Surely Mr. Anthony can look after him better than I, Gentry," Zaroff said. He grinned at Jim, who ignored him.

The elevator doors opened. A wall of service revolvers faced them. Jim held up his hands.

"Hello officers. How can we be of service?"

"Anthony!" Healy snarled, somewhere in the back. "Let 'em through boys! We're gonna need him!"

The police officers stepped back. The lobby of the apartment building was in shambles. Bullet holes dotted the walls and the windows were shattered. People were being helped up off the floor by police officers.

"What the hell is going on?" Healy said, slapping his leg with his hat. "Armed kooks and hairy monsters, tearing up one of the snazziest buildings on Fifth Avenue!"

"It's all connected, I assure you," Jim said. Tom and Mephito were already hurrying towards the underground parking garage. "What occurred, exactly?"

"Craziness. Insanity. However you slice it," Healy said. "About twenty minutes ago, desk clerk notices an awful lot of shifty guys-"

"Shifty?"

"Oriental-looking, some of them," Healy said. Jim frowned. Healy sighed. "Look, I ain't making judgments, I'm just saying-"

"Never mind. Go on," Jim said. Healy nodded jerkily.

"These guys, they're packing. Guns, knives, like they're planning on busting up stairs. They popped the doorman, took out the desk clerk as soon as he hit that security button you installed, made everyone else lay down." Healy shook his head. "The elevator—yours—comes down—ding!—guy runs out, the chi–"

"Tibetan," Jim said. Healy raised an eyebrow.

"The Tibetans," Healy emphasized, "Don't do nothing—Hell, supposedly they looked as surprised as everyone else—until the broad–"

"Fleur! Where is she?" Pike reached for Healy, but the detective danced back, throwing up a warning finger.

"Hands off the merchandise, buddy!"

"Healy, get to the point!" Jim said, pushing Pike back.

"The broad comes out, the Tibetans-" He gave Jim a look. "Grab her and hustle her towards a car outside. Meanwhile, the poor sap who came down with her has gotten out on the street by then and he's trying to hail a taxi."

"Which way did he go?" Jim said. Healy grinned nastily.

"Straight down," he said. He jerked a finger across his throat. "While two of 'em are stuffing the broad in the back of the car, two more of 'em apparently gut the poor bastard right on the street. We got here about then. Let the air out of one of 'em right there, knife in hand. The other chokes on that yellow stuff from before. Car with the broad heads uptown." Healy's nostrils flared. "You wanna give me the lowdown on what's going on now?"

"The animals responsible for the other four murders are upstairs in my penthouse. Dawkins will let you in," Jim said. "A rare species of ape, native to Tibet."

"Apes? Then what's with-"

"A cult, Detective."

"Some kinda Eastern thing?"

"Worse," Jim said. "I assume you had them followed?"

"How stupid do you think I am, Anthony?" Healy said. "Every bull who ain't here is in hot pursuit of those guys. Now-"

"Now, we finish this." Jim turned to Pike. "You, however, are staying here."

"What? No! Jimmy-"

"Pike!" Jim grabbed his shoulders. "Listen to me. Please. DeLancy is dead. You're the last part of the equation. The last tally to be made." Jim's eyes narrowed. "That's why they took her, Pike. To lure you…"

"Jimmy, I-"

"Trust me, Pike. You have to trust me."

"DeLancy trusted you. And he's stuck to the sidewalk by his own blood. And what about Eddie-" Pike said. Jim's mouth became a flat line. Before either Healy or Pike could react, Jim's fist thundered across his jaw. Pike toppled backwards into Healy's arms.

"I'm getting tired of arguing with people." Jim rubbed his hand. He pointed at Healy. "Now, get on the horn. Find us a location. I'll have our radio on. You know the channel."

"Yeah, unluckily thirteen," Healy said, trying to keep Pike from slumping to the floor. "What the hell is going on, Anthony?"

"The thin line between love and hate, Detective. The same as always," Jim said. He turned and strode towards door.

Outside, he glanced at the covered shape that had been DeLancy. As with Phipps, he pushed the flare of emotion down and tamped it out. But his hands curled into knotted fists regardless. To Jim Anthony, Death was the enemy. An opponent he could never truly defeat.

But that didn't mean he wouldn't keep trying.

"Jimmy," Tom said, waving a hand. "Ready to go?"

Jim looked up ad started towards the car. Tom got back in. Mephito was in the back seat, glaring intently at his medicine bag.

Jim slid in to the passenger seat and slammed the door. With a flick of his finger, he tuned the radio to the police band.

"Follow the birdies," he said, pointing. Tom threw the car into gear and they swerved into traffic, leaving a trail of honking cars behind them.

"I saw Zaroff sneaking off," Tom said. "He done for the day?"

"No, he's going after the last of the Yetis," Jim said. Tom frowned.

"He would," he said. "Hope it eats the snotty-"

"I don't. The creature is dangerous, for all that it doesn't belong here. Zaroff is one of the world's greatest hunters. If he can bring it down before it kills anyone else, more power to him."

"What if he can't?"

"Then it falls to us." Jim sighed. "One more thing to worry about."

Listening to the chatter, Tom deftly wove through the night-time streets, the snow falling around them.

"Why the hell did they kidnap her?" Tom said. "Ain't Pike the one they want?"

"Yes, but he has to come to them willingly," Jim said. "It's part of whatever arcane ceremony they're playing out. This isn't about revenge...not really."

"Could have fooled me," Tom snorted.

"Five by hate, one by love," Jim paraphrased. "Pike is the one. Six deaths required for the ritual..."

"But what's the point?" Tom demanded. He twisted the wheel, avoiding a car that was hanging off the sidewalk, covered in snow and ice. "Road's getting bad," he grunted.

"I'm not sure," Jim said. "But I'm almost positive that I know where they're going..."

"Yeah?"

"Yeah."

"Then point me the way, boss!"

"There." Jim pointed to a tall shape rearing up out of the night.

"Holy god," Tom said. "There?"

"If you were at home in the Himalayas, where would you go?" Jim said. "Besides, other than the Waldorf-Anthony, it's the tallest place in the city."

"Yeah, but it's not even finished yet!" Tom protested. "Ever since that loon in the blimp-"

"Even better," Jim said. "Less chance they'll be bothered. Especially considering the snow we've been having." His eyes narrowed. "They're there. I'm sure of it. Step on it."

"You got it boss. Chrysler Building coming up!"

* * *

A sea of multi-colored flashing lights surrounded the Chrysler Building. The reflected lights crawled up the darkened building, bouncing back down to illuminate the dozen black patrol cars. A thirteenth car was parked on the sidewalk athwart the doors to the tower.

"Healy said you was coming," a uniformed sergeant said. "Said we were to let you do your thing."

"And?" Jim said. He stood at ease, ignoring the wind and the cold. He had left his coat behind, and rolled up his sleeves, leaving his broad forearms bare. As he spoke, he was wrapping a length of white tape around each arm and hand in turn, the way boxers did before a fight.

"And we don't know how many guys they got in there, guns, nothing. The building's been deserted since about six months ago, that nut in the blimp-"

"The Rooftop Raider," Jim said, his lips quirking in a smile.

"Yeah, since his blimp smashed into the Cloud Club on the top floors."

"I remember. I was in it at the time."

"The Club?"

"The blimp." Jim flexed his hands.

"Christ. Anyway, you might want to hurry."

"Any reason?"

The sergeant shrugged. "The Chief is on his way. Mayor. Everybody."

"So we'll have an audience." Jim clapped the man on the shoulder. "I've worked under worse conditions."

"Yeah, I read the papers," the sergeant said.

Jim turned, his eyes finding his companions.

"So, what's the plan, Jimmy?" Tom said hefting the Thompson he'd pulled from the trunk. He checked the drum magazine and laid the barrel across his shoulder. "Guns blazing?"

"I was thinking of something more subtle."

"Yeah?"

"You sound disappointed."

"Let's just say I'm spoiling for a fight," Tom said. "I've been playing chauffeur all day!"

"Feel like playing it one more time?"

"What?"

"I had you bring the Ford for a reason." Jim went to the trunk and lifted the interior out, revealing an array of devices. Working swiftly, but surely, Jim began removing pieces and connecting them until an odd, squatty contraption almost the size of a man sat on the snowy street.

"That looks like the gyrocopter!" Tom exclaimed.

"That's because it is. Or, rather, a smaller version. Built for one person. And, in the event of an emergency, one passenger." Jim gave the propeller an experimental twirl. "I designed it with an eye for emergency rescue efforts, but I haven't had the opportunity to give it a whirl, so to speak."

"And you think now is a good time?" Tom sounded incredulous.

"Unless you want to fight your way up seventy-seven floors," Jim said.

"But the weather-"

A clatter of bones caused both men to turn. Mephito squatted nearby, peering down at a cleared patch of pavement where he had just tossed the bones he carried everywhere in his medicine pouch.

"Grandfather?" Jim said. Mephito looked up.

"The bones say, the wind is with you on this day."

"Oh, well, if the bones say, well, we just got to believe it right?" Tom said. Jim smiled.

"Indeed."

"I was being sarcastic."

"I know." Jim slapped Tom on the shoulder. "Up, up and away, as the man says."

"Aw hell."

With Jim's help, Tom clambered into the combination harness-seat of the micro-copter and stood. The weight of the device was taken up by the spring supports, and Tom leaned back, tightening the straps. He flicked the switches experimentally. "Toggles work the same?"

"Same old, same old. Standardization is the key to victory, my friend."

"Yeah, yeah, tell it to the Germans."

"You'll need this." Jim handed him a modified gas-mask, with thick goggles and an oxygen tube. "Wouldn't want you blacking out up there."

"Oh good," Tom said sourly. Jim checked the fuel gauges and leaned around, smiling.

"Ready?"

"No."

"Too bad. Grandfather, you might want to-" Jim stopped and looked around. Mephito waved at him from behind the car. "Ah."

"Is it too late for me to get back there?" Tom said. Jim grabbed the pull-start and said,

"Yes."

With a strong jerk, the engine coughed, grunted, and roared to life. The propeller, gently spinning, abruptly sped up. Tom felt himself bouncing for a moment and then, in a second of vertigo-inducing nausea, he was hurtling upwards!

A sudden weight caused him to look down. Jim clung to a specially designed web-like sub-harness that extended from Tom's own, his face hidden behind a gas-mask of his own. A bandolier of thick canisters decorated his torso, and he wore gloves and a flat, segmented cuirass over his bare chest and belly. One of his specially-designed pistols was strapped to the back of his waist, and a broad-bladed knife was sheathed on his hip.

"Isn't this great?" Jim yelled as they surged upwards.

"No!" Tom said grimly, fighting the controls. The micro-copter swung this way and that, suddenly buffeted by the cold winds. "We've got an updraft, it's moving us too fast!"

"The wind is with us!" Jim shouted.

"Right up until it slams us into the damn building!"

"You're too pessimistic, Tom!"

"And you're insane!"

"Only by the standards of society!"

"Why am I here?"

"Philosophy? Now? Tom, eyes on the prize!" Jim pointed. "We're being blown away! Get us closer!"

"Closer, he says," Tom muttered. "I'll give him closer." Gritting his teeth, Tom thumbed the switches and the 'copter bulled forward through the vicious winds. Snow curled around them, and Tom's teeth were chattering. Jim slapped his leg. Tom looked down.

"Almost there!" Jim said, pointing. Tom nodded jerkily.

"How you getting off?"

"Through the wall!"

"What?"

"Well, there's nowhere to land!"

"How am I getting down, then?"

"Same way you would the gyrocopter!"

"Prayer?"

"There!" Jim's muscles bunched. Tom grunted as he caught sight of the tarpaulin that marked the spot where the Rooftop Raider's blimp had crashed into the Cloud Club. The gaping hole was in the midst of repairs, and, as such, made the perfect spot for Jim to disembark.

Granted, he had to leap across the void, but Tom was confident in his friend's ability to defy certain death yet again. He looked down and gave Jim a thumbs up.

"Go get 'em, Jimmy!"

"Do my best, Tom!" Jim replied. And then, with a single thrust of his powerful arms and legs, Jim Anthony leapt the five foot gap between the micro-copter and the Chrysler Building!

* * *

Crashing through the tarp, Jim hit the floor and rolled to his feet, one hand already pulling one of the heavy canisters from the bandolier.

As expected, several gunmen were waiting on him. Even as they opened up, Jim tossed the canister. It exploded on contact, releasing a cloud of soporific gas. Men gagged and choked, stumbling, falling.

Swiftly moving towards the stairs, Jim palmed another canister. A Thompson chattered, and Jim swung aside, lobbing the gas canister in the general direction of his attackers.

How many men did his enemy have? Enough, most likely, Jim thought. Dozens. How many had been here waiting? How many had come to New York from Tibet?

Jim took the stairs two at a time, heading upwards towards the observation deck. The highest point in the city. Where better for a king to survey their kingdom?

A bullet ricocheted off of the stair rail and Jim ducked, tossing his next to last canister overhand. It thudded on the landing and someone gave a strangled cry.

Jim was up and moving a second later, padding through the cloud of knock-out gas like a bronze tiger. Bodies lay in enforced slumber, and he carefully stepped over them.

Something in him felt pity for the Tcho-Tcho. They had buried their kingdom, their glory, in order to prevent this very occurrence. He wondered what ancient madness had driven them to that last resort. The willful dissolution of an entire race, in order to prevent the rise of a mad king.

Unfortunately, kings had a way of returning. There was always a sword to be drawn from a stone, or a birthmark spotted in a market place. Always a group who thought things had been better when kings had ruled, and men were but servants to royalty.

And all too quickly, even the strongest dissenters fell into line. Or were killed.

Something snarled.

The hairs on the back of Jim's neck rose. Shaken from his thoughts, he turned slowly, watching the shadows. He closed his eyes for a moment, cursing himself.

Five beasts. Odd number. He'd thought so at the time, but hadn't thought it through. Numbers mattered.

A chair flew out of the shadows, and he jumped aside, grabbing his last canister.

Six. Not five. Breeding pairs. Three mated pairs. And the last was here. Guarding its king.

The snarl, again. A grunting cough that an imaginative man might imagine as words. The scrape of something across the carpet. Jim spun.

A hand closed around his, crushing the canister in his hand. Jim hissed in pain, but scrabbled for his pistol. It was only armed with mercy bullets, and those had proven ineffective against the creatures' thick hide. A side-effect of their evolution in high-pressure, colder climes, a part of him pedantically noted. The beast lifted him by his arm.

Jim drew his pistol and shoved it forward. The creature's other hand flashed out, slapping the pistol away. Then, with a roll of ape-like shoulders, it swung Jim up and slammed him down, brutally!

Jim hit the floor and felt his brain wobble in his skull. The Yeti dragged him up and tossed him aside. Jim crashed into a table and lay dazed in the shattered ruins.

The Yeti paced forward, sidling towards him and then around. It huffed, agitated. Then, the collar on its neck sparked and it shuffled back, eyes narrowing.

"Not yet," a voice said.

Clutching his side, Jim pushed himself up. He swept the shadows with his gaze.

"Of course not. You like to watch, don't you?" Jim said. Someone laughed.

The sound of clapping filled the empty observation deck. Clap. Clap. Clap. And footsteps. A slender form stepped out of the shadows, a yellow scarf fluttering in the wind that moaned through the shattered windows.

"Very good. Very cutting."

The voice was muffled. Jim shook his head and pulled his gas mask off.

"Fact, not sarcasm. You watched your beasts murder–"

"Vengeance is a royal prerogative, Mr. Anthony."

"Murder is never a prerogative, justified or not." Jim's eyes narrowed. "Where is Mrs. Pike?"

"Around. She is unimportant. A tool, to be discarded." A slender hand fluttered. "As are you all."

"That's a matter for debate," Jim said. He pulled his legs under him slowly. "Why kill them?"

"Five for hate, one for love, and Carcosa will be revealed," the King in Yellow said. "I am ready to retake my throne, Mr. Anthony. My exile has been long enough."

"Bertie Freis," Jim said, softly. "Which one was he?"

The King stopped. Head cocked. Thin, gloved fingers reached up and began to unwind the yellow scarf. It fluttered away and caught on one of the broken windows, where it rustled in the wind like a banner.

Fleur smiled, and said, "Which do you think, Mr. Anthony?"

* * *

Jim froze. Just for a moment, as his mind jumped tracks and started in a new direction. "Ah," he said. "I had assumed that you were part of it. But–"

"Misogyny, Mr. Anthony? How unlike you." Fleur smiled bitterly. "Elizabeth the First proved that a woman can be King."

"You are not Elizabeth," Jim said. Fleur laughed.

"No. I am not. I am King of a greater kingdom than some paltry, fog-bound island. I am the King of Lost Carcosa. The Golden Kingdom." She lifted her hands and seemed, for a moment, to be reaching for some indefinable thing. Then, she shook herself and dropped her gaze to Jim.

Knowing that every second she continued to speak was a second he could use to formulate a plan, Jim said, "Then your father-"

"A dreamer. A ruthless, terrible dreamer. But he knew. He listened to the old stories. The old legends-"

"The legends your people buried."

"Fools," Fleur spat. "Idiots."

"No. Wise. Heroic," Jim said. "They decided to bury the demons of their past en masse. A entire race committed cultural suicide in order to protect the world from the madness they had birthed."

"Madness? Madness! They were the mad ones!" Fleur hissed. "The King in Yellow was a god! Their god! And they uncreated him!"

"Some gods are better left buried."

"Maybe so," Fleur said. "But not me."

There was a drone in the distance. A thrum of engines. Jim ignored it, his attention focused on Fleur. "Bertie found it, didn't he?" he said. "He found Leng."

"Leng..." Fleur said. Her face went still. Jim rolled his shoulders, preparing himself.

"He found it. And he sent for you. You were too frightened of him not to go-"

"I was not frightened!" Fleur said. "Gods cannot be frightened!"

"But you were!" Jim said. "Frightened of your brother. His delusions. His madness. The same madness that gripped your father, and now grips you."

"No-"

"What happened, Fleur? Did he show the wonders-the terrors-that he had discovered? A ruined city, high in the Himalayas. Evidence of a civilization destroyed by some unknown calamity. The tattered remnants of a proud people. Did they worship you?"

"He—I—" Fleur stepped back, her face twisting.

"Or did they warn you?" Jim pressed. "Did they try and stop you? Is that how Bertie died?"

"He failed," she snapped. "He died because he wasn't worthy. Five for hate, one for love. The sacrifices a king must make!" Something came over her then. A shadow, intangible and invisible. She stood straighter. More regal. "He called me there to kill me, you see...but he couldn't." She laughed, a harsh sound, like the rustling of sail cloth. "Oh, he was clever, my brother. He nursed his grudges. He hated, where other men merely disliked. The five would be easy. But the one—ah, the one—that was harder." She smoothed down the front of her coat. "I was the only one he loved, other than our father."

"He called you to Tibet to kill you, but faltered," Jim said. "Because he couldn't destroy the only thing he truly loved."

"Because he was weak! So weak." She tossed her hands. "I was so afraid of him for so long, but he was weak!"

"How did he really die?"

"I shot him. I bought a pistol, you see. And I shot him." She withdrew the Mauser he'd seen before from her coat and aimed it at Jim. "Just like I'm going to shoot you."

"You suspected-"

"I knew!" she said. "Do you think I didn't read those books? Those scrolls? I am not some illiterate society flapper, Mr. Anthony. I knew what was required, and I went willingly!" She licked her lips. The drone was louder now. A grumbling thunder that seemed to rattle the shattered windows in their frames. Jim recognized it now.

It was the sound of an airship.

"Why did you come back?" Jim said, his mind working desperately. "Why kill the others? Did you really hate them?"

"I loved my brother," she said, softly. Her eyes sparkled like new-formed ice. "If they had stopped him, like I asked them, none of this would have been necessary. But they didn't! They failed me, like all men fail!"

"Your brother-"

"Failed to kill me. So I killed him. I had to kill him, because his friends, that damnable Club, failed to stop him! Just like I had to kill our father..."

Jim's mind hit a bump and stopped, just for a moment. Then it continued on, adding the new information, building a map of a mind twisted by hate and by love into something inhuman. "Your father failed you as well."

"All men fail. Even my husband," she said. "After all, he's not here to rescue me, is he?"

"Did you really want him to be?" Jim said. Splinters snapped as his weight shifted. The Yeti snarled. Fleur gestured with the Mauser.

"Of course. I wanted to say goodbye, properly." Fleur waved a hand. "Before I left to assume my throne. I have completed the ritual. The gate is open."

"You wanted to kill him."

"I-" Fleur closed her eyes, momentarily. Hesitated. Jim moved, a quicksilver lunge, muscles rippling as he jumped for her. The Yeti was quicker.

It hit him like a freight train, slamming into the far wall, rattling the windows. Claws slashed and the bandolier fell off, but they skittered off of the armor he wore. The Yeti reared back, growling. Jim drew his knife. The Yeti darted forward, jaws wide.

Jim gritted his teeth and stabbed the knife through the Yeti's forest of teeth. The blade shattered several on its path to the creature's brain. Black blood gushed down the length of Jim's arm and drenched him. The Yeti writhed, its body refusing to die. Finally, agonizingly, it fell still. Jim wrenched his arm free and kicked the creature off. As he stood, a bullet caught him in the chest, knocking him backwards!

* * *

Jim sucked air into his lungs. Luckily, his patented bulletproof armor had saved him yet again. He lay gasping from the force of the bullet as Fleur walked towards him. The entire deck was shaking now.

"Amazing creatures, aren't they?" she said. "Hundreds of them lurk in caverns in those ancient mountains. Bertie thought they may have been on their way to being human once. He captured six of them as part of his bid to impress the Tcho-Tcho. It was said that the King in Yellow could bend the demons of the heights—the Mi-Go—to his service. Bertie did it easily enough with those delightful collars dear Franklin devised."

"That was why you used them to commit your murders," Jim gasped. "To cement yourself in their eyes. To impress the ones who might not totally hold to their old traditions."

"Proof is ever the soul of power."

"Power corrupts," Jim replied.

"I'm ahead of the game there," Fleur said. She raised the pistol. "The head, this time, I think."

"Of course. Kill me. Then what?" Jim said. He hoped it would work. It was the last card in his deck. Fleur lowered the pistol a fraction.

"What?"

"Kill me. Then kill Pike. Just like you killed your brother. Your father. The others." Jim sat up, face blank. Psychology. "Kill every man who might even have the slightest hold on you."

"What are you-"

"All your life, men have held you down. Kept in your place," Jim said, keeping his voice mild. Indifferent. "It's only natural you'd lash out. It's what women do, after all."

"What women do?" she said. "This isn't about-"

"Granted, few have ever sought to usurp the male paradigm as thoroughly as you have. 'King'. 'God'. Freud would have some things to say-"

The bullet caught him in upper chest. The armor clanked as Jim was knocked back down. He took a breath.

"I'm not insane," Fleur said sharply, drawing closer. Jim coughed.

"Of course not. You're just hysterical."

Another bullet. His armor shuddered. She was standing over him.

"Gods do not get hysterical."

"You're not a god. Just a woman."

"Definitely the head. If only because you're insulting my intelligence with this pathetic assault on my gender." She squatted and pressed the barrel of the Mauser to his skull. Jim's hand flashed up. The Mauser went flying. Fleur rose awkwardly, mouth open. Jim followed.

"For the record, you are, indeed, insane," he said. "But not because you're a woman. Because you murdered—or ordered the murder of—numerous individuals in the pursuit of ephemeral goal."

"Ephemeral?" she said. "I have seen it." Her hand swung up, wrist twisting, a thin blade sliding into her waiting palm. She lunged, burying the blade into Jim's shoulder. Jim grunted and stumbled back, Fleur clinging to him, her eyes blazing. She leaned close to him, twisting the blade.

"And no one—man, woman, or beast—will keep it from me!" she purred into his ear. She yanked the blade free and slashed it across his face, opening his cheek. Jim smashed his forearm into her belly, propelling her off of him.

She hit the deck and rolled to her feet. With a snarl worthy of the dead Yeti, she flung the blade. Jim twisted awkwardly, the pain of his wounds slowing his reaction time. The knife sailed past, and Jim fell to one knee, off balance.

Fleur took advantage of his predicament and leapt towards the shattered window closest to her. Jim experienced a moment of shock as she sailed through the gap.

"No!" he said, staggering towards the window.

Fleur shrieked with laughter as she clung to the ladder that extended from the airship that hove into view beside the Chrysler Building.

Separated by a gap of more than five feet, she gazed victoriously at Jim. Overhead, the airship's engines thundered titanically. It was a compact thing, built for durability rather than speed.

"As you can see, Bertie's airship worked fine, despite the lack of funds," she shouted over the howl of the wind. "And now, I go to claim my throne, Mr. Anthony!"

"Not if I can help it!" Jim said. He climbed up onto the window and

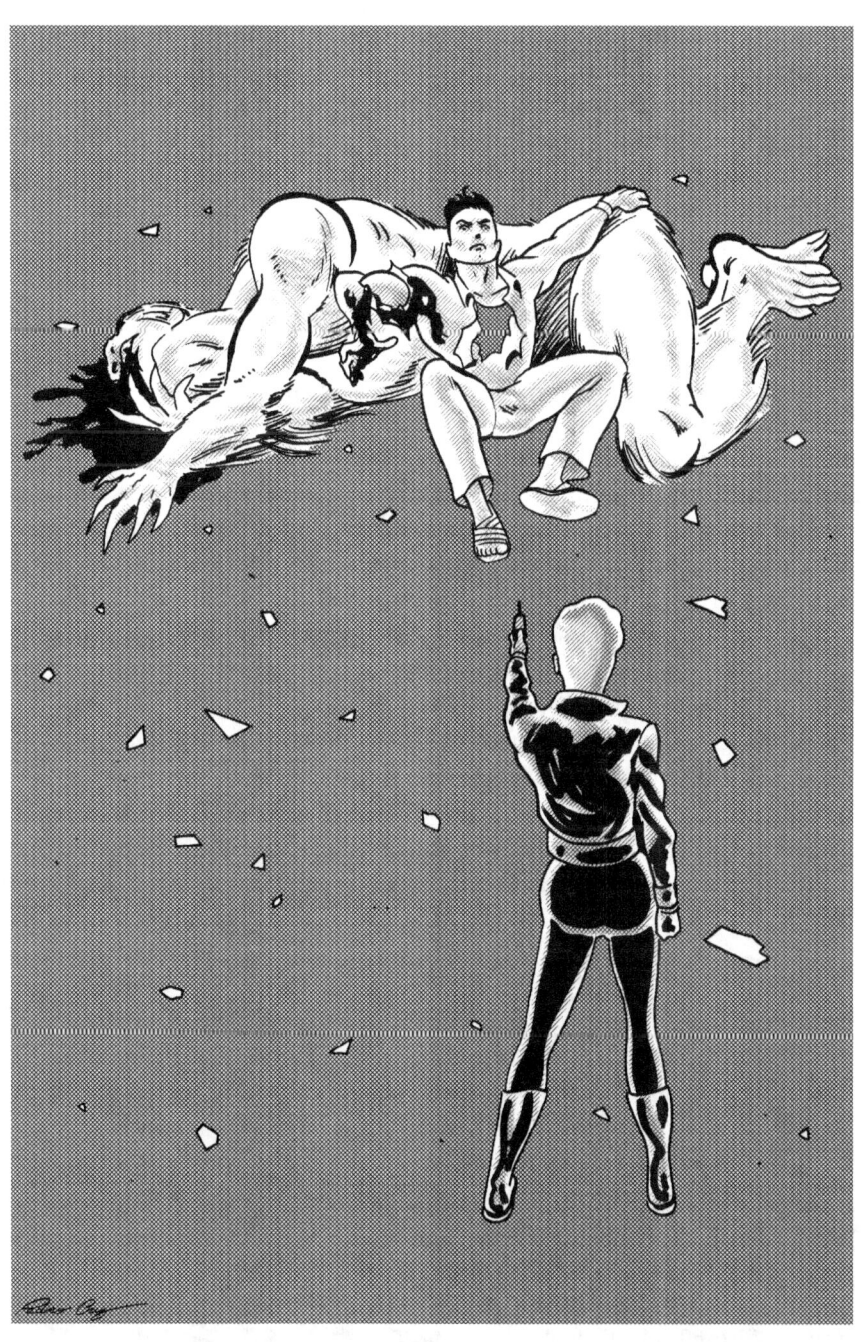

"Amazing creatures, aren't they?" she said.

sprang across the gap. Below him, the ocean of night was lit by the thousand deep stars of New York, a maelstrom of lights magnified by the reflective snow. He hit the ladder just below Fleur, his arm beginning to go numb from blood loss.

"This airship won't get far in this weather!" Jim bellowed. "You can't escape!"

"It will take me far enough, Mr. Anthony!" Her booted foot thudded down onto one of his hands. Jim ripped his hand away, fingers throbbing. "You, however, are getting off here!"

Jim didn't reply. Instead, he swung his hand up, grabbing her ankle. Fleur screeched and snarled down at him. The airship began to move, buffeted by the winds, heading away from the building. Spotlights cut through the snow, spearing the vessel. Jim began to haul himself up, slowly, refusing to give in to the pain.

"Get off! Get off!" Fleur shrieked, kicking at him. Her knee slammed into his chin and Jim momentarily saw stars. He released her and swung out over the city, hanging on only by one hand.

The airship chugged determinedly towards the harbor. Cold was seeping into Jim's pores. He felt sick. His jaw was numb. He glanced at his shoulder. Something yellow bubbled in the wound.

"Moon Blossom," he grunted. Fleur looked down at him, her classical beauty twisted into a Mephisthophelean mask.

"Of course it was poisoned, Mr. Anthony." She laughed. "How much longer can you hold on? Do you feel it yet? The moon-sickness?" She laughed again and began to climb. "I don't feel the need to stick around and watch you fall, Mr. Anthony. When you do though, give my regards to my brother and father in Hell!"

* * *

The wind screamed suddenly, picking up, rising to a devil's roar. Fleur said something, but the words were ripped away. The airship shuddered and listed.

Jim swung himself back towards the ladder, clutching for it weakly. His strength was draining away. Closing his eyes against the wind and the numbness seeping through him, he tried to marshal his remaining resources. Taking several short breaths, he brought his thoughts into sharp focus, willing himself back to alertness.

He coughed and his lungs suddenly felt heavy.

In the Amazon, there were tribesmen who could rid themselves of poison by sheer will. Jim had taken the time to study with them for a few months. In theory, he knew what to do. In practice, well, it was handy to have an antidote nearby.

Fumblingly, Jim reached into the thick belt around his waist, fingers finding the catch of the hidden, reinforced slot opposite his knife sheath. Inside, a thin vial rattled around. Plucking it free, he popped the top and tossed back the contents.

He coughed, gagged and nearly fell as a cleansing fire seemed to burn away the numbness that had flooded his system. Sweat popped all across his rangy form and his arms and legs trembled.

Nonetheless, one hand over the other, he began to climb. Above, Fleur was clinging desperately to the ladder as it whipsawed back and forth.

The airship rolled gracelessly in the steel and concrete canyon, buffeted by pressurized winds. Sparks and debris flew with a thunderous groan as the airship brushed too close to a building. Glass shattered in a continuous shriek.

It had been a good plan. The vessel had survived the conditions of the Himalayas, after all.

But New York was not Tibet.

The ladder wobbled wildly as the airship tried to scrape its way through a narrow gap. Fleur screamed in rage. She could go no further up the ladder, not without risking bodily harm. Her face swiveled down, eyes alighting on Jim as he crawled towards her, his face pale, but set.

"Why won't you die?" she shouted.

"Tell them to land!" Jim replied. "Or we could all very well die!"

"Gods don't die! They kill!" Fleur said. One handed, she shrugged out of her voluminous coat and it hurtled away, caught by the updraft. Her slender frame was clad in the same outfit she'd had on before, but it was decorated with a complicated and archaic looking harness-a veritable web of strange leather and brass clasps. Thin blades were sheathed at odd points across it, all ready to hand. Her thin fingers plucked one loose and then, with nary a sound, she allowed herself to slide down the ladder towards Jim!

Jim grunted as Fleur's weight hit him. His hand shot out, grabbing her wrist, holding the blade at bay. Normally, he would've had little difficulty in subduing her, but the poison and his awkward position made it difficult. Her face was inches from his.

"I thought about you, you know," she said, her teeth bared. "Rather than poor, foolish Franklin. But you left the country before I could so much as flirt."

"Sorry," Jim said. His arm trembled. He realized with a start that she was stronger than she looked. Much, in fact. "You wouldn't have been happy."

"Undoubtedly. I hear you have a hard time keeping it from playing tourist," she said. The blade inched closer. Overhead, there was a screech of bending metal.

"I do enjoy the company of women," Jim said. The blade pushed towards his face. Something glistened on its tip. "More poison?"

"The war harness of the King in Yellow. The leather is soaked in the juices of the Moon Blossom. Every blade in it is poisoned."

"Delightful," Jim hissed.

"Isn't it just?" she said. Her hips ground into his as she pressed herself close, suddenly. Jim was aware of the heat of her, despite himself, despite the situation. A deadly blossom was Fleur.

A sudden burst of light and heat was birthed above them. They both looked up in shock. Fire crawled across the bag of the airship. The engines groaned again, a sad, keening sound, and then, with a wail, they exploded!

"No!" Fleur screamed. With sudden savagery, she redoubled her efforts to kill Jim. He found himself fighting for all he was worth to keep the blade from his throat.

"This is your fault!" she said. "You did this! You-"

"Aren't gods omnipotent?" he said, trying to twist her wrist, to force her to release the blade. "You did this to yourself!"

Flaming chunks of debris showered them as they struggled. The airship was coming apart even as it burst clear of the concrete corridors of the city and wove ungracefully towards the icy waters of the Hudson.

Fleur's boots struck Jim's hips and he found himself falling away. He reached out desperately, grabbing the ladder with two fingers. She swung forward to meet him even as the ladder itself flew upwards, becoming parallel to the fiery ruin of the airship as it tumbled in a slow, wheeling arc towards the waters below.

At the apex of the arc, where gravity held the least sway, Jim let go. Fleur's blade hissed through the air, missing him, as he hurled himself backwards and away.

There was no time to think. No time to plan. Only instinct, an instinct honed by generations of fierce living ancestors, to guide him.

Jim twisted in the air, aligning his body, hoping that the layer of ice would be shattered by the airship's descent and heat before he hit. Arms outstretched, from a hundred and twenty feet, Jim Anthony hit the waters of the river smoothly. And then…nothing.

* * *

Jim awoke to the sensation of cold. His eyes fluttered open, only to be struck by the stabbing glare of multicolored lights. His fingers gripped the snowy bank of the river and he pulled himself up more fully out of the water. He was glad of the cold. It kept him from feeling what would most likely reveal itself as a full set of strained muscles later. Jim pushed himself up, spitting river water. He rolled onto his back and looked for the wreckage. A burning semi-pyramid was all that remained of the airship that had carried both Fleur and her brother to their destinies.

It took him several seconds to realize someone was sitting beside him.

Fingers gently probed the wound in his shoulder. He looked up into the face of a Tcho-Tcho. There was a familial resemblance to the others. The man had a round face and white hair, clipped short. The last pieces clicked into place as Jim met his eyes. Fleur's eyes. Bertie's eyes too, his sluggish memory recalled.

"Royal guard," Jim said, hoarsely. "Royal lineage."

"Yes," the man said simply. "Who better to guard kings than their own kin?"

"And when they've gone mad?"

"Who better to kill them?" the Tcho-Tcho said. "But when the king returns, we must as well."

"Returns?" Jim said. The man did not reply. Jim tried another tack. "Then the Tcho-Tcho never really left-"

"No. Only us. We exiled ourselves for our crime." He grabbed Jim's jaw and twisted his head. He blinked. "Antidote?"

"Yes."

"Smart man."

"I try." Jim looked back at the river. "Why?"

"Kings are hard to come by…" The Tcho-Tcho trailed off. "Even harder to keep satisfied."

"Your men…suicide?" Jim asked.

"Some. Others were killed when your police raided the building. And I-" He gestured. It was a mild thing, but spoke volumes.

"You came to see whether your king had passed the test." Jim said, weariness stealing the harshness from his words.

"She failed. The King is dead. Long live the king." The Tcho-Tcho stood. He smiled down at Jim and tapped the medallion that hung around his own neck. "The journey continues."

"Why did you pull me out of the water?" Jim asked.

"Why would I not?" the Tcho-Tcho said, with an eloquent shrug. Then, he turned and began to walk swiftly along the river, leaving Jim to stare after him. Soon, he was gone. Jim felt no urge to try and stop him.

For a moment, Jim found himself wondering how many of the Tcho-Tcho were left. How many of that duty-bound legion remained, scattered around the world in hiding? And whether they would go home now. Somehow, he doubted it. Who knew how many more heirs to the throne there were?

Had it all really been an elaborate game? A trap designed to weed out the recessive gene of madness in a family, to reveal the true King in Yellow to an inhumanly patient people?

Jim had a feeling he would sleep better not knowing. At least for now. Already however, part of his mind was planning to collect the maps, the clues. Pike had kept them. If Fleur hadn't surreptitiously destroyed them-

A squeal of sirens alerted him to police cars crowded the bank farther up. Fingers moved toward him, shouting questions. He had an image in his mind, of Fleur. Falling away. Disappearing beneath the dark waters. Was she dead? Few people could survive such a fall, or being dunked in icy waters. Jim was one. Was Fleur-

"Jimmy!" Tom said, sliding down beside him, grabbing him. "Somebody get an ambulance!"

"A towel will do, Tom. Maybe a cup of tea. Twist of lemon, dollop of honey, perhaps?" Jim said. He looked at his friend. "Any word from Zaroff?"

"Nope. Did you expect there to be?" Tom said. "Last I saw him, he was skedaddling off from the Waldorf-Anthony. Think he found the beastie?"

"It doesn't matter. If he didn't, what's one more monster in this city?" Jim said. Tom looked at him.

"You okay Jimmy? You look like hell."

"Nothing twenty-four hours of sleep and few stitches won't fix." Jim probed his wounded shoulder gently. "The Tcho-Tcho?" he said, making no mention of his savior.

"We got a few of them. But they were-unh-"

"Dead?"

"Yeah. The poison-"

"Of course." Jim rubbed his face. "Of course they did."

"The rest scattered-" Tom continued.

"Good." Jim nodded.

"What do you mean 'good'?" Healy snapped, coming down towards them. "Do you have any idea how hard it's going to be to track those-"

"Then don't," Jim said. "The ones who had a hand in the killings have killed themselves. The others, well, they'll disappear. Which, in its own way, is as much suicide as poison."

"What?"

"The Tcho-Tcho won't exist in a few generations. They're breeding themselves out. Blending in. Disappearing." Jim looked at the detective. It was a lie, but a necessary one. No need to start a hunt that would end in failure. Not when one man could do it much more effectively. "They tried to prevent this. But they failed. I suspect the ones who remain will take steps to ensure that such a failure does not occur again."

"What the hell are you talking about?"

"Sometimes, Camelot is best left to dreams, detective. The reality is never as satisfying."

"That dip in the river really scrambled your brains, hunh?" Healy said. "Jesus."

"I assume you're dragging the river?" Jim said. Healy snorted.

"Not until it thaws, we ain't." Healy stuffed his hat on his head. "It's going to refreeze quick, so-" He stopped and looked down at Jim. "The dame?"

"She's-"

"Jim! Jim, where's Fleur!" Pike bellowed, rushing towards the river, scattering cops with broad sweeping blows from his arms. Healy waved them away and stepped aside. "Where is she?"

"I'm sorry," Jim began. Pike's face crumbled. He fell to his knees.

"No. You promised-"

"She was dead before I got there. They killed her after they captured her, most likely," Jim said, as gently as possible. It was another lie, of course. Later, Jim would wonder whether it had been the right course of action. He would find no satisfactory answer. He would doubt as to whether there would ever be one.

"Who? Who was it?" Pike asked in a strangled voice. Jim looked out at the river, his gaze sad.

"The King," he said, finally. "It was the King in Yellow."

***

PART TWO

ON THE PERIPHERY OF LEGEND

by Micah S. Harris

"**T**his affair with these yeti, I must say Anthony, was quite something of—what is the current vulgar expression?—a 'panic.' Yes, that's it. Hunting these ape men has quickened my blood and whetted my palate for, shall we say, 'the grand entrée.'"

"And what would that be?" Jim Anthony asked, leaning back in his chair and sipping his champagne.

The two men sat in a private dining booth that looked over the dance floor of the members only speakeasy, *Old Knickerbocker's*. The member here was Jim Anthony and his dinner guest was the Russian expatriate Count Zaroff.

"Things unknown to the modern world. Creatures that are truly monstrous," the Count answered and took a drink of his vodka.

"That describes those yeti we've just finished off to a 'T,'" Anthony said.

"Formidable creatures, true; an exhilarating experience to be sure—but one which unfolded in the canyons of Gotham, Anthony," Zaroff responded. "They were not in their own element, which I maintain is necessary for a proper hunt. Further, as you demonstrated to me, these yeti were mind-controlled . . ."

"Yes," Anthony said a bit wistfully. "Dear, departed Fleur: 'the woman who would be king -- in yellow.'"

". . . so we were never pitted against the beasts left to their own instincts and cunning."

"I take it you will be off to Tibet, then?"

"Some place warmer, actually. I am speaking of big game hunting—*truly big* game."

"The most dangerous kind there is," Anthony said.

As though of its own volition, Zaroff's hand went to his face, fingers brushing gingerly the scar there. "Not quite," he said.

The two men made for a striking pair. Anthony wore white tux and black tie, long dark hair slicked back. That wild mane, despite the application of a fashionable greasing, still resisted the attempt at societal refinement. Further, the cut of his tux seemed the product of a sartorial conspiracy to emphasize his warrior's physique —broad-shouldered, muscular, lean of waist and only two generations removed from his Comanche grandfather. These apparently contradictory aspects in his countenance of the savage and the civilized were best wed in his face: keen, intelligent eyes and an aquiline nose simultaneously gave him the appearance of both a hawk and a sophist.

Dressed in black tux, his hair and beard white, Count Zaroff made a counterpoint to Jim Anthony. Or, more accurately, Jim Anthony and Zaroff were perfect and flawed versions of a single archetype. Zaroff wore refinement, as he did his tux, more comfortably than did his dining companion, yet Zaroff's propensity for yielding to unbridled passion was far greater than Jim Anthony's. Humanity, like the tux, was something that Zaroff took on, but could easily lay aside—as easily as he could take up then lay aside a rifle or bow. The mitigating compassion for his fellow human beings, present in Jim Anthony at his most savage, was absent in Zaroff. And Anthony intuited that absence had something to do with the scar slashed across his companion's face.

Still, there was a quality of greatness about Zaroff—a ruined greatness, like a bombed-out cathedral which Anthony had once picked through in the wake of the Great War; now he found himself picking over Zaroff, desperate to discover there was still something there that would justify redemption of the whole.

"Hiya, Tarzan," a peroxide blonde with arched, dark brows crooned as she glided in high heels by Anthony's booth, her willowy figure amply displayed in backless evening gown. Her fingers involuntarily arched, polished red nails sinking into her clutch: clearly, she longed to sink them instead into Jim Anthony's broad back. He smiled. "Evening, Madeline," he responded, raising his glass. But it was Zaroff whose steady gaze trailed her across the dancing floor.

"Zaroff," Anthony said, an undertone of caution in his voice. "I was under the impression it was a different sort of game you were talking about pursuing."

"Only now, with my blood still astir from the hunt, can I seek love, Anthony," Zaroff responded. "Every savage instinctively understands this equation."

Intent on his new prey, Zaroff rose and began to move across the dance floor. Unlike Zaroff, the couples there chose to express their desire by this socially approved ritual of sexual pursuit; the present form the ritual took was something called *The New Yorkers* as performed by Red Nichols and His Five Pennies. Anthony realized any attempt on his part to restrain Zaroff from his amorous pursuit would be resisted robustly, so he allowed him to go forth unchallenged and attempt to pitch woo. And though that accent may intrigue her in a seductive-foreigner way, like that Lugosi fellow was currently doing for the ladies at the cinema, the first and last word was that Zaroff was simply too old for Maddy's tastes.

Anthony pitied Zaroff. For all his talk of the savage nature of sex, it was clear that a woman of some refinement and polish was necessary for his satisfaction. He did not look forward to what kind of scene there might be when Maddy rebuffed the Count's advances.

"Relax," Anthony told himself. "Even Zaroff can't get away with hitting her over the head with a club. Not here."

"You should be more careful with whom you associate," a voice suddenly announced.

Anthony startled. Usually his almost preternatural senses alerted him to a hidden presence. He found himself looking at the back of a similarly white-tuxedo clad figure, tall and slim. Anthony tensed; how long had the man been there, right in front of him?

"Who are yo—" Anthony began, but the stranger was already walking across the floor, heading for Zaroff.

It looked like trouble had found Zaroff before he could find Madeline. Anthony could not get a good look at the man's face. When he addressed Zaroff, the Russian didn't appear to recognize him—at least at first. But a pass of the stranger's ringed hand before Zaroff's face and recognition instantly lit in his eyes.

Amorous pursuit was suddenly aborted as a sobered Zaroff seemed compelled to produce on his watch fob a small wooden case with the design of a cross carved into it. Zaroff opened it, then folded out a miniature triptych. Anthony could see two of the panels: a Byzantine Christ on one and Mary holding the infant Christ on the other. But it was the far right panel that concerned both Zaroff and the man who had approached him; it was also the one panel Anthony could not see. Then the triptych was folded back up in its casing and returned to Zaroff's pocket. Some sort of understanding had passed between the two men, something Anthony could not discern. Zaroff clicked his heel, made a curt bow, and then began walking back to the dining booth.

The mysterious man continued on across the dance floor. It was only then that Anthony got a momentarily look of the stranger's face in profile. Though he couldn't recall the name, Anthony recognized Zaroff's acquaintance as a globetrotting sportsman himself. Perhaps a disgruntled competitor of Zaroff's who bore a grudge?

"Who was that?" Anthony asked as Zaroff sat down, poured himself a new glass of vodka and downed it with one swallow, wiping his mouth with the back of his hand. The look in his eyes was fevered, and Anthony realized that he was seeing something there that's unfamiliar presence had succeeded in disconcerting Zaroff.

"You're afraid," Anthony said. "Actually afraid."

"Bah!" Zaroff grunted, waving him off with one hand as he poured another glass of vodka. There was now anger in his eyes, aimed at Anthony for daring to say to his face what Zaroff knew himself was the truth.

Then the anger was gone, his eyes suddenly cool, the glass of vodka halted on its way to his mouth and returned to the table.

"Answer me, Zaroff," Anthony repeated, leaning forward. "I've seen you staring down a charging rhino while you emptied a magazine into it. You barely broke a sweat. What possible sort of threat does a mere rival sportsman pose to you?"

"A 'sportsman?' That's his—what do you say? 'Story?' That's his story? Well, perhaps he is . . . now. But in Russia, before the Bolsheviks rose up, he, as I, was part of an elite inner circle constructed around the Czar. I did not recognize his face, but we were made known to each other in the exchanging of the signs."

"His ring and that icon you pulled from your pocket?"

"Allardravitch was the best of us. And now he has become the worst. It is the way of things, that the more brilliant the light, the darker the shadow."

"What has he done?"

"Betrayed his sacred trust! He now is one of them, one of the Communists. Or their pawn."

"But he's an American."

"Don't be naïve, Anthony. His citizenship is what makes him an ideal agent for the Reds."

"What hash does he have to settle with you? The revolution was a success—the Reds won."

"Exactly. When I saw the way the winds were blowing I absconded with a goodly sum of my fortune—a fortune that now belongs to the people, according to Allardravitch's new masters."

"So he is here to collect from you, then?"

"He will try. Listen, Anthony: it was my intent to issue you an invitation this evening before Allardravitch injected himself afresh into my affairs. His presence, however, means there is no time for you to weigh your options. You may be sure that you will be unlikely to have the opportunity again to hunt such game as I offer."

"I take it you would have me join you on this safari you were mentioning earlier?"

"I will make no pretensions of sentimental attachment," Zaroff replied. "But you are my peer in woodcraft. To hunt with such a man is a rare privilege, and I desire much that you should hunt with me, Anthony."

"I'm honored by your esteem, of course," Anthony said. Zaroff slightly bowed his head in response.

"My yacht is docked in the harbor," Zaroff said. "With Allardravitch lurking about, we would be best advised to quit the club and head there immediately."

"And from there, *where* exactly? I'm intrigued, Zaroff, and I understand the immediacy of your situation, but I have to know more. Where do we go to hunt? "

Zaroff smiled. "An uncharted island, far west of Sumatra. Once there we shall drop off the map—quite literally and, to be honest, for an indefinite period of time."

"Isn't that extreme?"

"You must understand that if Allardravitch is looking for me in New York, no doubt the Reds have agents all over the globe. On this island alone will be safer than my own."

"So the rumors are true; you *do* have a secret island."

Zaroff leaned back and templed his fingers. "Yes, a base where are stored the art treasures, icons, diamonds, and gold I took with me from Russia. I would be a fool to run there straight away and risk the possibility that I might lead Allardravitch directly to what he and his masters seek. The island that *I* am speaking of is one of which no one living has heard, not even by rumor. But should Allardravitch succeed in following us, the island itself will rise up and eliminate him."

"If it would eliminate Allardravitch, then why not us?" Anthony asked.

"As formidable as he is in the urban milieu of intrigue in which he thrives, Allardravitch could not possibly be our equal in the wilds. I do not say that the risks are not great, even for us two together, but they are not impossible. You see, Anthony," Zaroff leaned forward, "the jungle we would penetrate is truly primeval, as no other on this planet. Prehistoric animals still inhabit it."

Anthony's jaw dropped. "Dinosaurs?"

"Among other forms of atavism, yes."

Anthony, of course, was startled by Zaroff's revelation. The idea of dinosaurs surviving into the twentieth century was a pet theory of his own. Darwin's account of Galapagos had certainly established the survival of isolated species. Why shouldn't dinosaurs have survived? The crocodile, their contemporary, was still hale and hearty. The chance to study as well as hunt the legendary thunder lizards was an opportunity that he found heady.

Still, he had to ask the Russian: "You're serious?"

"When have I ever not been when discussing hunting? I have complete confidence in my source. Now you understand what I meant by 'big game.'"

"Dinosaurs . . ." Anthony's voiced trailed off with the thought.

"My yacht is already loaded with sufficient provisions, and is a veritable armory afloat, filled with such weaponry needed to bring down these brutes. Do you understand now the magnitude of this opportunity, Anthony? But I make it only this once, and I dare tarry no longer. I must have your answer *now*."

"Relax, Zaroff. The situation is not as urgent as you think. In fact, if we are to successfully elude your friend Allardravitch, we should begin by staying put."

Anthony picked up a menu and started perusing it. "What are you going to have? I'm thinking Peking duck."

Zaroff's eyes narrowed as he regarded Anthony, then took up his own menu and began looking over it. "What is your plan?" he asked.

"I take it you would have me join you on this safari you were mentioning earlier?" Jim said.

"It's possible this Allardravitch is already aware of where your yacht is moored. He will know the minute we step from the club, and, if he isn't right behind us,we may be certain he will meet us at the dock. You *do* have a wireless on board?"

"Certainly."

Still looking over the menu, Anthony slowly shook his head from side to side. Then he placed the menu down and looked up. "Waiter!" Anthony called, beckoning with one hand while pulling a pen and notepad from an inner coat pocket. He began scribbling something down.

"Are you ready to order, sir?"

"Yes—the Peking duck. But there's something else I'm not finding on the menu," Anthony said, tearing a sheet of paper free of the pad. "Care to help a gentleman out to the tune of fifty dollars?"

"Indeed, sir."

"Will you deliver this to the man in the gray, pinstriped suit sitting at that table for one over by the potted palm tree?"

"The one drinking milk, sir?"

"Ovaltine. Yes.His name is Tom. Go to the kitchen first, though, and see if his order is done. Probably a Dagwood sandwich. Intercept his waiter; here's a ten spot that should more than adequately compensate him for the tip Then *you* deliver my note on Tom's plate and tell him this is from Jimmy.. Then I want you to go back to the kitchen. Put on your coat, hat and galoshes and take the kitchen exit to the parking lot. You'll need to roll one of your serving carts out there. Tom will meet you and direct you to our car.I want you to put what Tom gives you on the bottom shelf of the cart. Roll it back into the kitchen, drape it with a table cloth so that it veils what's on its bottom shelf—don't let any other of the help see what you're delivering to me if you can."

"Take off your hat, overcoat and galoshes; brush off any residual snow on your person and the cart. Then put the largest Peking duck you have in the kitchen on top of the cart and deliver it to us, as though you are just coming from the kitchen with our supper. Leave the cart with us in our booth and pull the folding doors behind you. Then forget about this side trip. Are you game?"

"Indeed, sir. At once."

"Exactly what game are you playing, Anthony?" Zaroff asked as the waiter departed.

"The one we're both playing, Zaroff. I assume you play to win?"

"Always."

"We need to get a message to your captain, but I'm sure your yacht is being watched just as we are. So, we can't go ourselves or even send a messenger because Allardravitch will be on top of us or him in an instant. Still, your captain has to get word to weigh anchor and set sail immediately. Without us."

"What? I think not! I've told you what I have on that ship—it is necessary for the hunt."

"They're setting off without us, Zaroff. While we, in fact, remain here in the club—enjoying our repast. Relax. We are still taking your yacht to the island."

Zaroff cocked his head. "You intend that we should overtake my boat at some later point. Is that it?"

"No need to overtake it. I'm going to send them out of the harbor and to my secret Long Island pier. We'll shake Allardravitch and then meet up with them there."

"And you think Allardravitch cannot discover this location?"

"Impossible. No one knows of its existence but Tom and now you. Don't fill up on bread, Zaroff. Trust me: you want to have plenty of room for this bird I'm talking about."

Twenty-five minutes later, the waiter rolled the draped cart with the Peking duck to Anthony's booth.

"Dinner is served," Anthony announced with a smile. Despite the cold, the waiter was sweating. He had earned his fifty Depression era dollars: what he was rolling was heavy and unwieldy. Anthony leaned in, removing the lid from the serving tray to reveal a succulent drake. Returning the covering, he smiled up at the waiter and handed him a fifty-dollar bill.

"One more thing," he said. "There is a man with a prominent nose and a white tux about the premises. Please keep an eye on him and inform me if he leaves the restaurant. Here's an extra fifty for your trouble."

"Yes sir."

Anthony then handed him a hundred dollar bill. "And here's another hundred if you, uhm, 'clean up after us.' When we've gone, store this apparatus you've brought somewhere secure and wait for my pal Tom to contact you. And close the booth's partition as you go, please. Thank you."

The waiter nodded his head in agreement. Then, as instructed, he slid closed the partition, granting the desired privacy.

Anthony easily lifted the 15-pound roasted bird in its tray and put it aside. Now he threw back the covering, revealing what the waiter had brought them under Allardravitch's prominent nose: an unwieldy cabinet of radio tubes, a large battery, a coil-wrapped nail, and the rest of the mechanical elements that together made a wireless telegraph.

"You carry a portable wireless in your car?" Zaroff asked.

"It can be useful to have mobile communication in real time. Also, I can monitor police transmissions if I need to," Anthony said as he began unrolling a spool of wire that he took from the cart.

"I'm certain Allardravitch has the same capability at hand and can monitor your transmission."

"Doubtful. This machine has been modified according to my own design which I extrapolated from Tesla's theories. Anyway, he would have to know your particular frequency. Let's see . . . the harbor's only about fifteen miles away. An antenna of thirty feet should do." Anthony rolled off some more wire from the spool.

Zaroff cast a glance up at the ceiling. "You're about ten feet short."

"I'm not going up; I'm going *around*," Anthony said as got up and laid the wire in a large loop around their booth's floor. Then he broke it off from the spool and connected that end to the transmitter lug.

"What frequency is your wireless tuned to?" he asked Zaroff.

"Three hundred kilocycles."

Anthony began sorting through several small chunky metal boxes, each containing a crystal lathed to a different oscillation. Zaroff watched with interest as Anthony picked one and inserted it into the machinery in the cabinet.

"And I assume you have an alias you use?" Anthony asked.

"Yes. Be certain you introduce your missive as coming from 'Mr. Banks.'"

Anthony began tapping the key.

"Tell me, Anthony," Zaroff asked. "Why not just go to the wireless instead of going to such elaborate contrivance to have it brought to you?"

"Once we step outside, I suspect things will start happening fast. There simply won't be time to give the yacht the needed lead time which staying here will buy us. And besides, I've been looking forward to this duck all day."

Message sent, Anthony covered the wireless with the tablecloth and retrieved the roasted main entrée. Taking his knife and fork, he began to carve. "As I figure it, we should allow thirty minutes for your yacht to be at my pier when we arrive there.

"Eat up, Zaroff," he said. "I have a feeling it will be some time before either of us tastes a civilized meal again."

* * *

A half hour later, bundled in long coats, scarfs, and Stetson hats against the snow blowing through Manhattan streets abandoned to the winter evening, Jim Anthony and Zaroff made for Anthony's sedan.

Anthony opened one of the car's back doors, allowing Zaroff to slide across the seat. Once inside, Anthony addressed his best friend who sat behind the wheel.

"Evening, Tom," he said. "Looks like we've got a Red on our tail that we're going to have to shake."

"Well, there's a surprise," Tom said, turning and glowering at Zaroff, "considering the company you've been keeping lately. Guess you're glad now I wouldn't break bread with your new pal on general principle that I don't eat with killers —"

"Easy, Tom."

"—or I would've been pretty conspicuous leaving the dining booth to do your bidding." Tom shut his eyes, shook his head, and let out a heavy sigh. Then, rubbing his eyelids, he turned back to the car wheel.

"Where to, Jimmy?"

"Our secret pier."

Tom looked into the rearview mirror, his expression one of sheer incredulity. "You're trusting *him* with the location?"

"*Go*, Tom."

The sedan's wipers whispered to life, shifting to the side the snow that had piled on the windshield. Then Tom was pulling out of the parking lot. They were barely on the road when a limousine emerged from *Old Knickerbocker's* parking lot as well and headed after them.

"Allardravitch," Anthony said, watching in the rearview mirror. "I suppose he would have given us more of a lead if the snow wasn't blowing curtains between us. Speed up, Tom."

He did as ordered. Anthony continued to watch in the rearview. As expected, the limousine sped up as well.

"Press it to the floor, Tom—looks like he's making a bid to apprehend us right *now*."

The pursuing limousine came alongside Anthony's sedan. Standing on the running board, a dark figure under a hood, his black cloak billowing about him in the bitter rushing wind. He pulled a gun from within the folds of his cloak and took aim . . .

"Allardravitch!" Zaroff snarled.

Anthony was already reaching for his own pistol holstered under his arm, but not before Allardravitch fired into the front tire on the driver's side. Then he seemed to be gliding backward as the car carrying him slowed. At that same moment, Anthony's car swerved across the road toward a lengthy cement road-divider raised by a construction crew. Anthony realized Allardravitch had had his driver decelerate so that his car wouldn't collide with Anthony's sedan when it veered.

His muscles straining to maintain control over the vehicle, Tom gripped the wheel, and instead of smashing the front of the car into the divider, he brought it along side it. Using it as a ramp, he leaned the car over on the two wheels of the passenger's side, lessening a bit the encumbering of the flopping millstone that was the driver's side front wheel. Now Tom peeled off the concrete barrier, and, still driving on the passenger's side wheels, brought the car back into the proper lane.

"Tom!" Anthony shouted, struggling not to slide down on to Zaroff. "Find an alley and back into it."

"You don't ask for a lot, do you, Jimmy?" Tom yelled back, grimacing with the effort of maintaining the balance to keep from turning them over on the tops of their heads. Meanwhile, Allardravitch was again gaining on them.

Anthony saw an alley coming up on the other side of the road. He knew they would have this one opportunity to regain back any control over the situation.

"Tom!" he shouted. "Go back on four wheels --!"

"I get you, Jimmy!"

The resulting swerve took them again into the other lane. But this time it was according to design—the safety barrier had run out, so the nose of the car ran into the curb. Jimmy switched to reverse at the moment of impact, stripping the gears, but, bouncing the sedan off the curb, he brought the vehicle around by the one front wheel of which he retained control, placing the automobile's rear end into the alley as Anthony had ordered. Stuck in neutral, Tom through sheer will and the remaining momentum carried them halfway back up the alley, the sedan banging off its walls.

Allardravitch swooped in like a large black bird, jumping from the running board but forced to retreat because of the blinding glare of Anthony's automobile lights. They had reached a stalemate—at least, until the car's battery died. Allardravitch smiled. He could wait.

After long silent moments, Allardravitch heard a mechanical phlegm-hacking, choking, gasping—and then a motor took to chugging life, and a sudden revolving swirl of motion appeared in the air —

Anthony and Zaroff were rising from the alley's floor in Anthony's compact one-man gyrocopter, which had recently made its maiden voyage to the top of the Chrysler building. While the car lights had held Allardravitch at bay, Anthony had unloaded the flying contraption from the trunk, strapping Zaroff into the harness designed for use in rescue missions.

In a moment, they were clearing the alley's walls. And in that moment they were most vulnerable, for, once they were clear of the sedan's lights, Allardravitch could draw a bead and fire. Already his gun was raised, taking his aim --

A bullet sped up the alley, striking Allardravitch's firearm and sending his gun flying from his hand. Walking up the alley and out of the headlights glare strode Tom, his pistol aimed at his and his best friend Anthony's current nemesis. Allardravitch did not flinch but gripped his arm—which, despite the ache, was not bleeding but bruised. He was using mercy bullets. Allardravitch suddenly had an understanding of his new adversary. Jim Anthony was compassionate. A compassionate fool. The worst kind.

Allardravitch smiled beneath his hood . . .

Then the sedan's headlights failed, the car's battery spent, and the shadows owned the night.

* * *

Lifted into the blowing snow, Anthony and Zaroff felt wet flake after wet flake striking their bare faces. Zaroff could close his eyes and tuck his head, but Anthony was piloting and had to endure the repeated cold sting of the frozen precipitation, constantly blinking flakes from his eyelashes. The end of his nose was frozen, swollen to a puffy red he'd only seen before on the life-long, hard drinkers of the Irish side of his family.

The lights of Manhattan below were smothered beneath the layer of thick clouds. Veils of snow swirled tauntingly about the two men, draping then undraping them. But soon Anthony had made it high enough to be out of the thick of the precipitation and thus able to see the stars and navigate.

They had been in the air for almost twenty minutes when Anthony plunged them down through the clouds. They were over woodland and fields piling with snow. If Anthony had been looking for landmarks, the landscape was now altered, but he still seemed to know where he was going. Now a pine-lined shore came into view; stretching out from it was a long wooden pier, and just sailing up to it was Zaroff's yacht.

"Well done, Anthony," he shouted out.

Anthony brought them down onto the pier, and they disengaged themselves from their harnessing. As the yacht was mooring and Anthony was folding up the mini-gyrocopter in preparation for storing it, Zaroff already was striding down the pier.

Anthony had locked the gyro in the shed where his own speedboat was docked and was briskly walking to join Zaroff on board the yacht when he heard the *thrum-thrum-thrum* of what sounded like another gyrocopter—

He twirled around, looked up, and saw the black, flapping shape in the air, blades spinning above it. In another instance, the figure was descending, coming to land on the pier . . .

"Zaroff! It's Allardravitch!" Anthony shouted. The Count looked from the deck of his yacht, visibly stunned, then ducked below.

Anthony knew there was no point in running for the yacht. Should they succeed in casting off, Allardravitch would overtake them before they were beyond the range of his mini-gyrocopter. Instead, Anthony reached into his coat, took out his gun, and strode up the pier.

Allardravitch landed, his black cloak flapping about him, his red scarf making a scarlet slash across his chin like a bloody maw under his hood. In a quick gesture, he discarded the goggles he had worn, and then, in the same motion, the black gloved hand produced a gun from the cloak's folds. He began walking toward Anthony.

The two men stopped within ten feet of each other, guns drawn.

"Nice one-man gyrocopter," Anthony said. "My patent is pending, by the way."

"I warned you about the company you keep," Allardravitch said in a tone as cold and sharp as that of a steel chisel striking a sepulchre stone.

"How did you find us?"

"Your chauffeur told me."

Anthony tensed, his hand tightening on his gun. "What did you do to Tom?"

"I simply explained things to him. It seems he doesn't approve of your new friend either. His opinion was even worse when I confirmed what Zaroff has been up to on his private island."

"And what did you tell Tom about what *you're* up to, Allardravitch?"
Anthony thought he could discern a smile under the hood.

"Is that who Zaroff told you I was?"

"Are you denying it?"

"No. It's just I haven't heard that name in a very long time."

"What do your current Red masters call you, then?"

Allardravitch laughed—a sound that sent a chill over Anthony, even when it seemed the weather could not be more freezing. "It is *I* who am the master, Anthony."

"I don't care who you are or *what* your role is in all this. Do you understand me? You're not taking him."

"Why do you protect him? Do you know what he's done?"

"I've only heard rumors. Unless you can produce something to substantiate them, then it's just Rainsford's ravings and your word against Zaroff's."

"I have a clear sense of who's lying and who's not, Anthony."

"And I have no reason to trust you or your instincts. Only my own."

"And what are they telling you?"

"There's something worth redeeming in the man."

"He can be 'rehabilitated'?" Allardravitch said caustically. "A leopard can't change its spots."

"He might," Anthony said. "I suspect I will know by the end of our voyage. And if I discover what you're telling me is true, and he can't be reformed . . . only one of us will be making the trip back home."

"How will you do it? Do you plan to dispatch him with one of your mercy bullets?" Allardravitch sneered sarcastically and nodded at Anthony's own gun.

"Don't mistake me for the bronze man, Allardravitch. I've used hot lead when the situation required it."

A wild, strangely familiar roaring sounded down the pier. Anthony looked over his shoulder to see a white shaggy ape creature, propelling itself toward them on its hind legs and one forearm, the other arm raised against its breast.

Yeti!

Clearly, Zaroff had not dispatched the last one as he had led Anthony to believe. Anthony raised his gun and fired at the beast, as did Allardravitch.

The yeti did not slow down. Thrusting Anthony aside, its formidable weight slammed into Allardravitch, momentum carrying them both off the pier and into the freezing waters.

"Anthony! Come!" Zaroff shouted from the yacht.

Anthony glanced at the struggling forms bobbing up in the water that seethed with their struggle. He ran to the one-man autogyro, quickly thrusting his hands about the engine. Not completely the same as his own design, but close enough. In a few moments he had disabled the craft and then tossed it into the water over the other side of the pier.

Then he sped toward the yacht. "Cast off!" he shouted.

The boat was already out a good five feet from the pier when he reached it: easy enough space for Anthony to clear with the run he had behind him. He landed on the deck. As he suspected, Zaroff held the remote control device that Fleur had used to control the beasts she had unleashed on them and their fellow members of the Baltimore Rifle Club. He snatched it from Zaroff's hand, but before he could call the Yeti off Allardravitch, Zaroff shouted:

"Look!"

A soaked black figure was wading ashore, dragging a white shaggy one that was limp and still. His guns rendered worthless from their dip in the river, Allardravitch used his bare hands to twist the creature's head around from behind, snapping its neck. Any threat the yeti represented to him was over; any threat Allardravitch had been to to Zaroff had also now passed. Anthony had left him effectively stranded: were he able to break into the boathouse, he didn't have the ignition key of his speedboat or his mini-autogyro. He could, however, dry off to avoid catching pneumonia. Once they were far enough out to sea, he would radio Tom to come after him. Though he suspected by that time, Allardravitch would have extricated himself somehow.

Anthony turned angrily to Zaroff.

"What were you keeping a yeti around for?" he demanded. "And where did you get this?" he shook the control device at him.

"When I found the creature, it had an injured forepaw from a fall it had taken into an alley. I would have no pleasure in taking my prey under those conditions. I tranquilized it in hopes of healing it and eventually returning it to its natural habitat in Tibet, to hunt it there. When it was unconscious, I noticed that interesting collar about its neck. You explained what it was for, remember? When we met up at your penthouse after our adventure,and you showed me this remote control device. A quick survey of your laboratory while you were indisposed disclosed where you had stored it."

"You stole this from me, Zaroff?" Anthony asked, his tone indignant.

"As I recall, it wasn't your property either, Anthony," Zaroff responded coolly and lit up a cigarette. "Besides, what use would you have for it?"

"How long before you were going to tell me we had a yeti on board?"

"Technically, the proper, Tibetan classification is 'mi-go' . . ."

" 'Mi-go' then! When were you going to tell me about it? And how long were you planning to keep the yet -- 'mi-go!' -- in the hold? Until our dinosaur hunt is done? Then—what? We're off to Tibet? I didn't sign up for that, Zaroff!"

"The creature would have been transferred to other accommodations before our safari began," Zaroff said calmly.

"Where --?" Anthony began. Then he winced with realization: "Your private island. We were going to stop off there en route? I thought you didn't wish to risk leading Allardravitch to it."

Zaroff smiled. "I had confidence in your ability to outwit him. Of course, I had not planned sacrificing my mi-go, but it was evident a stand-off had developed on the pier. How could I have possibly turned my back on you after what you've done for me, Anthony?

"Now, I have dry clothes for you. Come."

* * *

The next two weeks at sea were more than leisurely compared to how their voyage began. To combat boredom, Zaroff had had a skeet device rigged to his yacht, and he and Anthony would fling clay pigeons over the sea and shoot in a competition that would always end in a tie. They also engaged in some deep-sea fishing, something that Zaroff had to school Anthony in, but which he quickly learned to relish: the adrenaline rushing moment with the rapid clack and whir of his line as it sped out to sea, the exultation of the taut pull of a leaping, bright marlin against his own straining muscles. At times, he thought of the rod as bending like a dowsing tool taken to violent life, wanting to abandon his grasp and go off to be one with the power it had discovered, a power humming through the line and up Anthony's arms as he maneuvered second by second to achieve and maintain the precise mix of dominance and grace it took to handle his catch.

At other times, he thought of the rod as a conductor's wand that arched and bent, come to rebellious life with the music as he attempted to direct a symphony that defied him, a wild music that sought to retain mastery of its own fate, threatening to charge madly and forever away from him at any moment.

When he or Zaroff had brought a large fish to the deck, its thrashing—and jousting, if it were a swordfish—put them in danger. Zaroff, to avoid the hazards of the giant fish wildly flogging the wooden deck, its body a living lashing barber's strap, would fire a bullet into its brain and end the threat. This coup de grace bothered Anthony. To have to go in and slit the fish while it went through its paroxysms, to risk a hard slap to the jaw, seemed more honorable somehow, somehow more fair to the fish. When he tried to explain this to Zaroff, he dismissed him with a contemptible "bosh."

"I suppose you would rather lose an eye?" he asked. "The creature would sooner see you maimed and dead yourself in its struggle for survival. I hope you do not plan to deal with the dinosaurs we shall hunt with such 'fairness.' It doesn't exist in the wild, Anthony."

"I know that, Zaroff. I'm not naïve. But even in the wild, we can't abandon our human qualities that set us apart from the rest of nature."

They were sitting in the comfortable padded leather lounge chairs in the yacht's combination library and den. From the gramophone, Pachelbell's *Canon D* played. The shelves were lined with classics: a quick scan revealed Dickens *A Tale of Two Cities*, Dostoysky's *Crime and Punishment*, Tolstoy's *War and Peace, Marcus Aurelius—The Complete Works*, and some volumes from more contemporary writers: Bierce, London, and Crane.

"Look around you, Zaroff, at the library you've built here," Anthony said. "Think of the music you're listening to: these are the finest products of our race; art is evidence that we have a higher dimension to our existence beyond mere nature."

"I am not unaware that culture has a unique significance. But art is a delicate treasure, hard won and to be preserved over the ages. I surrounded myself with it, even when *in* the wild, in such a little pocket of civilization as you see here. But the reality is that we are out on a sea that without discernment would dash us against the rocks and with us all this art and literature. It is not malicious: it is just the sea. Neither am I malicious, Anthony, when I take up the rifle and bow. I become but a force of nature within nature. At such times, I leave civilization behind completely—all the better that I may live to return and enjoy again its boons."

By the beginning of the third week at sea, they were on the ocean off the West coast of Malaya. Anthony, clad only in shorts under the sun, was enjoying another bout of deep-sea fishing. The South Sea's morning sunshine was making him pleasantly drowsy, as though he'd already put in a hard day and was enjoying the reward of a rest. He was thus relaxed when

To combat boredom, Zaroff had had a skeet device rigged to his yacht...

the fishing rod leapt from his hand and onto the deck, bounding toward the side. Anthony caught it at the penultimate moment, and the fight was joined.

He was suddenly very awake. It was a robust struggle and every cell of Anthony's body felt galvanized by the bout. He, however, was not prepared for what he pulled from the sea—and out of the past.

"Get over here, Zaroff!" he shouted.

For once, Anthony saw true spontaneous surprise form over the Russian's countenance at the creature's appearance. The large, still thrashing thing was eel-like, with a frightening jaw and large black eyes that were wild, ghastly. Anthony recognized it at once.

"This is a coelacanth," he announced, grinning widely. "They're extinct. *Supposed* to be. Are you seeing this, Zaroff? Prehistoric life still existing along with us on this planet. How far away are we from the island?"

"Close, obviously. Consider this beast but first fruits, Anthony. Bit of an ugly brute, isn't it?"

Anthony looked away from Zaroff and back down at the coelacanth. There were tears in his eyes, as though he had just encountered a unicorn in the woods. Zaroff flicked his cigarette butt into the sea and began walking back to the side of the yacht where he would return to his own fishing.

"A loss of the capacity for wonder," Anthony noted under his breath as he looked after his companion. "You worry me, Zaroff," he muttered. Then he cut the line with his knife, and dodging the paroxysms of the coelacanth, managed to take hold of it in his muscular arms, and toss it back into the ocean.

A sharp, keening whistle suddenly demanded the attention of all on board. It was then that Anthony and Zaroff first noticed the large ship in the distance.

Zaroff was peering at it through a small, hand held telescope when Anthony ran up to him. "See anything interesting?" he asked.

"Hmmph," Zaroff shrugged, passed him the spyglass, and lit up a fresh cigarette. "The usual. Merchant vessel, I suppose."

Looking through the glass, Anthony could make out the vessel's name painted on the hull: *Venture*

"Where could they be headed?" he wondered aloud. "I thought there was nothing around here for miles—except this secret mystery island." He lowered the spyglass and looked at his companion. "I thought no one else knew about it, Zaroff. Instead, it looks like another contingent for a convention is showing up."

"They could not possibly be aware of it," Zaroff said. "I have the only copy of the map and handwritten journal of the 16th century missionary who was the first white man to ever travel there."

"How do you know that? Where exactly did you come across these items?"

"I obtained them during a Black Forest hunting trip I took before the Great War. An old German I met put me up in his lodge—his name was Lidenbrock. He told me of encountering prehistoric animals on an expedition he took with his uncle many years earlier."

"To the island?"

"No. He claimed to have visited the center of the earth, believe it or not. The route there which he described would make it impossible to mount a proper safari. But his uncle, when he was nearing death, told him of a previous, aborted attempt to enter the earth's core, through an opening on an island described by this missionary to Malaya. That ingress was sealed, but not before creatures had migrated through it and populated this island. I traded the man's nephew my best rifle for the missionary's map and diary ..."

"*That* was your only evidence?"

". . . and an unfossilized dinosaur femur his uncle had brought back from the island. It matched perfectly that of an Allosaurus skeleton in the Royal Museum."

Anthony nodded toward the ship. "I'd still like to know what they're doing out here."

"Don't lose your focus, Anthony. It is better that we keep our distance, to take no chance of slipping knowledge of the island's existence to these people."

"I think I know how to keep my mouth shut, Zaroff. No offense, but after two weeks of seeing only your and your crews' mugs—it's starting to get monotonous."

By now, the *Venture's* crew should have spotted them as well. But as the yacht loomed nearer, there was still no sign of activity on board—the impression was that they had discovered a ghost ship adrift. This naturally intrigued Anthony more. Was this another *Marie Celeste*?

Then a shriek: a shrill, clear soprano, clearly that of a woman.

"Okay, Zaroff," he said. "We're checking this out."

Zaroff was now himself compelled to draw in closer. Through the spyglass they finally saw men aboard. Their backs were turned away from the sea to something that was happening on deck.

A man was cranking a large camera on its tripod. He was shooting through a pane of glass, which, though Anthony could not see the details, was partially painted over with a scene of temple ruins overrun with vines, trees and overgrowth.

Anthony was more interested in the subject of this shoot anyway, who stood between the glass and a canvas back drop painted blue with clouds.

Doubtless, she was the one who had screamed. Anthony, who had not seen a woman for half a month, made an eager appraisal: long, slim legs and full, firm breasts that rose under a doeskin brassiere. Her bare midriff exposed a tiny waist that curved out, rounding her hips under a loincloth of the same doeskin. Her skin was pale, but healthily so, a glimmering pale flushed with pink; her long blond hair in a wildly abandoned coiffure foamed from under a bejeweled headdress and over her shoulders.

"What has you so entranced, Anthony?" Zaroff asked. Anthony reluctantly passed the glass to him. He knew the moment Zaroff saw the girl: his lips parted with an involuntary in-drawing of breath.

"She looks like she could play Odette on the stage," he said, admiring her long limbs and elegant neck.

Perhaps we should just sail on by at that . . . Anthony thought.

But then, one of the sailors turned and noticed the yacht.

"Hey!" he shouted, pointing. "Look!"

Now all attention turned from the shoot—including that of the girl, who immediately abandoned character and looked toward the yacht as well.

"Luva Pete!" the man behind the camera yelled. "Who's queering my shot?"

* * *

The cameraman had now come to the side of the ship, to join the beautiful blonde and the sailors. Anthony was having a hard time taking his eyes off of her, as was Zaroff. She smiled at Anthony, and he felt his heart lift into his throat. Suddenly, a sun-ruddy, broad shouldered young sailor appeared at her shoulder, draping her with a pea coat which he was intent was going to completely cover her. He looked sourly down at Anthony.

The man who had been filming shouted down to them: "What are you doing out here in the middle of nowhere? Besides making me sore? I was waiting for the sun to be at a certain spot all day and now the moment's passed—we're a day behind thanks to you!"

"We apologize," Anthony said. "We thought you might be in trouble."

"We were doing just swell until you showed up! Who are you?" The man appeared in early middle age and in excellent shape. His lean, clean-shaven face under a pith helmet was deeply tan, and over his tall, lean body he wore a loose white shirt, jodhpurs, and calf-length leather boots.

At his question, Zaroff gave Anthony a furtive glance and said under his breath, "Careful, Anthony."

"Does Zaroff actually fear a Red informant among these people?" Anthony thought. Over the past weeks, he had wondered how much of Zaroff's story he had fed him was true. Still, having thrown his lot in with Zaroff at the desperate commencing of this adventure, he was completely committed now.

"We are sportsmen out deep sea fishing," he said, dodging precise identities for the moment. "Sorry about ruining your shot. But if you can't do any more filming today anyway, we would welcome some fresh social-ization—we've been out to sea for half a month."

"Don't know much about what goes into making the movies, do you, pal?" the man replied. "There's a lot more than rolling the cameras: there's rehearsals, and costume fittings . . ."

"From the look of it, there can't be *that* much costuming involved," Anthony responded with a grin, causing the girl to blush and sink into the pea coat—he noted with interest that his appraisal had made her self-conscious in a way her broad shouldered, self-appointed protector's efforts had failed to do.

"And —" Anthony added, "—we have a fully stocked liquor cabinet on the yacht. Last I heard, there's no prohibition in Malaya."

The man beamed under his pith helmet. "Brother, why didn't you say so in the first place? Welcome aboard!"

* * *

Zaroff groused about how free Anthony had been with his alcohol, but apparently decided it had been worth it when he saw the girl again -- up close this time. The man behind the camera intro-duced himself as D.W. Cecil De Cent. "If it's a De Cent, it's *decent* box office. Count on every *cent.*" He was now wearing a white yachting outfit and sipping wine at a dining table in the captain's quarters. Said captain was an elderly man with gray hair and a slim build, face and neck well lined and worn and deeply tanned from too many years at sea. He was enjoying a brandy.

Zaroff had returned to the formal dress he had worn at *Old Knickerbocker's* and brought his gramophone over from his yacht. Anthony had changed into fresh khaki pants and a loose fitting shirt. The only concessions he made to formality were shoes (slip-on canvas) and slicking back his long hair.

The broad-shouldered young man who had wrapped the girl in a pea coat turned out to be the first mate and he was not enjoying any alcohol, nor, apparently the company of Anthony and Zaroff. He was obviously possessive of the girl, though whether he had any right to be was something that was still to be established.

Then she entered—an entrance she had been preparing for nearly the hour that had passed since Anthony and Zaroff were invited aboard. Her hair was now set and freshly coifed about her face and neck, no longer floating freely over her shoulders. She wore a powder blue, short-sleeved, double-breasted blouse with a matching, just-above-the-ankle-length pleated skirt and bright high heels that made her legs appear even longer.

Anthony was pleased to see that up close her complexion remained flawless porcelain, flushed with a pink in her cheeks and lips that nullified any need for rouge and lipstick. Her eyebrows were plucked and arched but other than that and her hair there was little cosmetic about her appearance. Her large round eyes were blue as robins' eggs, bright and intent on taking in everything about the new arrivals—as they were her.

"Ah, here's our leading lady now," De Cent said. "Miss Dana Sparrow."

" 'Dana Sparrow' for the moment, gentlemen," she said. "Mr. De Cent suggested I try some different stage names on for size. There's a list. Tomorrow I'm 'Charlotte Duncan,' and coming up are . . . let's see . . . 'Joan Xavier,' 'Ruth Bertin,' and 'Eve Trowbridge.' But 'Dana Sparrow' is the flavor of the day."

Both Anthony and Zaroff had risen to their feet when she had come into the room, prompting De Cent to follow suit, though he downed the rest of his glass of wine first. The captain apparently felt that since he was too old for the young woman to express any romantic interest in him, no such manners should be required on his part. The first mate just sat, crossed his arms, and stewed.

"Oh brother," he moaned aloud when Zaroff raised Dana's hand to his lips and kissed it.

"There's no need for that," she said, quickly withdrawing her hand. "Thank you, though."

"Let me get your chair for you, Miss Sparrow," Anthony said, pulling it away from the table.

"Oh. How gallant. Thank you. But I'm afraid you have me at a disadvantage, sir."

"A disadvantage?"

"You know my name but I don't know yours—oh, that's right." She laughed. "I *haven't* told you who I am, have I?"

"You're Dana Sparrow—for the duration," Cecil De Cent said and smiled. "Miss Sparrow, meet Jim Anthony and Count Romanovitch Little Racal-something."

"Raskolnikov," Anthony corrected him, and Zaroff winced. "How do you do, Miss Sparrow?"

"Very well, thank you," she said.

"Have some hooch, Dana," De Cent said.

"I'm afraid I'm just a natural teetotaler, Mr. De Cent. I want to stay sharp anyway, keep my wits about me. Hi, Jack," she said and waved her fingers at the first mate. He grunted an acknowledgment.

"So, now that your star's here, Mr. De Cent, why not tell us what this movie you're making is all about," Anthony said. "What's it called?"

"Uhm . . . *Trader Horn*," De Cent said. "Either that or *Jamboree*. It's still up in the air. Or maybe not."

"And what's the story? Miss Sparrow?"

"I'll give you a hint," Dana said with a smile. "If you gentlemen had come floating by a few days ago you would have seen me being filmed in quite a different costume: a medieval, fairy tale gown. And that's what this story is based on . . ."

"Careful, Dana," De Cent crooned cautiously, regarding her over his wineglass.

Her eyes met his gaze and she tucked her head slightly at him in acknowledgment. ". . . and I, uh, was screaming that day, too," she said. "I'm sorry, Mr. Anthony. I guess you could say I have a contractual obligation to keep mum."

"When it comes right down to it, Anthony," De Cent said and rolled his wine over his palate, "'loose lips sink ships.' Even out here in the middle of nowhere I find it prudent to stick to that policy in regards to the project at hand. Sorry. You'll have to buy your ticket to find out like everyone else."

"That's fine, Mr. De Cent. I prefer figuring things out instead of looking up the answer in the back of the book anyway. The clues are slim, though. Hmmm . . . medieval gown, you said, Miss Sparrow." He smiled. "Those tend to reach from neck to toe, don't they? Well, I have to say I much prefer what you were almost wearing today. That costume should give the Hayes Code a conniption."

Dana smiled archly in response to the comment, clearly pleased with Anthony's estimate, but her cheeks were coloring as well.

"Can you at least tell me what your part is?" he asked her.

Dana opened her mouth hesitantly, giving De Cent a side-glance.

"White goddess of the lost city," De Cent said.

"Excellently cast," Zaroff pronounced, appraising Dana frankly. The pink of her cheeks darkened again. She gave Zaroff a slight, uneasy smile, then turned back to Anthony, one hand pushing a curl back over her ear.

"So, what *was* that screaming we heard earlier?" Anthony asked.

"She was practicing her battle cry," De Cent said. "Dana's character is a regular Brunhilde. So we were getting her into character with a war whoop."

"Can you tell us where you're filming? Besides in the middle of the ocean?" Anthony asked.

"We're headed for an island off the Malayan coast," De Cent said. "We're meeting up with the male lead there. And that, gentlemen, is all about the latest D.W. Cecil De Cent Production you're getting out of cast or crew."

"You'll have to forgive Mr. Anthony for wanting to dispel the mystery," Dana said, looking appreciatively at him. "He's a detective by trade. An international one. I thought I recognized him from the papers and the news reels, but I wasn't certain until I had a name to put with the face."

"What I'd really like to know more about is you, Miss Sparrow," Anthony said.

"As would we all," Zaroff said.

"My life story then? Okay. I'll bite—not that there's a lot to tell," she said, sliding back in her chair and looking from one set of eagerly intent eyes to the other, though not lingering for long on Zaroff's. "I'm from Illinois—at least, I grew up there."

"Chicago?" Anthony asked.

"I'm afraid not. Just a country gal through and through, Mr. Anthony."

"Please. Call me Jim. Mr. Anthony was my father."

Jack snorted "Bushwah!" and wiped his nose with the back of his hand as though he had sneezed.

De Cent smiled. Dana paused, then decided to ignore the first mate and turned her attention back to Anthony.

"Okay . . . Jim. My last name—my real one—is French. I was told the lady who brought me to the orphanage spoke French; she said in broken English that she had come across the Great Lakes from Canada. My father was unaware I existed, and he could never know. She never said why or why she had to let me go."

"That's tough," Anthony said. "I'm sorry."

"Well, you can't miss what you've never had, right?—oh, yes you can," Dana added quickly with a smile. "Going about my chores on that farm, I did a lot of daydreaming about my parents. That my dad was maybe, royalty, and my mother a commoner. She was afraid if I stayed with her, his enemies would track me down somehow. Typical little girl fantasy, I guess, to be a princess or the bride of a king."

"Wait --'farm?' I thought you said orphanage," Anthony said, confused but pleasantly so.

"The orphanage was a farm—self-supporting. I learned a lot about self-reliance there. We raised and grew what we ate. We sewed our own clothes, too. So I guess you could say I'm pioneer-hardy.

"But it wasn't *all* work," she was quick to add, reaching out and gently tapping Anthony's hand with two polished fingertips. "I don't want you to think my life has been pure drudgery. We threw parties. And there was a wonderful library there—we were just across the river from Hannibal —"

"Mark Twain country," Anthony said.

"Yes. Complete with the cave Becky and Tom hide in from Injun Joe. I can't tell you what a thrill it was when I was a little girl to go in there. It was fun and fascinating, but scary, too, because I was convinced that if the cave was real, then Injun Joe might just be, too. And then my little boyfriend sort-of reached out and grabbed my leg —"

"You screamed," Anthony said.

"I *caterwauled*," Dana said and laughed. "Maybe it was the echo in the cave, but I never knew I could yell that loud. And I ran, too. Since then, I've had recurring nightmares that I'm running hard in the dark with something after me —"

"Injun Joe?" Anthony asked.

"Injun Joe! Yes! But I always wake up before he catches me."

"I hope the experience didn't put you off Twain."

"Not at all. *The Prince and Pauper* I adore—and his novel about Joan of Arc? He said it was his best. That one's my favorite. Do you know it?"

"I only know of the historical Joan of Arc, of course. She was a brick," Anthony said.

"And someone who belonged to another world. I felt that way myself. Watching the flickers fed my fantasy. See, once a month we could walk to town and go to the theater. They were silents, of course. Not that I ever minded having to do some reading. I became so caught up, that I felt like I was up there *on the screen* with them. And with this Depression, there were more and more helpless children who needed the shelter and food of an orphanage. And I was a big girl by then. That's when I set off to New Jersey. Fort Lee. To get into the 'flickers.'"

"How long did you live at the orphanage?" Anthony asked.

"All total twenty-eight years, Mr. Anthon—Jim. I guess I'm just a late bloomer. And more comfortable dreaming about life than living it. I needed the Depression to prod me out of the nest, I guess."

"And in all that time, no further contact from the woman who left you at the orphanage?"

"No. Though I *am* supposed to have an uncle, one who was sending me money through a third party, so I never got an address. Then the third party disappeared along with any further funds. But the ladies who ran the orphanage had saved up most of the previous money for me, and I used that for my stake to get to Fort Lee."

"Is that where you met Mr. De Cent?" Anthony asked.

De Cent, who was now a bit tight, answered for her: "Not at all! I pulled her off the streets of New York where she was swiping food from street vendors to survive—I caught 'er Delicious Red handed."

Dana's cheeks became a richer blush as she winced against the memory. "Uhm . . . the Depression almost closed down the Fort Lee studios. I went to New York for work, and I had a little luck, but Long Island didn't lack for actors—most of them unemployed. Mr. De Cent helped me out of a jam. And I will always be grateful for that.

"And I guess *that* brings you up to date on the life of 'Dana Sparrow' from infancy up to, oh —" she glanced at the watch on her slim wrist— "five minutes ago. Any questions?" she chirped, now fully recovered from the embarrassment De Cent had caused her.

"Yes—may I have a dance, Miss Sparrow?" Zaroff asked, rising and bowing.

Dana hesitated for a second, looked from Jack, who was leaning forward with a grimace like he had a stomach cramp, to Anthony, who gave her a reassuring look and nod. She turned back toward Zaroff and smiled. "Of course, Count," she said. Zaroff moved behind her, sliding her chair out for her.

"Anthony—put on the Sleeping Beauty suite," he ordered.

Through the gramophone crackled a reproduction of a Moscow Orchestra performance. He made a regal figure, taking Dana's hands as the music struck up and whisking her over the floor, though Zaroff did not so much lead as *pull* her along.

The other men looked on, Jack still fuming, De Cent and the captain amused by Dana and her admirer. As her spin brought Anthony back around, her eyes sought his for reassurance, which his steady, watchful gaze gave her. He was sorry for her embarrassment, but, as he had at the nightclub, he also pitied Zaroff's futile attempt to pitch woo.

"It looks like Dana has quite the admirer in Count Raskolnikov," the captain said.

"Yeah?" De Cent, still tight, said: "A snowball has a better chance in Gehenna than he does with her." He squeezed the first mate's shoulder. "Don't worry Jacksie, ol' boy. Nobody's stealing your girl."

Scowling, Jack shrugged off De Cent's hand, and was ready to offer him a few choice sailor words when he caught sight of Zaroff's hand dropping to Dana's behind, causing her to startle.

Jack erupted from his chair, jerking Dana out of Zaroff's grasp, shouting, "Who do you think you are? You're a 'Count,' huh? You got the manners of a lug!"

"How dare you, you proletarian —" Zaroff snarled back, grabbing Jack by his lapels and leaning into him. Jack released Dana, and she stepped back, shouting, "Jack! Stop it!"

"Stand down!" the captain barked, rising.

But the mate had already pulled back a haymaker, and brought his fist into Zaroff's right temple. Zaroff staggered backwards and went down in his elegant tux like a bag of dirty laundry dropping ungraciously to the floor.

"Holy mackerel!" De Cent blurted, his alcohol-delayed reactions pulling him out of his chair five seconds after the fact. The first mate stood, feet spread apart , looking down on his felled opponent.

"What have you done, Jack?" Dana demanded of him.

"What do you mean 'what have I done?' The tramp was getting familiar with you!"

"And I would have guided his hand back to where it was supposed to be! I didn't need you to jump and break out a . . . a dance hall brawl! I—excuse me, gentlemen," she said and quickly made for the deck.

Jack's jaw worked mutely, his eyes flashing both bafflement and anger as he looked after her. De Cent shrugged and patted him on the shoulder. "Simmer down, kid," he said. "And give her time to calm down, too. If you *don't* give her time, you're just going to dig yourself in deeper. Get me?"

"A lot better than I'll ever get women," Jack said.

"C'mon then. Grab the Bolshevik's feet; let's get him spread out on the couch."

"I apologize for my friend, gentlemen," Anthony said.

"'s'all right," De Cent said. "Nobody's sore at you, Anthony."

"I'm not so sure about that," Anthony thought, looking at Jack. Seeing that Zaroff was being taken care of, he slipped out onto the deck where he found Dana looking over the railing, out to sea. It was twilight now, stars appearing in a deepening violet sky. The breeze was teasing at the strands of her light hair, and her fair skin gleamed softly in the gloom.

"Hi," he said, joining her at the railing.

"Hi," she answered in a small voice.

"So . . . what's the story with you and the first mate?" he asked.

Dana looked at Anthony. "There is no story, Jim. He had no business acting like the Count was infringing on his property—"

"Is that how you see it?" Anthony asked. "Seems to me he was just being, well, gallant."

"Why are you defending him? He doesn't like you any more than the Count, you know."

"Do you think?" Anthony asked with a grin.

He was gratified to see her laugh.

"I could have handled the Count perfectly well on my own," she said. "His fingernails may have been manicured but they felt just like the grubby ones I've had on me in the dance halls. I hoped to be allowed my dignity by everyone pretending they hadn't seen the Count grope me. But Jack made it plenty obvious, and the fight—it made it even more like something I thought I'd put behind me forever."

"You're being too hard on yourself, Dana. You've been in a tough spot. A lot of people have lately. And if the worse you've done was take a few dimes in exchange for a dance—"

Dana placed her hand over his on the rail and looked him in the eye. "It was, Jim. I'm not so naïve that I don't know that some girls got a lot more from their partners because they *gave* a lot more. But I never did."

Her small, pale hand on his dark large one all but paralyzed it, sending an electric hum up his arm. He realized that though he was by far the more powerful, he was, at the moment, at her mercy. It was a disconcerting feeling, but one that Anthony knew he could get used to very quickly. It was easy now to forget about Zaroff and even the promises of the incredible sport that awaited them on the island. Suddenly, none of those things seemed as important as they had been just that morning.

Dana laughed and looked out to sea again.

"What is it?" Anthony asked, feeling an irrational alarm that she had read his thoughts and was mocking him.

"When I was reading at the library in Illinois, there was a nook with a window that was my favorite spot. Looking out from it in the spring and summer, you just saw acres and acres of green corn stretching away to the horizon. I would pretend, then, that I wasn't in a library but on a ship out to sea and the fields were the ocean. And now that I am out to sea, I want nothing more than a really good book. I guess I'm the kind of girl who just can't be satisfied."

Anthony smiled down at her. "The Count has a library on his yacht," he said.

Dana turned and leaned on her side against the rail, facing Anthony. "Do tell," she said and smiled.

"And I think he owes you a volume or two for being such a masher. Miss Sparrow, will you accompany me to the yacht?"

"Indeed, I think I shall, Mr. Anthony," she said.

He escorted her to the rope ladder.

"Wait a minute," she said and slipped off her shoes. "These heels aren't made for climbing."

"Ready?" Anthony asked.

"Um-hmm," she said.

He swung over the side and began descending, anxiously watching Dana as she followed. His fear, he quickly saw, was unfounded: she climbed down the ladder with the confidence and pluck of the Tom Boy she must have once been, playing on that farm. Anthony was unexpectedly and delightfully impressed.

Also impressive: from his vantage point below her, he enjoyed the sight of her rounded behind descending toward him. The sea breeze blew her skirt up about her knees, exposing slender, curved calves that hovered before his face. The temptation to reach out and touch the silky white skin glimmering before him was a strong one. Then he remembered her childhood boyfriend who had done just that and conjured the ghost of Injun Joe. He didn't want to startle her and send her—caterwauling— into the ocean.

As he touched down on the yacht, he eagerly reached out as she turned to descend and took her in his arms, lowering her pale bare feet to the deck. Having her held against him, even just for a few seconds, gave him a heady rush.

Zaroff staggered backwards and went down in his elegant tux like a bag of dirty laundry...

"Oh," Dana said. "Thank you. But I could have gone the rest of the way on my own."

"Where would be the fun in that?" Anthony asked with a grin and was rewarded with a charming blush. Smiling, she cleared her throat and stepped away from him—though only two or three feet. All Anthony would have to do, he realized, would be to reach out and grab her and pull her back into him. His pulse was quickening at the thought, but, lest she think he was an equal heel to Zaroff, he resisted the urge.

"So, skipper, where's the reading room?" she asked.

"Right this way," he said, taking her hand and leading her below deck.

Dana's eyes went wide when Anthony opened the door to the library, and she "ooohed" at the sight of the shelves of books ascending the walls.

"Please tell me they're not all in Russian," she said.

"Only the ones written in it originally. So, in less you have a yen for Tolstoy . . ."

"Read 'im already," Dana said as she slid a book out partially from the shelf. "So," she said as she regarded its cover. "Your pal with the Russian fingers is named Romanovitch Raskolnikov?"

"Yes. That's right."

She pinned Anthony with her bright blue eyes, grinning triumphantly. "I've read *Crime and Punishment,* too," she said.

Now it was Anthony's turn to blush. "Uh, that obvious, huh?"

"I think it's unlikely that anyone in the *Venture* crew has ever read it. And Mr. De Cent doesn't care if his name is fake as long as his alcohol is real enough. If it's at least 80 proof, your secret should be safe with him."

"And am I safe with you, Dana?" Anthony asked.

"I think the question is, am *I* safe with *you,* Mr. Anthony."

"Please don't think I lured you over here to —"

Dana smiled and held her palm up to silence him. "If that's not the case, please don't say so; be a gentleman and allow me to continue flattering myself."

"I just don't want you to think I'm a masher or a wolf, like Za—Romanovitch."

"Why, I don't think that at all, Mr. Anthony," she said. "I came with you, didn't I? At least, I don't recall you dragging me by my hair."

Anthony smiled. Dana tilted her head to continue reading the book spines, hands behind her back. "Hmm . . . Noel Coward . . . Shakespeare. It's so nice to be in the presence of some appreciation for the theater— even if it *is* the Count's. I've had the best time of my life with the guys on that ship, but it's not exactly a cultural Mecca over there. I mean, could you imagine Jack writing a play?"

"Where did that come from?" Anthony asked, bemused.

"I know. It's a ridiculous notion. I'd be surprised if he's even seen one. Ah—Gaston Leroux, *The Phantom of the Opera*." She pulled it completely from the shelf and held it out with both hands, regarding the cover. "I've always wanted to read this one. Somebody checked it out at the library back home and never returned it."

"You like that gothic stuff, do you?" Anthony asked, smiling and leaning back against the shelves and crossing his arms.

"'Heaving bosoms' and the like? Guilty as charged. I'm just a romantic at heart, I guess," she said. "Yourself?"

He smiled, regarding her frankly. "With the right girl. The right situation."

"And what would those be?"

"Oh, I'd say a blonde with big blue eyes —"

"Don't forget a handsome, mysterious adventurer —"

"— whose paths cross on a voyage at sea. Would that be about right?"

"It sounds heavenly."

He stepped in close to her. "And they're alone. On a tropical night."

"I like this story," she said. "What happens next?"

He reached out, pulling her against him. His senses were suddenly awash with her scent, the feel of her body, and that perfectly beautiful face so close to his own.

"Luva Pete!" Anthony gasped softly. And then his hands were behind her head, cradling it, his fingers in her soft golden hair, bringing her mouth to his. Dana responded eagerly with her own full, soft lips.

Then she withdrew just a bit, took a deep breath, and said, "This is all quite out of character for me."

Anthony smiled. "Just keep following my direction, and you'll be fine."

Now Anthony's hands were around her waist, drawing her tightly into him, kissing her again. He had known many beautiful women in his life, but precious few of this *kind* of beauty—one combined with purity and a character seasoned in the depths of despair. And to have *that* beauty in his hands, willingly giving itself to him . . .

It was a rush, but then suddenly he remembered where they were in this story: the villain's lair. And he had brought her here. What if Zaroff came through that door right now? And what was he going to do anyway when he came to? How exactly would he avenge his insult? Anthony was letting his own desires put everyone in jeopardy. He had to stop it. *Now.*

"Dana . . . Dana . . .," he said pulling away as her lips nipped after his departing ones. "I was wrong."

"What?" she said, frowning at him.

"This isn't the time or place. I need to get you back on your vessel . . ."

"My . . . did you say 'my vessel?'"

"And then I need to get Romanovitch back on his yacht and away from you all. Look, you told us 'Dana' wasn't your real name; you didn't ask why my companion is using a pseudonym . . ."

"I don't need to know . . ."

"Yes you *do*. You need to know that he's potentially a dangerous man."

"You can protect me," she said, stepping toward him.

"This isn't like one of your books, Dana," he said sternly, stepping back. "No matter what you do, good people get hurt in real life."

"I think I know a little something about that, Jim," she said, tears starting to shine in her eyes. "And while I haven't lived the glamorous life you have, there's no need to be patronizing." She was suddenly prim and straight.

"I just think it's worth a pound of cure if we get you in your cabin, and I get Zaroff —"

"Who? Zaroff? That's his name . . . his real name? Zaroff? Why does that sound familiar?"

"Forget it. It's out of another story, one that you don't want to be part of. Believe me. The Count needs to be back on the yacht and far away from the *Venture* by the time he wakes up."

"'Far away'—you're going? Just like that?"

"I think it's best. You'll be all right. I'm sure Jack will see you're taken care of."

"*Jack* will see --?"

"He's scruffy, but he's got your best interests at heart."

"But when will I see *you* again?"

"I can't say. I don't know how long I'll be gone or even exactly where I'm going at this point."

Dana construed her pretty features into a scowl.

"You do understand why I'm doing this don't you?" Anthony asked.

"I think I do: you're a coward, Mr. Anthony."

"Wha—you think I'm yellow? Who am I supposed to be afraid of?

Jack?" Anthony asked, flustered.

"No! Not *Jack*. Excuse me."

"Wait, I'll walk with you. I don't want you to fall off that ladder —"

"I can handle myself just fine, Mr. Anthony," she said, making for the door. "I'm not Pearl White in some movie serial!"

Still, Anthony watched her carefully as he followed her up the rope ladder. He had been impressed with how sure-footed she had been before, true, but now she was upset and that could result in a slip.

As he came over the side, he found her slipping her heels back on, confronted by Jack. "Where did you go?" he demanded.

"I don't want to talk about it, Jack," she said in a huff. "I'm going to my room. Don't follow me."

Jack leaned into Anthony. "What did you do?" he demanded. Anthony merely raised his hands passively. "Easy. We just had a misunderstanding. Here," he handed him the copy of *The Phantom of the Opera* that Dana had left behind in her anger. "Give this to her tomorrow after she's had time to cool down. She'll appreciate it."

Jack took the book in one hand, shoving Anthony away with the other. "You and your Red buddy have made enough trouble. You both need to go, and, brother, I mean *right now*!"

"I concur completely," Anthony said. "Just give me my friend, and we two trouble makers will be out of your hair for good."

"Go on, then," he said.

Zaroff, Anthony was glad to see, was still unconscious. He threw him over his shoulder while D.W. Cecil De Cent looked on in a liquored daze. "Thank you for your hospitality," Anthony said. "Please keep the booze as our way of apologizing for any untoward behavior you've suffered from us."

He carried Zaroff past Jack, who, Anthony noticed with a sharp pang, was still holding Dana's book. Then, Zaroff across his shoulders, Anthony put one leg over the railing, then the other, and descended the ladder.

Zaroff's crew exhibited unease over their unconscious captain. Clearly, they wanted to delay leaving to receive their orders from him. "We're not welcome here anymore, fellows," Anthony said. "And we're going right now. Back on course. You have the charts. Do it."

Jim Anthony's authoritative stance, unyielding as it was, carried the day, and the crew obeyed.

Zaroff was still out when Anthony saw the distant lights of De Cent's ship wink out over the horizon. Only then did he go to bed himself. For a long time he stared at the ceiling of his cabin, thinking of Dana, replaying their moment. But now, he was certain, it was a moment that had passed. He would probably never see Dana Sparrow—or whoever she really was—again except on a movie screen. And if he did see her in person, she would probably give him the air.

As the saying went, "That ship had sailed."

Literally.

* * *

When Zaroff came to, Anthony was squatting on his haunches by his bed. The sun was just rising. Zaroff blinked in confusion, stared at Anthony, then began struggling to his feet, clearly ready for a fight.

"Where is that scruffy Cossack? How dare he put his hand on —"

"Simmer down, Zaroff," Anthony said. "They've gone. Or we have. Which ever version suits your pride."

"Who brought me here . . . who gave the order to sail?"

"I did."

Zaroff sat up straight. "You had no right to deny me satisfaction! We're going back —"

"Of course, that's your call. But before you make it, you should know something . . . ."

"What? What should I know?"

"Those people were all hiding something."

"Explain."

"'Dana Sparrow' wasn't the only pseudonym floating around last night. I don't know how often you get to the cinema, but 'D.W. Cecil De Cent' was a pastiche. I didn't recognize who he really was until we were up close. I guess that director's outfit threw me. You're familiar with Polish 7th Air Escadrille?"

"You mean the Kościuszko Squadron?"

"Right. He was a pilot with them. Long before he got into 'flickers.' And even though that was after you left Russia, there was no love lost between Poland and Russia under the Royal family was there? When you and Allardravitch served the Czar? He *seemed* friendly enough while you were supplying his booze, but if he's nursing a grudge, it would probably come out eventually. I took the opportunity of your being knocked out to get us out of there—before 'De Cent' lost his good mood."

Zaroff was silent as he let what Anthony had said sink in. Then: "You acted in my best interests. And I thank you. Still, I would welcome a chance to settle the score with that first mate . . . and to renew my acquaintance with the delightful Miss Sparrow. Who knows, eh?"

A knock on the cabin's door sounded. Zaroff barked "enter" in Russian. The captain stepped inside and said something else in his and Zaroff's native tongue.

"What is it?" Anthony asked, hoping that the yacht had not been secretly trailing "D.W. Cecil De Cent" and his ship.

Zaroff smiled. "The island," he said. "We are approaching it. Come!"

They went topside, and Anthony saw their destination for the first time. Its jungle went right down to the ocean, or, rather, it seemed the over and under growth swept up from the shore in a verdant wave, thinning out halfway up the highest mountain which crowned the island with a denuded stone cranium. Opaque in the mist, the island occluded itself in layers of various densities of cloud, making its interior even more of a mystery.

"It looks like something out of Dore's *Paradise Lost*," Anthony said. Zaroff passed him the spyglass which Anthony brought to his eye. Almost immediately he gasped: what looked like bats careening about the stone mountain were revealed up close as pterodactyls, riding the wind currents that whipped about the precipice.

"They look like they could snatch up a child and carry him off—maybe even a woman," he said. "Zaroff, how are we getting on the island? I'm not seeing any available ingress."

"When we round the island a bit more, we should come to a sound, and from there into the mouth of a river that will take us into the interior."

The route unfolded just as Zaroff had said. By noon, they were sailing inland up a brackish river. Anthony noted crocodiles sliding on their bellies down its muddy banks into the brown water. These were, surprisingly, smaller than their cousins in the modern world.

He was awed to see a living archaeopteryx skim over the water's surface in a movement that was a combination of flight and a running motion that made it appear to be walking on the water. It snapped at the large insects that swarmed there.

Perspiration soaked through the men's shirts. Anthony would have shed his already and slipped into some shorts except he wanted protection against insect bites and what illness they might induce. He had also put on a cap, as had Zaroff and the crew, that included mosquito netting hanging about their heads.

As the river opened up and widened, they came across a herd of brontosauruses who were partially submerged, enjoying the easing of gravity upon their massive bulk that the buoyant water granted. From the shore, its huge tail sliding behind it like a serpent in its train, a duck-billed dinosaur, trying to escape the heat, waded in up to its hips, then continued to submerge by degree until only the hollow dome of its skull crowned the surface

Anthony remained in awe. Zaroff, however, lit a cigarette, and dismissively waved off the smoke he puffed out. "These creatures are cows; torpid, dull things. They are not worth the expenditure of one bullet. The game of merit will be the predators of these creatures. Our brains and woodcraft against their brute strength and ravening. I will not rest, Anthony, until I have brought down the greatest of these."

Zaroff closed his eyes and inhaled, his mouth open a little as though he were savoring a fine wine over his palate. "Imagine one elegant shot into the tiny brain, the resulting magnitude of the collapse of its bulk.The dust shall rise in a curtain at the felling, and the island itself will be moved out of its place."

It was still early afternoon when Anthony and Zaroff went ashore and began pushing their way through ferns and scrims of vines. Zaroff had supplied them both with Lugers, which were holstered on one hip, and long knifes sheathed on the other. They carried rifles held at the ready. Two of Zaroff's men from the yacht followed them, each bearing a case of ammunition.

Not thirty minutes into the jungle and they saw for the first time the Great Gray One.

The Tyrannosaurus Rex loomed before them like a mountain of flesh rising in the middle of a glade, a scaly mass supported on girthy haunches which were planted among the strewn limbs, viscera and blood of some creature that was now impossible to identify. The carnivore stood there lazily, sated, its tiny eyes hooded.

Does it dream? Anthony wondered.

Zaroff was already taking aim with his rifle's scope.

"Are you insane," Anthony asked him. "You're only going to make it mad and bring us to its attention!"

"Not if I can place a bullet in its puny brain," Zaroff said. "Not if I can fell it with one eloquent blow."

He fired and the tyrannosaurus flinched, jarred out of its reverie. At the sting of the bullet, it exhaled a hissing sound like a crocodile or a swan. It slowly turned its head, a large, gray revolving stone. Its nostrils pumped the air. Then, with a contemptuous turn of its massive back, it reentered the jungle on the opposite side of the glade, pushing into the trees, their trunks snapping as though against the surge of a great, gray tidal wave.

Anthony laughed: "Well, Zaroff, I suppose he told us."

"He will come to respect me," Zaroff said. "I will have the mastery of this Great Gray One."

Suddenly, the trees about them were trembling from all sides. An upright creature the size of a small man, erupted from the scrim of greenery, snatching up and carrying along with it one of Zaroff's men who shrieked in terror and pain. It opened him with fore claws that weren't the dangling delicate things of the tyrannosaurus but instruments as rapacious as its maw. This was the dinosaur that would one day be classified as "velociraptor."

Anthony and Zaroff whirled and opened fire on the beast, their bullets striking then spewing flesh, taking the raptor apart. It dropped the already dead man and collapsed into the underbrush: one of the bullets had penetrated its skull.

Now there was more rustling in the trees and overgrowth. Zaroff tossed his remaining man his Luger. They and Anthony went back to back and began to rotate clockwise, arms at the ready.

The early afternoon heat pressed close. The jungle became eerily silent—so much so that they could hear the blood of the slain man dripping from the limbs and branches where it had sprayed: red droplets left after a violent storm of claw and fang.

Then from three sides sprang the raptors, the talons of their upright legs aimed for the men's abdomens. Anthony, Zaroff, and Zaroff's man opened fire, sending hot led into the creatures' own viscera, causing their leaps to go off target. One went down on its side, and Zaroff's man delivered the *coup de grace* by implanting a bullet from his Luger into its brain. Another of the creatures was bleeding so heavily from its own stomach wounds that it fell prone, landing before Zaroff's boots as though prostrate in supplication. The Russian shot a bullet into its skull to insure its threat had passed.

The other creature swayed on its talons, hissed and again charged. Anthony shot through its neck, severing its jugular vein. Violently spewing blood from its throat, the raptor hissed and screeched shrilly as it spun about before falling dead.

Another rattling of branches and leaves. Anthony and Zaroff raised their rifles. *This* raptor, one who had remained hidden and off to the side until now, did not charge. Anthony immediately noticed the mottling on its snout that looked like the death's head on a moth. Its nostrils flared, taking in the unfamiliar scent of these men. It studied them with the sinister lozenges of its eyes. Anthony had the uneasy feeling that they were being committed to the creature's memory for future reference.

They fired, but the raptor ducked back into the overgrowth and ran.

"I think we'd better get back to the boat—he might have gone to bring back some more of his friends," Anthony said.

"I want the body of at least one of these," Zaroff said, then pointed with the end of his rifle to the raptor that was least mutilated from their gunshots. "That one," he said. Since Zaroff's man was now encumbered with two boxes of ammunition, Zaroff indicated that Anthony should take up the burden of the beast. Anthony shook his head.

"I'm not leaving your man's body here to be ravaged by these creatures," he said. "I'm afraid you're going to have to carry the raptor yourself if you want a trophy, Zaroff."

The Russian scowled. Then: "I can carry Igor," he said, "if you insist on being sentimental. You are, of course, endangering us who still live by this pointless charity. Will you then bear the dinosaur, Anthony? It is more the burden and you have superior physical strength."

"Under those conditions, certainly," Anthony said. Heaving the reptilian heap onto his broad shoulders, he led the way, Zaroff carrying the dead man and his servant struggling with the two boxes of ammunition. In this manner they returned to the ship. Zaroff had the raptor taken to his taxidermy chamber while Anthony saw to the burying of the dead man.

* * *

Anthony never completely got used to living alongside dinosaurs. It was like they each were on separate but overlapping planes of reality—almost as though, in their presence, he was standing in front of a Hollywood process screen. Still, in the days that followed, Anthony got over his initial awe enough to begin to mentally make notes about the dinosaurs he observed on the island.

The larger ones appeared to be the most ancient—and the Great Gray One seemed the oldest of all. The older ones' motions seemed strangely jerky more times than not, which Anthony thought indicated some form of arthritis. Still, they possessed a certain ponderous quality, a weighty presence with which the younger dinosaurs were not endowed. The latter's movements were more fluid; they were quicker, more agile, but, strange as it seemed to say, the younger thunder lizards seemed *ephemeral* in comparison to the older ones. They also tended toward a pack mentality.

No doubt it all had something to do with the inbreeding that had to be the state of reproductive affairs on the island. In any closed system—whether dealing with genes or ideas—everything became derivative, and the result was a loss of robust individualism.

Yet, his detective's sense told Anthony that there was something else at work here. Their journey up the river, ever deeper into the jungle, began to be like some kind of excavation into the heart of the island's mystery. . . .

* * *

They were pressing into the interior—literally pressing with chests thrust forward through more scrims of vines and overgrowth, resilient branches and briars. On this excursion, the first after their initial, disastrous altercation with the island's wild life, the men carrying the boxes of ammunition were armed. Additionally, two armed men alertly guarded their perimeter to ward against further ambush.

For raptors continued to shadow them through the jungle. The men learned to tell they were there with the snap and crack of under- and overgrowth about them. Anthony and Zaroff would catch glimpses of the upright lizards slipping through foliage and vanishing as quickly as they were spotted.

When the raptors *did* sweep in, they were taught to respect firearms. Still, they would return, even when a fore claw dangled uselessly from being shattered by bullets. *They are some tenacious cusses,* Anthony thought. When a raptor became too wounded, useless for the hunt, the pack devoured their own for strength to continue stalking their prey of choice.

Anthony noticed again the solitary raptor who had observed their first attack, identified by the death's head mottling on its snout. He concluded this one was not part of any pack. Rather, it used the hunting packs to bear the burden of eliminating deadly resistance so that it, unhurt, could swoop in to finish the wounded and dying for its prey.

Anthony thought to point out the death's head raptor's modus operandi to Zaroff, then refrained, on the chance Zaroff had not himself noted it. His motivation for this restraint took him to a dark, grim place he did not relish visiting. It was the same reason why Anthony had never enlightened Zaroff as to the duel clothing / weapon nature of his belt.

For, despite the camaraderie they apparently had established, Anthony had meant it when he told Allardravitch that, if Zaroff turned out to be a cold blooded killer who proved irredeemable, then only one of them would be coming back. In the event of that scenario, Anthony fully intended that "one" would be him. He expected that the two of them would reach a crisis at some point on the island, and if things fell a certain way, he suspected he knew already how Zaroff would attempt to dispatch him.

So he studied the death's head raptor even as it studied him, with the intention to turn the stalking dinosaur into his ally against Zaroff if need be.

They had discovered spoor that Zaroff was certain belonged to the Great Gray One—at least they had not seen another dinosaur which walked on its hind claws large enough to leave those prints. The Russian was intent on following the trail to the end, even though it meant risking breaking the safety rule of not being in the jungle after dark. Anthony pointed out that the sun was about to sink under the horizon, but the prints were fresh—judging by a mangled archaeopteryx in one of them, its blood fresh, its tiny body free of rigor mortis and not yet scavenged in a jungle that wasted no time in taking care of its dead.

They came to where the trees divided on either side of a sparsely veg-etated clearing, a sandy plain marked with various large stones jutting out from it. While the perimeter men skirted the surrounding jungle, Anthony, Zaroff, and Zaroff's armed ammunition bearers stepped out of the trees, rounded a mountainous outcropping of stone —

-- and they were upon him: the Great Gray One!

Zaroff swore, aimed, and fired up under its chin. The bullet pierced the flesh and muscle and exited the tyrannosaur's cheek, prompting a hissing like steam spewing out from a boiler under pressure. The dinosaur looked down at Zaroff, its diamond shaped pupils narrowing into slits. One of its great hind claws went up as it moved to stomp the vicious mite into the ground.

The Russian leapt backward, barely avoiding the tip of a talon, and, quickly recovering, sent more bullets into the creature. Anthony had al-ready fallen back and opened fire. The bullets stinging the great inner thighs and belly provoked the tyrannosaur into a frenzied twirl, its tail lashing out --

The men who had been carrying the ammunition were caught in between dropping their cases and unholstering their Lugers. The tail slapped one of the men full force and his head twisted over his shoulder with a sickening snap that reported like one of the fired rifles. Zaroff's other man was sent flying headlong and the boxes of ammo were swept far away into the jungle's brush.

Now the two perimeter men were running in from the jungle, unloading on the Great Gray One. The tyrannosaur surged out onto the plain at the charging men. Suddenly, Anthony and Zaroff were in the on-coming path of the behemoth. The beast's haunches carried it along in great strides over them, so that Zaroff and Anthony were compelled to run along under the dinosaur to avoid being trampled beneath its back claws.

Zaroff's men ran along on either side of the tyrannosaur, their shots keeping the creature distracted and unable to focus on whom to attack. But neither Anthony nor Zaroff could pause to aim up into the giant's guts since they would quickly be crushed under foot.

The sun had disappeared; darkness was absorbing the plain and the jungle.

And then the raptors attacked.

From either side of the jungle they came, one leapt up and took down one of Zaroff's men from behind. It landed on his shoulders, and he fell prostrate. Flaying talons raked out the screaming Russian's kidneys and tossed them onto the ground. The other perimeter man turned in time to shoot the raptor that was encroaching upon him, hitting it right between the eyes.

The tyrannosaur now came to a stop, its hind legs spread in a great stance, surveying the melee about it. Zaroff's ammunition man who had been thrown headlong with a sweep of the Great Gray One's tail had recovered and came running in, firing into the raptors from behind. One turned and charged at him, but his bullet slammed into the creature's skull and it dropped.

Zaroff, Anthony and Zaroff's surviving men were caught between a quickly narrowing Scylla and Charybdis. The raptors' charge pushed them back toward the tyrannosaurus. They fired into the Great Gray One snapping down at them, gyring at the stinging of its belly. The beast's spinning compelled both the men and the raptors to duck and dodge the sweep of its giant tail.

Anthony dropped his emptied rifle and reached to his hip, in the confusion drawing his long knife instead of his Luger. There was no time to correct the mistake as one of the raptors ducked the tyrannosaurus's tail and sprang upon him.

When a raptor became too wounded, useless for the hunt,
the pack devoured their own for strength to continue
stalking their prey of choice.

Anthony's powerful arm flew up, catching it across the throat and keeping its jaws snapping and lunging at his face instead of making fatal contact. A hind claw struck out, slicing the gun belt and causing the still holstered Luger to fall to the ground. Anthony had no time to think of reclaiming it. Before the raptor could rake him again and this time dis-embowel him, Anthony brought the long knife up with his free hand and thrust the blade between its ribs, finding its heart. The raptor's vicious life gone, the Great Gray One's sweeping tail hurled it into the brush.

"Run, Anthony!" Zaroff shouted, dropping his own rifle after firing its final shot into the tyrannosaurus. "If we stay here, we *will* die—struck by our own fire or brought down by these things!" At that moment, the tyrannosaur's tail caught Zaroff across his back, sending him careening. Then its great maw dipped down, swallowing the ammunition carrier to his shoulders. It rose with a wild fling, the man's body separating with his decapitation and sent flying among the treetops.

Anthony sprinted for the dark jungle. The remaining raptors were now distracted as they fought for their survival against the Great Gray One who had taken their charge on the men as an attack on itself. Anthony was thus free to crash through the brush—into a jungle potentially seething with flesh eaters the equal of those he had just fled. When he stopped at last, drawing deep breaths, the full realization of his predicament weighed upon him. He was alone in this prehistoric jungle, armed only with his knife.

He heard a rustle in the trees along side him --

The death's head raptor!

* * *

A nthony had no desire to have a flesh eating dinosaur so close to his face that he could count its teeth. Once that evening had been plenty. If he had retained a gun, avoiding another such an encounter would have been easy enough. He wasn't going to risk throw-ing his knife at the creature, so it was useless *unless* the fight was up close. And, spent as he was from the battle he had just been through, he wasn't sure he would have the strength to again keep the dinosaur simultaneously at arm's length with one hand and drive his knife into its heart with the other.

Holding his knife by the hilt between his teeth, his hands dropped to his belt and began undoing it. The smoothly textured but sturdily woven rope belt was more than a mere article of clothing: it was a weapon in his arsenal, its buckle a steel ball the size of a baseball. In an instant the belt was slipped free and the buckle was spinning over his head.

The death's head raptor erupted from the brush. Anthony let the steel ball fly but held to the belt's other end. The ball smacked the raptor— *hard*—in one eye. It screeched in pain, momentarily halted in its tracks.. Anthony seized the opening, retracted the ball, and looked up into the boughs above him. Up shot the steel ball and the end of the belt it was on wrapped around a sturdy branch. After a quick, strong tug to be certain his purchase would hold, Anthony began pulling himself up among the tree's limbs.

The recovered raptor repeatedly leapt after him, powerful jaws snapping. Anthony's legs battered the predator, each thrust backed by the strength of a stallion's kick. He was thus able to deflect the dinosaur's attack until he was out of the reach of the death's head raptor and any other predators that might be hunting below. In the event that he encountered the Great Gray One again or another of the larger carnivores, he would drop down to the jungle's floor and make for any sheltering "briar patch" -- or reasonable facsimile thereof.

He traveled along from tree to tree via the branches. It was from this vantage point that he first saw the domes of the city, looking like half-moons trapped among the treetops, caught in their ascension back into the sky.

He knew he should concentrate on reuniting with Zaroff, but here was a mystery, something he knew would give him cause to toss and turn for sleepless nights yet to come if he didn't investigate it.

Zaroff can fend for himself, Anthony thought, and he began swinging through the branches in the direction of this silent city. Its cold lunar domes the color of sable and ermine, he half expected it to exist only by the moon's light and hastened to reach it before sunrise.

The sky was growing lighter when Anthony descended to the jungle floor that went right up to the city but did not penetrate it. At first, Anthony took this as a sign that the city was inhabited, but his subsequent investigation showed this not to be the case. Nor was it over run with fauna— there were no signs that the city's broad, ivory flagstone highways had ever been fouled by bodily waste. Nor had men plundered the gold that trimmed the seams of the flagstones.

Besides the domed buildings, there were towers like alabaster obelisks that tapered upward, crowned as often as not with tiny cupolas. Like

Herod's temple in Jerusalem, gold embroidered the large ivory stones that made up much of this architecture. And all the buildings seemed to be converging on a common point: a minaret-like structure taller than all the other towers.

Man-made fountains still sent their waters gamboling upward. The sound of their splashing was eerie in the quiet that held a serene yet oppressive sway over the city. These fountains were arranged about a large open mall, their water's spray making the flat stones that made up the mall's floor perpetually wet and shimmering. Anthony had walked through the deserted city in a state of wonder. He was now crossing the mall, refreshing himself from the splattering water that seemed to leap with alacrity to his mouth, eager to quench his thirst.

This open mall and its fountains led to the minaret central to the city. Its place of prominence indicated to Anthony that it held prime significance to the city's former inhabitants. Indeed, though Anthony could not know this, it was the repository of knowledge for the people who had discovered the island long before Anthony and Zaroff.

These people were visionaries, wise in their secret arts. They were the people of Co 'op' O'bi.

Jim Anthony could not read the records that were left of these people. He thus could not learn their history nor that of their city. No amount of inductive and deductive reasoning would reveal it. Nor could he appreciate the irony that the record of the people of Co 'op'O'bi among the books in the tower was not left by one of them but one of their successors in an act of confession and contrition:

We were not the first to come to the island. Before us were the people of Co 'op'O'bi and before them the natives, whose ethnicity makes it clear that they also came from elsewhere. According to the inscriptions they left in their abandoned city in the island's interior, these natives claimed to have been here even before the dinosaurs.

These creatures were considered the brood of the natives' evil deity, sent from that divinity's underworld domain to plague them. They believed they were championed by one of their own demigods, whom they identified with a giant anthropoid dwelling among the other forms of atavism here.

When the people of Co 'op'O'bi came to the island, they found the natives pushed back to the coast of their island by the prehistoric life. The people of Co 'op'O'bi fortified the wall the natives had built to protect themselves against the ravenous beasts. These life forms, however, were degenerating, having reached the limits of breeding the confines of the island allowed them.

With the humans on the island now protected, the people of Co 'op'O'bi used their arts to revitalize these prehistoric creatures. The basic structure of their cellular life was made again robust, and their precious breeding stock thus invigorated.

Greatest of the Co'op'Obi's accomplishments, greater even than this city that remains ever pristine after their departure, was their realization of the natives' mythical demigod. It is said that this beast was first seen in a vision by the great Co'op himself, in pitched battle with dragons whose prodigious spawn wearied him. With his court alchemist O'bi and the demiurge D'el Gado, Co'op followed his vision to the island and found there the giant anthropoid near dead.

O'bi and his acolytes did fortify the beast's skeleton with an armature of strangely tempered metals. Then the secret arts of O'bi endowed the anthropoid with strange alchemical life. Greater in height he became and able even, so it seemed, to alter his size at will. For now the beast had become god and taken on the dimension of myth. And as for all his mighty acts, are they not written in the book of the Rose?

So the beast god became the island's true king, the greatest achievement of the Co 'op'O'bi, whose every accomplishment was that of the Visionary. Yet the fame of their beast god went out moreso than that of his creators so that it has come to seem that their creation has always been in the world. Yet the beast-god was not and then was only by their secret arts.

Great is the work of the C 'op' O'bi and their work is an everlasting one as long as the earth continues. Yet the people of Co 'op'O'bi themselves were not immortal. Their arcane knowledge was passed to a few acolytes and their efforts were great, yet none as great as that achieved at the first by the Co 'op'O'bi.

Then, at the last, my people, the Weta-people, came to the island.

We sailed Westward from the Gray Havens, far west of Sumatra. It was after the return of the king; we went forward in triumph. And on this island we found all the works of the Co' op'O'bi preserved.

We had not the vision of the Co 'op'O'bi, but still found much at fault in their work. For we of the Weta-people follow a two-thirds-matriarchal triumvirate, and the will of the women weighed heavily in all that we did.

As long as the king could indulge in his permutations and fancies concerning the indigenous atavistic life, he was content. Thus, he stood by when the matriarchs deposed the natives' shaman and replaced him with a witch-woman of their picking. No longer were the women sacrificed to the beast god victimized at the hands of patriarchal men but rather at the hands of matriarchal women, which was much more to be desired.

With their strange hand sigils, our matriarchs sought to bind the beast-god, so that he became only beast and no god. Great were the follies that were now spoken of him. They taught him via their secret signs to express his own feelings, for expression of feelings is very important to women. But in the end they taught him only sorrow. Regarding the powerful wisdom of all the Co' op'O'bi had done, the matriarchs made only token acknowledgement and even held up their precursors' greater work to be mocked, derided and redacted. Because the Co' op' O'bi's wisdom was beyond their ken, they regarded their forbearers' works with contempt at worse and indifference at best.

Neither were things good with the rest of the island's denizens now under the sway of the Weta-people. Under the Co 'op'O'bi, the natives thrived in their margin of the island and their culture, while pagan, was robust and self-sufficient. Under the dominion of the Weta-people, the natives' society disintegrated until they were gray-skinned, zombie-like creatures, living among the tombs like those possessed of unclean spirits.

Our tampering with the island's fauna produced innovations, but more was lost than gained, so that the dinosaurs we bred became wraith-like things, loud but only hollow echoes of their ancestor beasts. We also brought forth-strange creations of our own, unnatural bat-like things that were once pterodactyls.

And now, due to the machinations of we, the Weta-people, the island itself is sinking from sight. Ultimately, our greatest accomplishment will be to have obscured and effaced the works of the Co 'op'O'bi people, a people far greater than our own, of whom we have shown ourselves unworthy as we board our great ships from the Gray Havens and pass once more into the West.

All of this was lost to Jim Anthony; for him, the city of the Co 'op'O'bi would be one more mystery the island refused to give up. But another enigma was presenting itself to him. As he surveyed the canopy of tree-tops on the island below him from the vantage point of a balcony on one of the city's towers, he saw a man and woman break out of the jungle, running for their lives.

His first impression, one that startled him, was that they were white. They were both in ragged clothing, but the woman was nearly naked, her long blond hair spilling over her shoulders. And in the next instant, Anthony's hawk sharp eyes recognized them:

"Dana! Jack!" he shouted at the top of his lungs, flinging the call out over the stone maze of the great city. It arrested them. They stopped, seeming to notice the city for the first time, Jack clutching Dana by her waist to support her. She was obviously at the point of swooning. Anthony shouted out again and began the run down the tower's flights of steps.

By the time he had crossed the city and was outside it, they were nowhere to be seen. Anthony twirled about on his heel. At least he could trail them once he had found where they had reentered the jungle. . .

"Jim!"

He turned at Dana's imploring, despairing voice. She and Jack were emerging from behind a large column that made part of the entranceway to the city. She was still supported by Jack who, despite their desperate, disheveled state, did not seem happy to see Anthony.

"I told you," he said to Dana. "We need to keep moving. Stopping here is a bad idea."

"Jim is a friend, Jack," she said. "And with just a little rest, I won't need you to carry me; we'll make up the time we lost. Jim! I don't know why you're here, but I am so glad you are!"

"Dana —" Anthony asked in near disbelief, staring at her as he would an apparition, "what on earth happened to you?"

"What *are* you doing here, Anthony?" Jack asked.

"Uhm . . . big game hunting."

"Yeah," Jack said grimly. "I've seen some of the local fauna."

"But what are you two doing here? Were you shipwrecked? What about the movi—" Then Anthony realized. "This island was where you were coming to film."

"To film what's on it," Jack said.

"You *knew* there were dinosaurs here?"

"No. I can truly say *that* came as a complete surprise."

""Well, if not the dinosaurs, then what *were* you expecting to find here? And, for the luva Pete, what *happened* to you two?" Anthony asked again, noting that, at his questions, a shadow seemed to settle over Dana's face.

"What we're running from happened to us. And that's why we've got to *keep* running. So it doesn't happen again." Dana buried her face into Jack's chest at that, and Anthony felt a shard of jealousy pierce his heart.

"But you can't keep going on like you are," he said. "These insects will give you hell where your torn clothes bare your skin, and Dana's almost completely exposed. It won't matter if you escape what ever is after you if you succumb to some kind of prehistoric malaria our bodies have no defense for. She doesn't even have any shoes! Listen to me: there's plenty of fabric in this abandoned city. Let's see if we can't find something to cover you. And you both obviously could use some water. There are fresh fountains here."

"Oh, *please*, Jack. Let's listen to Jim," Dana said, raising her face from Jack's chest and turning it toward Anthony. Her eyes were sending such a look of appeal for succor to him that it was all Anthony could do to keep himself from forcibly taking her from Jack and gathering her protectively into his own arms.

Jack saw what was passing between them and scowled. Then, taking his thumb and forefinger, he turned her head back toward him. "Listen to me, honey. I know you're tired but like I said, I'm strong enough for the both of us. I know it's got to seem like a nightmare now, like something that couldn't have possibly happened, but it did! And it was a lot worse than some bleeding feet and malaria could ever be!"

Dana's eyes were now glazing with fear at the remembrance of some horror that had apparently all but consumed her. "I thought I'd be torn limb from limb! And then the way he would toy with me. I've never felt so powerless in my life. So . . ." she looked down, regarding the rags that were all that hung from her nearly nude body, ". . . so *humiliated*. I think . . . I think he thought he was skinning me. What . . . what would have happened if Jack hadn't come when he did?" Her voice was now rising with the beginnings of hysteria.

Then she begged Jack: "You won't let him take me again, will you, Jack? You promised!"

"That's why we can't afford to wait any longer, honey," Jack said, embracing her shoulders and pulling her to him while shooting a triumphant look at Anthony.

"'Him?' Who exactly are you two running from?" Anthony demanded.

"Believe me, brother, you don't want to be around here to find out when he shows up. You'd best get back to your safari, and let us get off this island. We're going now."

Anthony reached out and laid his hand firmly against Jack's shoulder. "You won't make it. You can rest here, and there's plenty of room for shelter from whatever you're running from."

Jack shrugged off Anthony's hand. "Stand down."

"You're not taking her with you," Anthony bristled back.

And then Zaroff's cry from the jungle: "Anthony! Anthony!"

Anthony felt a bolt of panic jolt him: if Zaroff should find Jack and Dana here, and neither he nor Jack with firearms . . . .

* * *

"**S**ounds like your Russian pal is looking for you," Jack said sardonically.

"Listen to me, Jack. You're right. You need to go. *Now!*"

Jack immediately began pulling Dana along. She looked back regretfully over her shoulder at Anthony, and that look broke his heart. They slipped away among the trees while Anthony trotted out to meet Zaroff.

Zaroff saluted him and smiled. When they stood face to face, the still smiling Russian clamped his hand momentarily on Anthony's shoulder, a gratuitous gesture that surprised Anthony as a somewhat affectionate touch.

So, do you really have a heart in there after all , Zaroff old boy? Anthony thought. He was thus doubly glad that Jack and Dana had managed to get away. Sexual lust and a desire for revenge would have easily obliterated Zaroff's yet too tenuous toe hold on humanity.

"Anthony! So happy to see you are well, my friend. I have been searching for you this entire day. When I saw the towers of this city spiraling out above the jungle treetops, it seemed a certainty they would draw you to them."

Anthony briefly grasped Zaroff's upper arm to reciprocate and said, "This place is the ninth wonder of the world, Zaroff. I've been exploring it. Let me show you —"

"No, no, my friend," Zaroff said with a smile, removed his silver cigarette case from his breast pocket, and tapped out a cigarette into his palm. "It will have to be regulated to tenth place, for I have already discovered evidence of the ninth elsewhere."

"What exactly have you seen?"

"Only this ninth wonder's handiwork so far, but such handiwork!" Zaroff enthused as he lit his cigarette, put it to his mouth, took a leisurely draw, and expelled the smoke with a look of joyful speculation. "To wit: the Great Gray One we have stalked is *dead*, its jaws snapped and broken apart."

Anthony's own jaw dropped. "That would require hands with opposable thumbs, hands the size of . . ."

"—a giant! Yes! An anthropoid! A creature no one suspects of even existing, perhaps the only one of its kind. I must seize this opportunity to slay it and take its head. And you, my friend, I desire much to accompany me on this, the hunt of my life!"

Zaroff was beaming, and Anthony, knowing the invitation to be the highest compliment Zaroff could offer, struggled to hide his own revulsion at the thought of killing an anthropoid. Anthony knew apes were capable of emotions such as spite and sadness, feelings too close to a human's for him to personally desire to slay one. Of course, Zaroff had been accused of hunting *men*.

Yet, this same Zaroff, who could have abandoned him to the jungle, had risked his own life to find him.

"Zaroff," he said, "you and I together couldn't bag the Great Gray One; how could we hope to bring down an animal that was more than its equal?"

"I *must* face it, Anthony! Even if it means my death, to die at such a beast's hands in the jungle would be a glorious way to take leave of this mortal coil, much more to my liking than to die peaceably, full of years, in my own bed. If I am to face my end, let it be against such a magnificent adversary and not in the humiliation of being destroyed by an ignoble germ or virus!"

--*Or the ignominy of the electric chair*, Anthony thought. *Or a bullet from Allardravitch.* Had Zaroff also sensed from the beginning of their journey what Anthony had told Allardravitch on the pier—that only one of them would be returning? Was the proposed hunt a hidden plea from the Count to let him die on his own terms?

Anthony placed a firm hand on Zaroff's shoulder. "Sure, Zaroff. We'll —"

A cry in Russian came out of the jungle along with the swaying of trees and branches. Zaroff turned at the salutation. His eyes went wide, as did Anthony's, at what he saw:

One of Zaroff's perimeter men was coming out of the trees, herding at the end of his rifle Dana and Jack. As the two were marched to Zaroff, Anthony saw a look of pleasure beyond expectation form over the Russian's features. His gaze rested mostly on the barely clothed Dana—Anthony felt again his own desire quickened by this revelation of disheveled, vulnerable beauty. Anthony, however, wanted to protect as well as possess her. Zaroff's lust, like his desire to kill, was unmitigated by sympathy.

Dana and Jack were marched right up to them. Zaroff felt free to look the girl over, offering a frankly admiring appraisal. Dana's entire body colored with her embarrassment; she quickly dropped her own gaze away from Zaroff's—she was, in a fashion, fleeing from him. Ever the hunter, a delighted Zaroff took pursuit and captured her chin, turning her to face him. Her eyes gleamed desperately at Anthony, appealing wordlessly for his help. Frightened as she had to be, having fled in fear of one horror only to fall into the hands of another, she managed to keep enough presence of mind to not say anything that would give away that Anthony was an ally.

He made a slight nod at her which he hoped was reassuring.

Then Zaroff smacked Jack in the face with the back of his hand, his knuckles splitting the first mate's lip. Dana screamed as Jack lunged for the Russian, only to have Zaroff's man grab him and pin his arms tightly behind him.

"Let it go, Zaroff!" Anthony shouted.

"Relax, Anthony. I merely evened the score with this Cossack."

"Since the score is even, then you won't have any objections to letting them go now," Anthony said.

Zaroff shot Anthony a confused look. " 'Go?' Go where? Back into that savage jungle? How can you suggest sending a woman alone into it, unprotected?"

"She'll have Jack with her. And you can spare him a gun."

Zaroff laughed. "Hardly! Besides, our tally is not quite even yet. Miss Sparrow still owes me a waltz. We were not allowed to finish, remember? And I most certainly intend to collect. My man will grant her safe passage . . . back to my yacht."

"And what about Jack?" Anthony asked.

"I am not entirely without compassion. Give him your knife, Anthony. And I will give him an hour's start into the jungle."

" 'An hour's start?'" a scowling Jack asked, narrowing his eyes uncertainly at Zaroff as though he hadn't heard right.

"Before I come after you," Zaroff said coolly.

"*Hunt* Jack?!" Dana said in repulsion and disbelief. "Like he's some animal? You can't do that to him!"

Anthony blanched. Despite his own growing suspicions, to this point, it had only been Rainsford's and Allardravitch's word against Zaroff's. But now, to see him so casually state he was going to hunt Jack . . . clearly, this wasn't the first time.

"So the stories were true," Anthony said.

Zaroff smiled. "Yes, Anthony. They were. They *are*. I suppose you feel obligated to try and stop me now. But let me point out that any resistance you might offer is doomed to fail. My man and I are armed with guns and rifles; I have another man nearby in the jungle, similarly armed. You have a knife that the reach of our guns will not allow you close enough to use; these two," he nodded at Dana and Jack, "hardly even have the clothes on their backs. A charming state of affairs where Miss Sparrow is concerned, to be certain, but it leaves them all the more vulnerable.

"So there is no shame, Anthony, in your submitting when I have you taken back to the yacht with Miss Sparrow. My sole intention is that you should not come to harm, my friend; we still have a hunt to make together, yes? The greatest hunt of our lives!"

"So, that's been your angle, then," Jack all but snarled at Anthony. He nodded at Dana. "You've played things so that you can come across as her protector."

"Anthony," Zaroff asked, "what is he talking about? Played *what*?"

"Take it easy, Jack . . .," Anthony began, raising his hand.

"You let us go knowing we'd be recaptured, but you'd come off smelling like a rose!"

Zaroff's expression, to Anthony's surprise, was a wounded one when he turned it on him. "You tried to help them escape? You would have denied me the satisfaction of my honor? Or the pleasure of Miss Sparrow's company? Why, Anthony? Did you think I would not share her with you?"

" 'Share her?'" Anthony said, revolted, as he stepped protectively between Dana and the Russian. "Zaroff, I was a fool to think there was something worth redeeming in you. If I had thought for one minute it would have come down to innocent people getting hurt . . . I would have let Allardravitch have you."

"Your betrayal pains me, Anthony," Zaroff said. "By casting your lot with this first mate who sees you as an enemy and not the man who saw you as a friend, you have proven yourself unworthy of joining me in the hunt. But you may have use yet . . . as the hunted. At least you will make things much more interesting than Jack would be capable of alone."

"Listen, you fool!" Jack barked. "There is something right behind us that will be as about impressed with your guns as a pea shooter! It's on its way while we just stand around and wait for it to catch up --"

"NO!" Dana cried out, so desperate that she stepped out from behind Anthony and approached Zaroff. "Please, Count, let . . . Jim and Jack go. And I'll go with you. I'll do whatever you want. Just . . . let's get away from here. I . . . I couldn't stand to be in its hands again!"

Dana and Jack were marched right up to them.

"Did you say . . . 'hands?'" Zaroff asked, smiling eagerly at Dana. "Not 'claws,' but 'hands'? Hands perhaps large enough to rip apart a tyrannosaur's jaws, my dear? Yes?"

Dana staggered backwards at the memory, bursting into sobs. Fearful that she was in a swoon, Anthony stepped forward and pulled her to him to give her support.

"It was terrible, Jim," she said. "I was thrust up so horribly close, closer than anything human was ever meant to be to creatures like that, and there was nowhere for me to go! All I could see were surging waves of fur and scales going back and forth into each other and then they swept up against the tree I was in! The next thing I knew, the ground was rising up to meet me, and I was pinned down! I knew I was going to have the life crushed out of me at any moment! Then I heard a sickening cracking as loud as a large tree being ripped up from its roots . . . . I looked back over my shoulder, he grabbed its jaws and pulled—and the blood! The blood, Jim! The blood wouldn't stop gushing from that terrible, frozen rictus he had made of its mouth!"

Zaroff's eyes had widened with excitement as Dana described the battle she had witnessed, confirming his conjecture of how the Great Gray One had met its end.

"Then he took me from under the tree, and the way that thing looked at me—it was never going to let me go." She began to sob against Anthony's chest.

"And now the beast is coming to reclaim you!" Zaroff enthused. "Ha! Well, why not? I understand very well how you can become an obsession, Miss Sparrow. But do not fear, my dear. I do not intend to share you with this monster. You shall be safely kept on my yacht."

"Are you sure about that, Zaroff?" Anthony said, seeing a possible opportunity to keep Dana under his watch and out of Zaroff's floating fortress. "The beast obviously has her scent. If you send Dana to the yacht, he will follow her there. Do you want to risk this monster sinking your only way off of this island?"

Zaroff's eyes narrowed as he thought. Then: "No. We shall see to it that his pursuit ends *here*. Despite Miss Sparrow's fears, this beast apparently prizes her. So there should be no danger in tying her to a tree —"

Dana cried out, and Anthony drew her to him.

"—rather like staking out a lamb, I suppose. But don't worry my dear; I will fire on the beast before it can touch you. And then it will never threaten you again."

"You're crazy!" Jack snarled. "You won't kill it with a rifle! It's chaos when this thing cuts loose. You get me? Your bullets could strike Dana, or the monster could fall over onto her and crush her while she's tied to that tree!"

Anthony, however, had been thinking. "And besides, Zaroff," he injected. "What are you going to use to tie her?"

"Rope, of course," he answered.

"That coarse rope you brought from the ship? She's almost naked—that rope will lacerate and scar her soft skin. You really are an uncivilized brute aren't you?" Anthony responded.

Zaroff frowned and was silent. Anthony waited; he was playing Zaroff's desires against each other, waiting for him to reach the only conclusion that would accommodate both his lust for blood and lust for beauty. . . .

Then Zaroff smiled. "If you and Jack will be so kind as to remove your belts and lash the girl to that sturdy trunk there—the soft leather of Jack's belt should hold her without laceration, as will the silken cord of your own belt, Anthony."

Dana screamed and tried to bolt from Anthony's grasp. He held her tightly, giving her a couple firm shakes:

"Listen to me, Dana!" he said. "We have no choice but to do what he says. But trust me; I'm not going to let that monster get you again. I promise."

Dana's tear-streaked face looked up at him, and her deep, sharp breathing began to slow as she though she were drawing strength from his touch. Finally, she nodded her head in mute consent.

His arms around her waist, Anthony walked her to the tree Zaroff had indicated. Zaroff nudged Jack forward with the nose of the rifle in his back.

Anthony positioned Dana against the tree's trunk, smiling reassuringly down at her. Jack joined them, and the two men went behind the tree. Zaroff and his man were now standing about ten feet away, their rifles lowered toward the ground.

"Jack," Anthony said, "you tie her upper body. I'll secure her legs." The first mate grudgingly began to loosen his belt. Anthony had his off already and was crouching at the bottom of the trunk.

Then Anthony sprung up, twirling his weighted belt above his head. Zaroff startled, but before he could raise his rifle, the bola belt had already spun across the distance between them and caught him, snaring his arms to his sides. Zaroff's baffled man stepped haltingly toward his master to assist him.

"Shoot the men!" Zaroff shouted at his lackey. But in the man's hesitation, Anthony, threw his knife, and Zaroff's lackey fell headlong, the blade protruding from his chest.

"Move! *Now!*" Anthony shouted as he grabbed Dana's hand and pulled her after him into the jungle.

* * *

The three of them ran at breakneck speed, pushing through the trees and hanging tangles of vines. Behind them, a rifle fired but they already were out of its range. They had run non-stop for more than a mile when Dana suddenly stopped, yanking Anthony back.

"Please! Just let me catch my breath."

"Dana, you're bleeding," Anthony said, raising her face, and gently dragging his thumb over a cut to her cheek a resilient branch had dealt her.

She smiled. "You keep calling me 'Dana.' I'm 'Eve Trowbridge' today."

"You'll always be 'Dana' to me," Anthony said. "That's how I got to know you."

"Her feet are a bleeding mess, too!" Jack said, stepping over and yanking Dana away from Anthony and up into his arms. "I'll carry her, but we've got to keep moving. If either Zaroff or this monster catches up with us first —"

"You two keep on the way you're going," Anthony said. "I assume you're trying to reconnect with 'D.W. De Cent' and his crew?"

"Yeah, that's right,"

"I'm going to double back and take care of Zaroff," Anthony said.

"Jim! No!" Dana protested from Jack's arms. "Please don't go! Stay with us!"

Anthony smiled reassuringly at her. "Jack will make sure Injun Joe doesn't get you, honey. Just get off this island and never come back."

"Brother, you don't have to tell us twice," Jack said.

"But what about you, Jim?" Dana asked pleadingly. "We can't leave you behind."

"She's got a point there, Anthony," Jack said. "You're falling out with Zaroff pretty much guarantees you've forfeited guest accommodations on his yacht. You're not going back with him except as a trophy."

"It'll require some negotiating, that's for sure," Anthony said, his tone communicating a confidence he didn't feel. But he wanted Dana to make it to safety. And he believed he had a chance to eliminate two of the obstacles to achieving that goal.

"Don't worry about me," Anthony said, grinning. "I'll meet back up with you guys. Now, *go!*"

Jack took off, still cradling Dana. And Anthony allowed himself one lingering stare after them; he felt his heart bound when he saw Dana's blue eyes looking yearningly at him from over Jack's shoulder.

Then he turned to the task at hand.

He began to circle around back the way they had come. Zaroff would be following their trail easily enough. Anthony intended to maneuver himself behind the Russian. And then—Anthony set his jaw—then he would do what had to be done to make certain Zaroff would never take another human life.

All conditional, of course, on his successfully eluding what was trailing *him* at the moment. Still, he had to smile that it was following him, just as he had hoped, and not Jack and Dana.

Then he felt a sudden tremor under his feet and heard gunfire in the near distance. The gunfire ceased abruptly but the tremors were becoming more violent—and closer! A frantic rustling in the brush surrounding Anthony announced the creature trailing him had chosen the better part of valor and fled what was coming. Anthony was having difficulty staying upright as the ground convulsed. And now the higher branches were cracking, each with the sharp report of a rifle as they broke in the path of what thrust against them: Anthony saw entire trees torn loose and flying forward in the face of what was coming: harbingers and heralds of a disaster which was rapidly descending upon him.

Anthony managed to throw himself out of its path and back against a pillar-like trunk just as the terror propelled itself through the trees surrounding him. He had expected merely another gigantic atavism of prehistoric life, something anthropoid, even simian. He was not prepared for the numinous, to find himself in sudden kinship with Moses who had once clung in the cleft of the rock as the presence of Yahweh passed him by.

With a blasting roar and sweep of its long arms the god of the island pushed past, ancient trees snapping and sending large splinters like shrapnel flying before an incarnate hurricane honing in on Dana and Jack. Anthony was stunned, his initial impression that he was lucky to still live, though he sensed it was only because he was beneath contempt of such a being.

He was thankful that Dana's scent had not been strong upon him. If that beast had caught him up expecting Dana and been disappointed, Anthony knew he would now be dead. His immediate emotion after this great sense of relief was fear for Dana and Jack should this holy terror succeed in descending upon them.

But there was nothing he could do at the present to make any difference in how that entity's pursuit of them turned out.

And there was someone else who demanded his attention now. Someone who had unwisely engaged the beast-god's attention when he had passed him by.

Anthony followed the swathe the creature had made through the jungle back to a clearing. And there he found Zaroff, sprawled like a broken mannequin, one disjointed arm thrown back over his shoulder, a leg broken so that the bone pierced through the flesh and jutted out. Blood soaked his scalp, and he appeared unconscious. The Russian's rifle had been tossed clear of him. Anthony claimed it, cocked it and approached Zaroff with its barrel trained on him.

Zaroff made no movement, and Anthony had no trouble in unholstering his Luger and unsheathing the knife at his side. He felt for and found a pulse in his throat. He then alternately slapped each of the Russian's cheeks. "Zaroff!" he said at the top of his voice. "Zaroff!"

Something stirred among the trees near the edge of the clearing. Anthony looked in the direction of the noise. His plan had worked; now he steeled himself to follow through with it. He reminded himself that Zaroff had ordered him shot and before that had planned to hunt him down like an animal along with Jack. And he knew what he had in mind for Dana after the hunt had stirred his passion. How many more had Zaroff put through this kind of terror before taking their lives on his island? Still, the thought of putting a bullet in him while he was helpless and unconscious rankled Anthony's sense of honor. Whatever Zaroff had done, he was still a human being and worth some according of respect.

He smacked Zaroff again, hard. "Wake up, you vicious bastard!" he ordered him.

"Anthony . . ."

At Zaroff's intake of breath upon awakening, Anthony had reared back as though an adder had hissed at him. He rose to his feet and looked down at the Russian who smiled up at him.

"It would appear I acted without discretion," Zaroff said.

"So did I," Anthony said grimly.

Zaroff stretched out the hand of his unhurt arm up toward Anthony. "Fortunately, we have both survived to learn from our mistakes, eh?""

"Indeed," Anthony said but made no move to take Zaroff's outstretched hand. After a long moment, Zaroff withdrew it. "I see," he said. "I understand your position completely, of course. Will it be with a bullet?"

Anthony tossed him the knife. Zaroff looked at it quizzically then grasped the handle. "I am to have a chance, then?"

"Only the opportunity to go down fighting. The word from Rainsford was that you gave your victims on your island that much."

"But Anthony—with a broken leg and a useless arm . . ."

"Odds only slightly worse than someone with only a knife against a long bow or a rifle, wouldn't you say?"

"But how can you expect me to make it through the jungle like this?"

"You won't get that far."

Again, the rustling and stirring like an impatient wind in the trees.

"What is that?" Zaroff asked and craned his head in the direction of the sound.

"You executioner," Anthony said coolly and began walking to where the jungle resumed on the other side of the clearing.

The death's head raptor parted the trees that had concealed him until now. Anthony knew the creature had been shadowing him throughout his time on the island, waiting for a moment of isolated vulnerability as it had demonstrated when Anthony had found himself alone in the wake of the botched slaying of the Great Gray One. He had kept the death's head raptor as his ace in the hole in the event Zaroff attempted to hunt him. When the island's god had passed by, Anthony feared the death's head raptor's flight had aborted his plan to come behind Zaroff and lead the stalking dinosaur right to his *other* stalker.

But the raptor had found him again, after all.

And now he had found Zaroff—vulnerable and alone.

Anthony heard quickly hastening hind claws beating the ground behind him, and the triumphant shriek of the raptor. Its skull-like markings added an unexpected but appropriate medieval touch as its scythe-like claws fell upon Zaroff.

The Russian screamed once.

Anthony was glad it had been quick.

* * *

Anthony hadn't forgotten that Zaroff had claimed *two* perimeter men when they met outside the lost city, though only one of these had actually appeared, herding Jack and Dana. It was possible the other man had made contact with Zaroff between Anthony, Dana, and Jack fleeing Zaroff for their lives and Anthony coming across the wreckage the island's god had made of the Count.

Only Zaroff was to be found, though.

Had the island's god killed then tossed this perimeter man far away? Or had Zaroff's man deserted his master during that fateful encounter? Another possibility: Zaroff had sent him back for more ammunition to be better prepared for his assault on the beast god which he would resume after he himself had dealt with Anthony, Jack, and Dana.

At any rate, Anthony did not like having unaccounted for a man who had been loyal to Zaroff and may still be—especially if that man was armed.

Anthony approached Zaroff's yacht furtively. As he was no longer under the deceased Count's auspices, he had doubts about how welcome he would be. Hopefully, they would believe his feigned ignorance regarding Zaroff's fate. No doubt they would insist on seeking out their master, and he was glad that he had let the island take care of Zaroff: a bullet in his corpse could only be explained as suicide or murder. As things stood, any inferences concerning the cause of Zaroff's death could not lead to him. And he needed to be held blameless, for only then could he hope to be allowed free access to the Russian's yacht.

For, if the island's god had succeeded in recapturing Dana, Anthony knew he would need to avail himself of the armory Zaroff had on board in order to free her. On the other hand, if it turned out that Jack and Dana had made it successfully back to their ship, they and the other members of the De Cent expedition were unlikely to have waited around for him to meet back up with them. Which meant he needed passage on the yacht.

Not that he resented the De Cent expedition if they had left him behind; in fact, he *hoped* Dana was already far out to sea, long out of reach of the island's god and never to be tormented at his hands again. If the man calling himself D.W. De Cent had survived his encounters with the creatures on this island, if he had gotten on film what he wanted, surely he would have departed with no further delay.

The sun had been setting when he had left Zaroff to his fate, and Anthony was glad to have the cover of darkness as he approached the yacht. He found it still anchored where they had left it the day before. He was crawling through the brush, trying to remain concealed until he had a better feel of the mood among the men on the yacht. The boat was not lit except by the moon and starlight—they had always kept it dark at night to keep from attracting the attention of any dinosaurs.

A flood light from the ship's deck lit up the jungle about him, the startling brightness transfixing him as a bullet whizzed by his head and into the trunk of the tree behind him. Anthony rolled as the leafage and ground about him were repeatedly pelted. Using the undergrowth for cover, he crawled back quickly out of the range of the spotlight, then rose to his feet and beat an even faster retreat.

The light that had shone on him made it unlikely they had mistakenly thought him one of the island's beasts encroaching upon them. At any rate, he wasn't about to shout out or wave and remove all doubt—theirs, or his own.

Now his only hope of escaping the island was the *Venture*. Though he wished Dana safe above all else, the fact remained that her true circumstances—and his own—had yet to be ascertained.

He began a brisk jog back the way he came.

When he got back to the open glade where he had left Zaroff, he skirted it, circling through the trees to retain the cover they offered rather than follow a straight line and appear openly to any predators who stalked by night. The roundabout path he was taking meant he was steering clear of the spot where lay Zaroff's remains. Or where they had lain. For, if the beast that had killed him had left behind any part of the corpse, its remaining members had no doubt been torn apart, dragged over the glade, and otherwise defiled by scavengers. It was an ugly fate for an ugly man, yet Anthony had been the closest thing to a friend Zaroff had on the planet, and he took no pleasure in the thought of his body's ravaging.

When he was on the other side of the glade, all his intentions to the contrary, he found himself looking back in the direction where he had left Zaroff. He saw a night-shrouded form lying prone there, some smaller, saurian shapes at work on what was left of it. He shook his head from side to side, a regret as heavy as lead weighing on his heart. Then he resumed his brisk trek through the jungle.

Weariness was hobbling his steps like ankle chains by the time he reached the spot where he had parted ways with Jack and Dana. He had been going for two days now and had to stop and get some sleep or his dulled alertness increased the odds that he wouldn't survive his remaining passage over the island. He climbed into a sturdy tree, wedged himself into a receptive bough and passed out of consciousness.

His head was throbbing with the noon sun when he came to. A quick look over the lengthening shadows of the trees told him he had slept past noon. He jolted upright, finding himself being regarded quizzically by a feathered lizard. He would have been amused, but fear that he had missed the opportunity to connect with the De Cent expedition and escape the island sent him scurrying in a panic down the tree. He dropped the last ten feet to the ground, landed in a crouch, and then sprinted up the trail that could have been cleared by a cyclone but represented instead the wake of the island's god.

By mid-afternoon, he came upon a wall taller than any dinosaur, with cyclopean gates blasted outward out of their jambs. Right above the gateway, what looked like a giant, metal gong hung askew. Anthony passed through cautiously, holding his rifle at the ready. The only signs of life were numerous pairs of yellow eyes that gleamed sinisterly at him from the tenebrous inner reaches of what looked like a maze of aboveground catacombs. He found most disconcerting that these orbs were set in gray, dusky faces that were still identifiable as human.

"Who did this to them?" Anthony muttered to himself in disbelief.

Anthony kept his distance, as did they: apparently they had learned to respect gunfire. This he took as an indication that De Cent's interactions with the locals had been less than cordial. He moved on down to the shore where he found outrigger canoes, but no sight of the *Venture*. He saw that there were scraps here and there of lumber that had been cut with Western style saws and which bore the marks of a hammer head that could have come from *Montgomery Ward's* hardware section.

De Cent's group had been busy with something, and what seemed obvious to Anthony conjured up a surreal scene which, given the fury that had pushed through those gates, was frankly unbelievable.

Still, he had no time to puzzle it out. He didn't know what kind of lead the *Venture* had on him, but it was getting further along every minute. He hated stealing the outrigger, but his only option was to throw himself on the mercy of the island's denizens.

He shoved off into the surf, over and beyond the breaking waves, and, crawling into the outrigger, he began to paddle like mad.

He was half a mile out to sea when he saw the ship on the horizon. In desperation, he shot off a round of fire into the air, hoping to signal them.

Then the ship dropped over the edge of the world.

Suddenly, the sheer enormity of his isolation fell upon him: the ocean and sky went on forever and the magnitude of his prison assured that he would never escape it.

Not alive, anyway.

His rowed frantically, putting every bit of his considerable strength into propelling the canoe forward. Onward he pushed himself, the muscles of his arms burning to the degree that he felt that they would be ruined should he survive his ordeal.

And then a gun firing a round in the distance, apparently out of nowhere.

"They're signaling back!" Anthony shouted out and whooped with joy. He fired again into the air, wishing he could trade every bullet for a single flare, then returned to his frantic rowing . . .

And then the horizon drew in to him, and there was the ship, a huge, tarp-covered barge trailing it. He had little time to think of the significance of this, afraid as he was that the ship might once again dip beyond his reach—forever, this time.

But it quickly became clear that the ship was anchored, that they were in fact waiting for him. He knew what had to be on that barge—a giant raft hewn together back on the island's shore. It was unbelievable, but there would be plenty of time to hear that story on the long trip back to the United States.

A lifeboat dropped over the side of the ship, and two sailors rowed out to meet him. He continued to row himself, and soon the two wooden boats were knocking their sides against each other. Exhausted, he crawled out of the outrigger and collapsed into the bottom of the lifeboat.

"Are you all right, Mr. Anthony?" one of the sailors asked him.

"Happy to be alive—and to see you guys."

"Well, you look pretty spent, brother. Just lie back and leave the rowing back to the ship up to us."

"You'll get no argument from me. But—the girl—Dana? Is she all right?"

" 'Dana?' Oh, yeah. She and Jack are doing just swell. More than swell, I'd say—they're engaged."

Anthony felt the earth suddenly revolve away out from under him.

"How. . . how did that happen?"

The sailor laughed. "You mean 'when,' don't you?"

"Yeah. Sure. When?"

"Back on the ship when the rest of us lugs were building that raft."

"What do you have under that tarp?"

"Biggest ugly ape I ever seen. Bastard wiped out half our crew."

"*How* was it done, exactly?"

"Gas bombs put him out. Every hour on the hour, somebody now has to crawl out over his body while we're at sea, pull back the tarp, and give him a fresh hit. Only volunteers for that detail, though they'll get a bigger slice of the pie when we get to New York."

"What pie?"

"The million dollar one that we're all getting a piece of!"

Anthony nodded his head, laid back and closed his eyes, still stunned at the news of the engagement. As they neared the *Venture*, he saw Dana's face among the ones looking over the side at him. She leaned forward anxiously, as though eager to see that he was all right. Then she looked at Jack at her side and quickly muted her enthusiasm at Anthony's arrival.

"So what's the story, Dana?" Anthony thought, glad that his sunburn was hiding his coloring at the sight of the newly official couple. "Why did you do it?"

Anthony climbed up the rope ladder over the side of the ship, but by the time his feet were planted on the deck, Dana was nowhere to be seen. Jack nodded at him and offered a welcoming smile—of course. Why shouldn't he mind seeing him bob up out of the ocean, now that he had the world on a string—*Dana*, on a string.

"Hello, Anthony!" The man calling himself D.W. Cecil De Cent greeted him and firmly clasped and pumped his hand. "Jack and Dana told me they'd run into you out there in the jungle—you, and your 'pal' the Count—the dirty rat!"

"So, you knew he was rotten, and you still didn't send out a rescue party for me before you weighed anchor?" Anthony asked.

"Now, don't be sore, Anthony. Dana wanted to send some guys out, but they weren't exactly lining up for the detail after they heard that their crewmates who had already ventured out beyond the wall wouldn't be coming back. And then, of course," he nodded toward the raft, "they experienced first hand some of the local fauna themselves. You could've been dead already, for all we knew, but if you survived the jungle and the Count, you had his yacht to get off the island."

Anthony leveled his eyes with the director's: "The Count is dead. A victim to the 'local fauna.'"

De Cent's jaw went slack. "You don't say? Son of a gun! So, why didn't you take his yacht instead of striking out in that outrigger?"

"Because when I went back, they shot at me."

"Holy mackerel! With the Count dead, they took over his boat for themselves, eh? Pirates and scamps! I didn't say anything before because it looked like you and the Count were pals, but Russians don't rank too highly with me. I fought with the Poles against them after the Great War. In my opinion, you should be glad that you're washed up with that ilk. Now, come on, Anthony ol' pal, and let's get you into a bath and some clean clothes."

Anthony nodded his head in agreement. The first thing he *really* wanted to do, of course, was have a talk with Dana. But she had made herself scarce. That was okay, though.

There are only so many places and so far to go on a ship out in the middle of the ocean, he thought.

* * *

Freshly washed and clean-shaven, wearing a change of clothes from among the effects of the sailors who were killed on the island, Anthony went looking for the woman he knew as Dana Sparrow. Feeling no inclination to be shy, he went directly to her cabin and knocked. She opened her door and took a sharp, involuntarily breath at the sight of him.

"Hi, Dana," he said.

"Hi, Jim. I'm so happy to see you're well."

"I'm alive; I'm in good health; I wouldn't say that I am 'well,' though. I understand that congratulations on your upcoming nuptials are in order."

She sighed deeply and pushed her back up against the door to allow him to pass inside.

"Who told you?"

"A sailor in the life boat that picked me out of my outrigger."

Dana winced and shut the door. "When it comes to gossip, those hardened salts are as bad as the society matrons in an Illinois beauty parlor."

He felt his heart bound. " 'Gossip?' You're saying it's *not* true?"

"No. It's true. Do you wish it weren't?"

"What do you think I wish, Dana?"

Her cheeks and lips colored into that rich blush that made him want to grab her and kiss her face again and again.

"Well, I really wouldn't know, would I?" she said. "Before we were unceremoniously reunited in the jungle, the last I saw of you, you couldn't wait to get out of a very nice clinch that I thought we were both enjoying!"

"Are you all right, Mr. Anthony?"

"I told you why I had to do that!"

"Yes! But to just leave for parts unknown with not so much as a forwarding address --"

"They don't exactly have addresses in parts unknown, Dana—that's why no one knows where the parts are!"

"I wasn't speaking literally, Jim! And that includes when I describe the clinch as 'very nice!'"

"So, what? You get engaged to Jack to spite me? Isn't that just a little juvenile, Dana?"

"What we have is *not* juvenile. It's something that was building between us long before you showed up. It was a gradual attraction—like a mature relationship always is."

"Well, you weren't giving Jack the time of day is how it looked to me. Or were you just using me to make him jealous?"

"I was *not* using you. You can be incredibly charming, as if you didn't know. And romantic—'Jim Anthony, Super Detective'—you're like a modern day knight-errant, like that Doctor Savage in the pulps or Douglas Fairbanks. If anything was juvenile—and shallow—it was my attraction to *you*. If you had asked me then, I'd have told you Jack and I were only friends. Well, I've learned a lot about what love really is since he put his life literally on the line for me time and time again in that jungle. I would be a fool to walk away from that kind of devotion—any woman would!"

"Yeah, but you're not 'any woman,' Dana! You're incredible! This ship has got a veritable *god* in tow on his back because he couldn't let you go. Do you want to talk about devotion? *That's* devotion!"

Her color deepened again, but now it indicated anger: "Don't you dare make light of that creature's fixation on me!"

"Who's 'making light?' That was a compliment!"

"A *compliment*? To remind me that I was terrified for my life moment to moment for 24 straight hours—and don't think that I haven't realized that if that thing wakes up because someone doesn't give it enough gas, then it's *me* it's coming for! And in the process it could overturn this ship and drown everyone on it—even the 'super detective!'"

Anthony expelled a burst of breath, tucked his head, put his hand on the back of his neck and kneaded it. "That sounds like you almost care, Dana."

"Almost --? Of course I care about you, Jim! Just because I love Jack doesn't mean I don't . . . . But what I feel for you, it isn't coming from a sound place."

"Don't say that, Dana," he said, taking her by her upper arms. "It's coming from a place as sound as the rock of Gibraltar. Just like . . . just like my love for you."

Dana looked up at him, her eyes shining.

"You . . . love me?"

"Look, Dana, I wasn't making light of what you went through on the island. And I appreciate what Jack risked to get you back to safety. He's a brick and a good egg and all that. But I recall putting my life on the line for you, too. Who got you away from Zaroff? Don't think I didn't notice the yearning in your face back in the jungle when you looked at me—*me*, not Jack, even though his arms were around you. I saw how you looked at me, too, when they brought me to the ship. You just naturally respond to me, Dana, as I do you. That's the long answer to your question: yes, Dana Sparrow or Eve Trowbridge or whoever you really are, I love *you*."

"Then why did you leave me like you did back on Zaroff's yacht?" Now her eyes were brimming with tears. "How could you drop what was the most tender, most ecstatic connection of my life and just take off? Kissing you was like everything those kisses in the movies promised a kiss could be. And then, you just turned it off and were gone!"

"Luvva Pete, woman! How many times do I have to say it? I left to keep you safe from Zaroff! You saw what he was really like on the island! I didn't want you to have to go through that with him."

"But I *did* go through it, didn't I?" she said quietly but firmly and drew up her shoulders. "Forgive me for continuing to be such a foolish, romantic child. You're right, of course. You *were* right to leave as you did. In fact, it . . . it would have been better if our paths had not crossed again."

Anthony flinched as though she had slapped him. "Dana, you don't have to go that far with it. When you were in danger, I was glad I was there."

"And I so wanted you to take me up in your arms and save me then. But afterward, when I had time to think, I had to admit that it was my faithful Jack alone who had done nothing but kept me safe, while all the dangers I needed *you* to save me from were dangers you had brought on me *yourself*."

Jim Anthony's jaw dropped. "What are you talking about? I didn't sign you to a movie to be filmed on the most unsafe terrain on the planet outside of a war zone! And I sure didn't hand you over to any giant ape!"

"No, but you didn't exactly save me from that creature either, did you? That would be Jack. And he was right—you only held us up and increased the risk of my recapture and his being killed—as well as yourself. We were barely inside the gates before that thing came lumbering up behind us! And as for Zaroff, it was only because of your association with him that he found Jack and me at our most vulnerable. Once more, if you had not delayed us, our paths would not have crossed Zaroff's again."

He stood, stunned into silence for a long moment. Then he shook his head slowly from side-to-side and released her arms.

She was right.

"I'm sorry, Dana," he said softly. "You've been through hell, and life with me would mean you would be constantly in danger—as you said—by association. I have enough enemies to know I can't promise your continued safety. So I don't deserve you. Jack will see you are looked after like you should be. He's rough around the edges, but his heart is in the right place when it comes to you. I was out of line to confront you like this. I had no right. I hope you will forgive me?"

"Of course," she said softly but firmly.

He stepped to the door, opened it, and paused.

"I understand that you tried to get a rescue party organized to help me. Thank you."

"I wanted you to be all right. You . . . you *will* be all right, won't you, Jim?"

"Never better," he said through clinched teeth and walked out of the room.

* * *

For the rest of the voyage, Anthony was not inclined to watch the happy couple. So, when he wasn't in his cabin, he was in the one spot on the ship where he would definitely not see Dana.

He was at the rear, observing the unconscious beast-god.

An IOU for $50,000 bought Anthony the opportunity from one of the sailors to release the gas in his stead into the beast-god's nostrils. He could more than afford it and would have paid twice the amount gladly.

And, truth be told, having lost Dana, he was inclined toward recklessness.

Then his bitterness gave way to enchantment.

He inhaled the animal's musk—it was nothing like he had ever smelled before or would smell again. Like the odors of the dinosaurs back on the island, he found the beast-god's scent forlornly poignant, like hearing a melody that had passed out of the world forever, only to be unable to share it with anyone else, and hearing it ever afterward only in memory.

As he crawled between aureoles as large around as automobile radials, he thought of what his shaman grandfather's reaction would be when he saw this magnificent creature bound. Indeed, it was how he felt himself: this was an indignity inflicted upon no mere beast but an incarnate spirit.

Anthony had now reached the large flaring nostrils. Staring into the black wrinkled flesh was to peer into a dark cauldron of wonder, to see the face of a god and still live. He also felt not unlike Ulysses hovering over the face of sleeping Polyphemus and experienced a jolt of fear at the thought of this behemoth's *two* eyes suddenly opening upon him. He was poised not to impale, however, but to administer a draught of Lethe.

Having made certain his gas mask was secure, Anthony opened the valve on the small tank he carried. "Drink deep, old man," he said. "It's better that you be unaware of your new condition for as long as possible."

He clipped a few sample hairs, which he wrapped in paper and stored in his pocket. Then, before he turned to go, he gave in to an impulse of playful awe and reached out and sank both hands into the thick, black mane of the sleeping god.

* * *

The *Venture* docked in New York in the early hours of morning. Anthony slipped away under darkness while Dana still slept. He told only the second mate that he was disembarking. Not caring to wait for the gangplank to be extended, Anthony leapt from the ship's railing and onto the pier. Then he began the walk home in his bare feet. It was winter when he and Zaroff had taken off; now it was officially Spring, though still cold enough that no one else would be venturing outside without a heavy coat, let alone without shoes. Almost two months out of his life to try and reform a hopeless sociopath. Allerdravitch had called it right as a fool's errand. Was it worth it?

He thought of the night he embraced and kissed Dana Sparrow. And he smiled.

Absolutely.

When he entered his penthouse for the first time since mid-February, he wasn't expecting to be greeted by a pistol aimed at him.

"Jimmy?" Tom asked, partially lowering his gun and straining his eyes in the still dark morning hours.

"It's me, Tom," Anthony said with a broad smile and a wave of the hand.

"Luva Pete!" Tom whooped, already heading across the penthouse living room toward his best friend. "Hey!" he shouted. "He's back! Jimmy's back!"

He and Anthony embraced with liberal slaps on the other's back. Then Anthony was startled by the sudden apparition standing by ghostly white curtains in the pre-dawn shadows.

"Grandfather . . .," he said.

"Welcome home, son," Mephito responded with a smile. "I'll get the hot chocolate brewing. Tom, will you start the fire back up? I'm sure you're as eager as I am to hear where Jim's been and what he's been up to."

"You got it—hey, Jimmy! We won't be playing host to that crazy Russkie, too, will we? 'Cause, brother, it's just a bit too early in the morning for me."

"Not a problem, Tom. Zaroff is dead."

"Good riddance. That Allardravitch guy and me were on the same page about him— the right one, it sounds like. Hope I didn't make you sore, giving him the pier's location, Jimmy. But to my look-out, you had a viper in your bosom."

Anthony clamped his hand down on his friend's shoulder. "You're a better man than I am, Gunga Din! Now, get that fire going, let me get a shower, and the three of us will sit down to that hot chocolate. And do I have stories to tell."

"Hey—I'm bettin' that smile on your face means a beautiful tomato was involved."

"Beautiful. And the bravest girl I've ever known."

The sun was up and bright by the time Anthony finished relating his adventures to his grandfather and Tom.

"There's no doubt about it, Jimmy," Tom said, "you have to get her back. While there's still time. And that means you get dressed and get down to that ship while you still have a clue where to find her."

"I can't do that, Tom. Every atom in my body is aching to—it was all I could do not to kidnap her from her cabin and carry her back here with me—but it's like I told her: she deserves to be safe. And even if I turned over a new leaf starting today, you and I already have too many old enemies."

Mephito was staring deeply into the fireplace's flames as though trying to divine something from them. Then: "How long before we can see this beast god, grandson?"

"Let's see. They won't be moving him until they can do it under dark, so he's staying under that tarp for the time being. Once they get him secure on land, it's all going to be top secret. The best I could get from De Cent is the promise that a backstage pass will be held for me whenever opening night happens—which will probably be while its still early spring."

The old man turned his gaze again into the fire. "Spring will not come early this year," he solemnly pronounced.

Tom chuckled and nodded toward the Maxfield Parish calendar on the wall. "You're a couple days late, Mephito; Spring came on the 21st."

* * *

Although the vernal equinox had arrived on schedule, a late snowstorm blew in the first of April. The natives of Manhattan awoke to layers of ice and snow, winter unwilling to give obeisance to the turning stars. Anthony knew of his grandfather's preternatural abilities, always more reliable than that famous groundhog's, so he wasn't too surprised on that account. Rather, what made *his* jaw drop was a story in the morning edition of the *Times*.

There already had been a steady stream of articles leading up the premiere of what the press was calling "The Giant Terror Gorilla." Dana, under another name (he had no idea whether it was her real one or just the stage name they had settled on), tended to be featured prominently. The upcoming event was drawing an interesting amount of celebrity attention. One was none other than the Celebrated Feral Child of Africa who had a personal interest in apes, giant or otherwise. Famous monkey-trial lawyer Clarence Darrow had also come forward, claiming to be none other than Dana's missing uncle. He called on her to express solidarity with his concern that the proper rights and dignity be accorded this evolutionary offshoot who was cousin to our race.

But the article Anthony was reading now, published on occasion of the unveiling of the mystery beast that evening, outdid anything yet for sheer audacity. It was a distorted re-imagining of the island adventure, purporting how Dana, about to be eaten by the beast who had taken her captive, improvised a series of vaudeville style pratfalls and cartwheels which so charmed the monster that he could in no way ever think of her as lunch again.

A knock on the door drew him away from the fireplace and his paper. "Who would try to pass something like that off on the paying public?" he asked himself, still regarding the article with disbelief as he lay it aside into his chair.

His visitor turned out to be none other than the woman of the hour, whom he still knew as "Dana Sparrow." Her slender fingers curled into a ball, she had her small fist raised and ready to knock again when the door opened.

"Dana?" Jim said, stunned.

"Hello, Jim. May I come in?"

Anthony wanted nothing more than to grab her, pull her into his apartment and claim her as his own.

Instead, he said, "After our talk on the ship, I thought there was nothing more to say, Dana."

"Obviously, I disagree. May I come in?"

"Sure," he said, stepping aside to let her enter.

"Thank you," she said as he shut the door behind her. She was wearing a coat and hat, both trimmed in leopard fur and fresh snow. She shivered a little and rubbed her gloved hands together. "May I avail myself of your fire, Jim?"

"Of course," he said. "I'll take that wet hat and coat if you like."

"Please," she said, unbuttoning the garment.

"Where's Jack?" he asked as he slipped the coat from her slim shoulders.

"Sleeping off last night's bachelor party with all his sailor buddies in Atlantic City."

"So, today's the big day," Jim said as he hung her coat on the stand by the door. Dana gently tugged at each fingertip of her gloves and walked toward the fireplace. As he had that night at sea, Anthony again admired her well-rounded behind—twin ovals undulating. She sat down and leaned toward the flame, stretching her hands out toward its warmth. She looked back over her shoulder and smiled: "To which day are you referring? Tonight's unveiling of 'the giant Terror-Gorilla,' perhaps?"

Anthony joined her, sitting down by the fire. "You know what I mean, Dana."

She sighed. "Yes, I know. It's tomorrow. I know the wedding is usually the day after the bachelor party, but C.D. —"

"Don't you mean D.W.?" Anthony asked and smiled.

Dana smiled back: "—wanted to make the wedding announcement part of the opening night's festivities. But . . . I can't go through with it, Jim," she said, and there was moisture on her eyelashes that was not from the melting snow.

"Shouldn't you be telling that to Jack?"

"He's still passed out from getting so tight last night."

"Well, it's not like you haven't had opportunities before."

"I wasn't certain myself. I do love Jack. And I had put you out of my mind for the reasons I gave you on the ship. At least, since we've been off the *Venture*. Your constant proximity to me at sea meant I could never remove you completely from my thoughts—you can be quite infuriating, by the way. It was rather the same with that ape creature. I couldn't wait to finally put some physical space between me and both of you."

"I'm glad to know you've placed me in such august company, Dana. Does Zaroff get a posthumous induction into our little club?"

Dana reached across and lay her hand on his. Anthony felt again through her simple touch an exercise of the electrifying leverage this petite girl had over him. He knew he should withdraw his hand, but he was suddenly very weary of doing what he should where Dana was concerned.

Her hand stayed where it was.

"I wasn't relieved to get away from you for the same reason as I was the ape, Jim," she said. "But your presence, to me, on that ship was in its own way just as oppressive as that monster's. And when I finally *was* away, and it was just Jack and I, I was convinced the two of us could work. Until . . ."

"'Until?'"

"Jack and I are to appear on stage with the monster on opening night. Knowing my apprehensions, they wanted me to come down and see the beast since they'd broken and chained him. Regardless, they knew it would still be traumatic for me—but that would only be exacerbated if I were next to him for the first time in front of an audience. I do owe so much to C.D. that I couldn't *not* agree to appear the opening night, no matter my feelings.

"We were almost there. Then my heart started pounding, and I began to hyperventilate. Jack had to have the cab turn around. The odd thing was,I never felt that degree of panic on the voyage home when I was in constant proximity of the creature, even with nowhere to go if it broke loose.

"Do you understand, Jim? I tried to tell myself *Jack* was responsible for my being able to hold it together; after all, he had rescued me. What I didn't want to admit was that I was only able to sleep at night because *you* were aboard. You. Not Jack. I love him. I do. But you and I, we're like lock and key: there's only one fit."

Anthony felt his heart bolt, but he forced himself to rope it back in.

"Back on the ship, I recall you dismissing that notion as all romance and moonbeams. And when those faded in the cold light of day, you knew the reality is that with me you'll be in danger for the rest of your natural life. This appearance on stage tonight—this will be *one* night, one in which your adversary will be chained in chrome steel. Zaroff is dead. With Jack, no one need ever trouble you again. You'll be safe, Dana."

"I'm tired of playing it safe, Jim."

Her moist lips parted slightly; her large blue eyes shone longingly at him.

Jim Anthony took the delicate wrist of the hand that touched his and pulled her to him as though she were light as air. But her body proved deliciously solid and firm against his own. Their mouths pressed together, they finished—again and again—the kissing that had begun at sea.

"Can you forgive me, Jim?" she said softly, her lips to his ear. "When I rejected you on the ship, I wasn't thinking clearly. I was still traumatized from my ordeal. It was all too fresh."

"There's nothing to forgive, Dana. I'm just glad we both came to our senses before it was too late."

He pulled her on to his lap, and she slid back happily against his chest. He locked his arms around her slender waist. "I was foolish to hold you responsible for Zaroff's behavior,"she said. "You couldn't have had an inkling of his true character until *after* you two were out to sea, or you would never have been with him to start with. "

Anthony colored at that and was glad that she was turned away from him. "I don't think you'd be as charitable if I hadn't gotten you away from him" was all he said.

"But you *did*. You see?" She turned around on his lap, cupped his face in her hands, and, smiling sweetly, kissed him again. "I'm here. Safe and sound."

"When do we tell Jack?" Anthony asked.

"I'll tell him privately. I owe him that, poor Jack. And, besides, I don't want another fight to break out between you two. That's not fair to either of you, and it won't change anything anyway."

"I don't know," Anthony said. "I've been in Jack's place before, and it would have felt good to punch his mug. Look, honey, I don't want to look like I'm hiding behind your skirt. I have *some* pride, Dana."

"Swallow it," she said as she slipped off his lap and went for her coat and things.

"Are you going to tell him right now?" Anthony asked. "If so, I'm going with you --:"

"To the beauty parlor? I have an appointment to make sure I look my best for tonight—and for you, when you see me again. You *are* coming to opening night, aren't you? You have to, you know. I can only go through with it if I know you're there."

Anthony now stood behind her, helping her put on her coat. She turned around to him, still smiling.

"Of course I'll be there for you, Dana, But if you talk to Jack without me, I'm going to be angry with you," he said, cautioning her.

"Well, then, we'll be even. I still haven't forgiven you for slipping off the ship without so much as a good-bye. I'll see you tonight, darling," she said. She stood on her tiptoes to kiss him. With one broad arm he pulled her into him, the other hand going to her hair.

"Don't muss me," she said laughing as she disengaged herself. "A girl doesn't want to show up at the beauty parlor looking like she needs it."

"You know, I *still* don't know your name. Is the one in the papers . . .?"

"It doesn't matter—after tonight, I'm changing it to 'Dana Sparrow.' That was who I was when I was happiest. It's who I want to be again."

"For the interim only," Anthony said.

"The interim between what?" she asked, trying to look innocent and not break into a smile. She was losing that battle, and so, with a kiss on her gloved fingertips, which she then touched to his lips, she slipped out the door.

And out of his life forever.

* * *

Anthony's grandfather looked in awe upon the manacled island god.

Behind the stage's heavy curtain veiling the "Giant Terror Gorilla," C.D., a.k.a. D.W. Cecil De Cent, stood proudly in his tux and tails beside the wizened Indian shaman, his grandson, and Jim's best friend, Tom.

Mephito knelt, removing a handful of bones from a leathery patch attached to his belt. He tossed them to the floor, and they scattered out between him and the beast god. Tom and C.D.'s jaws both dropped when they saw the bones that had landed at random realign themselves into a specific pattern.

"Holy Mackerel!" C.D. said. "How'd you do that? Were you the magician in a Wild West show or something?"

Mephito looked up from his kneeling position, and, his face solemn, pointed an accusatory finger at the movie director.

"What you see is no trick. There are hidden powers you have disturbed by bringing that island's god here."

"Oh,boshwah! Save the hooey," C.D said and waved him off.

Mephito rose, his gaze never wavering. "You know that there are such powers which hold sway in ancient places, do you not, sir? You have traveled into what dark spots remain on this globe. Do not tell me you have not seen things outside all rational experience. I *know* you have."

C.D. tugged at his suddenly constricting collar. "Uh, well, an . . . exorcism by a missionary in the Yucatan of a man the villagers said had sold his soul to the devil. Something moved past me on the way out of him—a sound of heaving breathing, like horses that had been run long and hard. I swear, I felt it . . ."

Mephito stepped closer to the director. "The forces here dwarf what passed by you then. Why do you think we have this snowstorm, eh? You moved him and the seasons were pulled out of joint. You must stop this; return him or there will be dire consequences on this island of Manhattan."

"What?" C.D. asked, starting to recover. "Winter's going to go on forever or something? Give me a break! Besides, the kind of things we're talking about—it doesn't happen in the civilized world. We drove all that stuff out —"

"—with the Indians?" Mephito asked. "There are those who dwelled in America *before* the Indians. Their strange monoliths and ruins stand in New England to this day . .

"Yeah," C.D. said, "I get you. Matter of fact, I've filmed the ones in Dunwich."

". . . and before *them* were older things yet, which shall remain bound unto their appointed time. But the ruin you will bring down upon this island will come from your attracting dark forces of disorder from elsewhere—where they were content to dwell in desolate places, in the tombs among a dying people."

"Hey, Jimmy—Jimmy! Are you getting all this?" Tom asked, trying vainly to get his attention. Anthony had been distracted since they arrived, looking for Dana. And now she stood in the stage's wings, a stole around her bare, white shoulders, a gown of pale blue elegant simplicity clinging to her slim but curving body. Her hair was up, and the overall impression was regal—an ice princess stepped in from the snow.

Anthony's reverie sundered when Jack walked in and joined her. He did not look upset, so Anthony took it that Dana had not told him yet. Perhaps there had been no appropriate opportunity because of Jack's hangover or her beauty parlor appointment going over. Which was swell with Anthony. He would be there with her now to face Jack like a man. Though he didn't like the thought of hitting his rival between the eyes in public with how things had changed, it was more cruel to let him go on believing Dana was his. Anthony began walking toward them . . .

Dana saw him approaching and shook her head "no." Anthony stopped in his tracks. Clearly, she was telling him now wasn't the time. Maybe there was something else . . . something that would make him the biggest heel alive to break the man's heart publicly. And what if Jack stormed out? It would be selfish to throw a, well, monkey wrench into this evening that so much was riding on for so many people.

So he turned his back toward Jack and Dana before Jack could recognize him, and exited backstage via the opposite wing. But after the show, he wasn't waiting any longer.

Anthony found his seat between Tom and his grandfather. In a few minutes C.D. walked out to give his opening spiel, followed by the curtain rising on the Giant Terror Gorilla, which was accompanied by a chorus of gasps and "ahs." Then Jack and Dana were brought on stage—though she was not presented as Dana Sparrow but by a name that he still didn't know was assumed or real. He rankled when C.D told the press that the two "are getting married tomorrow," setting off a series of pops and flashes of light, followed by the cracking and crunching of bulbs dropped underfoot . . .

And then the screech and groan of the first of the island god's chains pulling free, and the loosing of all hell with him!

Anthony was on his feet at the breaking free of the first manacle. "Tom! Get my grandfather out of here! I'm trusting you to get him safely through this riot without being trampled!"

"Will do, buddy! C'mon, gramps!"

As though calmly regarding a tornado in whose path he stood, the old man was looking stoically into the storm that was the beast god raging on the stage. "I warned him," Mephito said as Tom took his arm and pulled him into the chaotic rapids that was the rush of human bodies for the doors.

Anthony, meanwhile, was fighting upstream against that surge of people who kept sweeping him back, back from the stage and Dana. By the time he had made his way to the front, Dana, Jack, and C.D. had fled the theater via a backstage exit, and the beast god had completely shed

"What you see is no trick. There are hidden powers you have disturbed by bringing that island's god here."

his chains and followed in pursuit, bursting through a large wooden door, which, when raised, had allowed for trucks to dock and unload directly behind stage. Anthony climbed the stage and sprinted in the monster's wake after Dana.

The creature had now emerged onto the snowy streets, sending automobiles careening into one another. The chaos greeting his arrival barraged his senses: unfamiliar electric lights streaked blindingly over his eyes, and a cacophony of car horns blowing and people screaming assailed his ears.

Fortunately, this new world's overwhelming revelation of itself to the beast god made it impossible for him to draw a bead on Dana, whom Anthony caught sight of, with Jack, just slipping through the revolving doors of the hotel across the street.

Anthony ran after them. But the monster now was between him and the hotel, long arms reaching out and grabbing a Model T Ford, one massive paw on each end of the car. He sent it skidding and careening sideways over the street and onto the sidewalk, plowing down people in its path.

Then the cyclopean horror began mounting the hotel, using the window niches and ledges for finger and toeholds —

-- A rifle cracked!—its ricocheting bullet just missing the climbing ape as its black mass slid up the hotel wall.

Who was risking a bullet going through a window and hitting a civilian? Not a law officer! Anthony looked back in the direction from which the bullet came, his eyes meeting a sight more difficult for him to accept than that of the giant rampaging over the streets of New York:

"*Zaroff!*"

At his shout, the Russian, who had again been training his rifle's sights on the climbing giant ape, turned toward Anthony and smiled at his stunned friend turned adversary.

To answer Anthony's silent question, Zaroff pointed to his waist —

-- at the reptilian-skin belt with the mottling in the shape of a *death's head.*

In the next instant, Anthony was drawing his pistol from the holster under his arm, and the Russian turned and fled into the crowded, chaotic night.

Recovering from his shock, Anthony knew that it wasn't mere chance that put Zaroff near-by the theater with a loaded rifle when the monster broke out onto the street. Somehow, he was responsible—and would be liable for the lives the beast god would take this night.

Anthony looked up at the climbing monstrosity. Jack would keep Dana safe. To deal with the escaped beast god would require the New York National Guard. He couldn't make a difference in that regard. But Zaroff was another monster loose in the streets of whom no one else was aware, with equal disregard for human life.

Anthony checked his gun's chamber to confirm it was fully loaded— and *not* with mercy bullets:

Far past time to use Allardravitch methods.

* * *

Zaroff had tipped his hand too soon; now he wasn't free to shadow the giant monster as he would have, because as he hunted it, Anthony stalked *him*, and the beast god's location would make an all too obvious beacon as to Zaroff's whereabouts. But at the same time, Zaroff would not just abandon the unique opportunity of this hunt, not after coming back from the dead for a second chance.

Throughout the night, Anthony searched, but things were much too complicated amidst the carnage and destruction. The icy streets were strewn with corpses: frozen husks of fathers, mothers, children, sweethearts: lives casually discarded by the beast god in his wrath. Cars wrecked and abandoned in the roads made an obstacle course whose navigating took precious time from Anthony. He would have leapt from the top of one automobile to the other, but Zaroff could be lurking behind any of them, ready to shoot.

New York City had turned over night into a war zone, stitched raggedly by stretches of barbed wire, blighted like the venerable cities of Europe were in the Great War. America had been spared the like then—but tonight, her portion had come. The declaration of martial law meant avoiding the soldiers. This also hindered his progress. Fortunately, the local flatfoots always looked the other way whenever their paths crossed that night.

He occasionally crossed refugee shelters that had been improvised in stores and businesses, where he could get food and water to restore his stamina. While there, he tried to pick up on the news of how the battle was faring. He missed the advantage of his mobile wireless to monitor police transmissions. Then he would have been spared spurious word-of-mouth gossip of the beast god's movements, such as the story that the giant ape had been spotted ice skating on his rump in Central Park.

He didn't have time to sort through such absurd fabrications and was relieved when the honking of a car horn alerted him to his sedan, which he hadn't ridden in since fleeing *Old Knickerbocker's,* coming down the street toward him. It had still been in the shop being repaired when Anthony returned home. When Tom brought the car to a halt, Anthony threw open the back door and was delighted to find the longed-for wireless had been returned to its place.

Tom passed him a wax paper wrapped sandwich, but before Anthony could begin devouring it, the wireless was picking up a police transmission. And his heart immediately began pounding his temples when he heard the name he had never known was a fabrication or not; not even when C.D. had used it to introduce to the theater's audience Jack's fiancee . . .

"Tom!" he shouted, stepping onto the running board. "You get us as close to the Empire State Building as you can *right now!*"

Immediately they sped toward the world's tallest building. The local police recognized the heroic, copper statue that was Jim Anthony, erect and alert on the running board and waved him on. Already, in the distance, he saw the dot that was the beast god ascending the skyscraper. An anguished Anthony couldn't make out the beast's burden, the most precious person on the planet to him.

Nearing their destination, he saw the National Guard setting up a roadblock. Anthony knocked on the window for Tom to slow down, then leapt from the running board, hitting the ground on the run. When the first guardsman moved to intercept him, he tossed the man aside and kept moving. Other soldiers converged on him, but by now he had reached the base of the Empire State Building.

The men who attacked him couldn't stop him, but they were succeeding in slowing him down, robbing him of precious minutes. Then C.D., who was just outside the entranceway to the Empire State Building, recognized him.

"Hey!" he shouted out. "Anthony! Let 'im through you buncha palookas!"

Anthony shot out from the soldier's grasp the moment they loosened their hold on him. He bolted past the movie director and through the revolving doors.

"Go, Anthony!" C.D. shouted after him. "Jack is on his way! Our girl could sure use both of her suitors about now—and how!"

Anthony erupted from the revolving doors and across the lobby.

Elevators would be too slow, so he quickly found the stairwell and began bounding up it, taking three stairs at a stride. He reminded himself that if he fell and broke his leg, he would be of no help to Dana. Still, he couldn't see subjecting himself to the comparative snail's pace of the elevators, not when a second could make the difference in her falling to her death.

At the fiftieth floor, the stairwell entrance door flew open, and Anthony found a rifle barrel imposing upon him.

"Zaroff!" he said, compelled to come to a halt. "Whatever grudge you have against me, be enough of a human being to allow me to help Dana first, and then you and I will --."

Zaroff's features were cold, his smile mirthless as he interjected: "I was under the impression that my lack of humanity was something you had come to accept about me, Anthony. Wasn't that why you abandoned me to the island? Now, slowly take off your holster with the gun still in it and drop it down the stairwell. Do it!" he barked, poking the rifle's end at Anthony, ready to shoot him directly in the heart if need be. "My recent mangling at the hands of that ape has left my aim at times unsure, but I won't miss this close."

Breathing deeply, trying to recover from his jaunt, a perspiring Anthony did as ordered.

"Move, now. Inside! And walk straight to the elevator. Hands held behind your head."

He herded Anthony out on to the floor. The elevator was open and waiting, its wire gating folded aside. Once inside, Zaroff, whose cocked rifle had never wavered, made Anthony slide the gate closed, then hit the button for the 102nd floor.

"So, how did you pull all of this off, Zaroff?" Anthony asked as they ascended. "Starting with, how did you survive, busted up and with only a long knife against that dinosaur's talons and teeth?

Zaroff smiled behind his rifle. "I had only the one chance, a split second. It was enough. I thrust the blade up to the hilt through the dinosaur's eye and into its brain. The scream you heard was not faked; it mauled me in its death throes. But I lived."

"You were still in no shape to get back to the yacht on your own."

"You'll recall I had two perimeter men in the jungle with me that day. You killed the one. After you, Dana, and that mate fled, I fired in the air to signal his comrade. When he arrived, I sent him back to the yacht and ordered him to wait. I told him I intended to hunt you, but if he saw you making your way back to the yacht without me, he was to assume you had defeated me and fire upon you on sight. Then he and the others were to search for me in the event that I had survived."

"I saw small, scavenger dinosaurs picking at what I thought was your corpse," Anthony said. "I take it they were eating the remains of the death's head dinosaur?"

"True. I left them quite a repast—except I skinned the mottling off its head to make my trophy. Then I crawled into the bushes and awaited my men."

"Why come back to New York to enact this crazy scheme and risk alerting your enemies that you had survived?"

Zaroff smiled again. "I had been defeated by that ape and you; only here could I redress both humiliations. And to have opportunity to hunt that magnificent brute again was worth risking all!"

"Even out of its natural habitat—'in the canyons of Gotham' as you put it once. What happened to your sportsman sensibilities?"

"My previous encounter with the beast revealed I was at too much of a disadvantage in its natural habitat; on Manhattan island, the odds were more in my favor."

"How did you manage to release him?"

Zaroff shrugged. "It sometimes happens that, in the cooling of cast metal, some pieces are not allowed the necessary time. Weak places form. Or maybe iron was substituted for certain of those chrome steel links, the difference imperceptible to the layman's eye."

"Who did your dirty work, Zaroff?"

"In these times, when every laborer is just a breath away from him and his family being abandoned to starvation, the offer of 50,000 American dollars does not lack for takers."

Anthony felt his face burn with anger, but he tethered his rage.

"And you had to have gotten here before the blockade was set up. How did you know the ape was headed for the Empire State Building?"

"You showed me how, friend Anthony: a radiotelegraph in my limousine, intercepting police transmissions in real time, while allowing me the needed mobility. I thank you."

The sting of his taunt was a poignant one for Anthony: here, again, his doings had meant unnecessary complications for Dana's crisis, further endangering her life.

"Don't thank me—if I could do it over, I would have handed you over to Allardravitch that night."

"Ah, but life allows us no opportunity to correct past failings, eh?"

Anthony smiled at him grimly. "I don't know. You've got a second round with the island's god."

The elevator door opened and Zaroff nodded him out into the unseasonably wintry air of dawn. Two shadows swept over the observation deck, accompanying a rattle of lead about them. Both men threw themselves back against the wall. Above them, the island's god roared his defiance, and a woman screamed.

"Dana!" Anthony shouted and ran back out onto the platform to look up and survey the dome which crowned the skyscraper. Dana lay prostrate on the base of that dome. She was sobbing, no doubt hysterical, but miraculously unwounded from the strafing.

He wanted to call out to her again, but he was afraid she might startle and fall. There was a metal ladder bolted to the side of the building that reached the dome. He it, grabbed on -- and immediately a bullet rang off the rung just above his hands. He fell back and whirled around to see Zaroff training his rifle on him.

"No, Anthony," he said. "I did not bring you here to facilitate your rescue of the lady fair from the ogre. Such foolishness! This is nothing like a fairy tale: simply the law of nature, 'red in tooth and claw!' Now, as I said, my aim is not as sure as it once was. Don't make me risk another shot in your direction. I prefer not to kill you just yet."

"Zaroff—let me get her before those planes swoop back in. It's a miracle she hasn't been shot yet. There's no time —"

"Yes, time *is* limited—before the planes return. I have only moments to claim the honor of felling the beast myself! But this triumph is nothing without the witness of someone who is my peer to appreciate my achievement. Then I will kill you, too, of course, and both my humiliations will be avenged!"

A woman's wild, desperate scream m sounded over their heads. Anthony looked up to see Dana in violent paroxysms of fear, struggling to escape the paw that now grasped her; traumatized, she was unable to care that to succeed would mean falling to her death.

"You madman! If you hit Dana —" Anthony began, seeing Zaroff leaning back to take aim—

-- and Anthony leapt across the observation deck, both hands coming down onto the rifle as it fired. Anthony now raised the weapon high above the Russian's head, but Zaroff would not relinquish his own vise-like hold on the gun, gripping it for his life.

The shadows of the biplanes in their death-dealing spiral were again winding dizzily over the observation deck and the struggling men. Mounted machine guns spat bullets over the dome at the giant beast god, who roared in unyielding, yet doomed defiance; in a swoon at his feet lay the captive, slender beauty for whom he ached with a longing equally doomed.

On the periphery of the unfolding legend, Anthony and Zaroff struggled, Anthony bending Zaroff back over the observation deck's wall. Zaroff barked a stream of insults in Russian into Anthony's face when he wasn't biting at it, but the Irish-Indian's superior strength was winning.

Then Zaroff jabbed his knee into Anthony's groin, and the jolt of numbing pain made him relent involuntarily. Zaroff was able to push him off, Anthony dropping back, but already poised again to charge —

—as Zaroff aimed his rifle upward —

-- two shots sounded, Zaroff himself wheeling with the impact of one of them and falling to the deck. Anthony whirled around —

As though one of the biplane's shadows had taken on a third dimension unto itself and arisen on the observation deck, Allardravitch stood there dressed in black, his cloak flapping about him in the wind, his pistol still held out, aimed at where Zaroff had stood just a moment before . . .

-- and then the sudden dark-as-pitch torrent rushing down past them, a blackness so large that it plunged the men on the platform into darkness as it momentarily passed between them and the sun on its journey far, far below.

"The airplanes got him," Allardravitch said coldly.

"It . . . wasn't the airplanes . . ." Zaroff croaked, smiled, and gasped, his eyes clinched tightly in pain. Then a violent tremor shook his body, and he was dead—truly dead—beneath the single hole in the side of the dome where his bullet, fired at the beast god, had struck, thrown off his aim when Allardravitch's bullet had found its own target.

Anthony bounded for the metal ladder to climb to the base of the dome where the island's god, in his last act, had carefully placed a fainted Dana before he surrendered and fell. As Anthony reached the rungs, Jack popped up through a hatch in the floor, still open from when Allardravitch had used it. Dana's two lovers had reached the ladder at the same time, both men suddenly arrested at the other's presence.

Anthony heard again Zaroff's mocking words, like his ghost whispered them at his shoulder: "*Ah, but life allows us no opportunity to change past failings, eh?*"

This, however, was his. He and Dana had barely been reunited when his past choices once again yielded consequences which were potentially fatal ones for her. With Zaroff and the beast god dead, there was no need that Dana should ever be endangered again—unless it would be by further association with him.

"None of this," Anthony said to Jack, indicating with a jerk of his head Allardravitch and Zaroff's corpse, "ever happened. *We* were never here. Understand? Especially not me. If she asks, you haven't seen me." He nodded up toward the top of the dome. "Go to her. Always take care of her. You . . . you're a good man, Jack."

Anthony extended his hand and Jack took it. "Same to you, brother," he said, and then scurried up the ladder. Anthony ducked down the open hatch, eager to be away before Dana awakened. He paused, however, to poke his head back up and address Allardravitch:

"I assume you will see to it that there is no body to explain?"

Allardravitch nodded affirmatively.

And Anthony was gone.

In the days following the Empire State Building incident, those events that took place in the margins of the legend remained unaccounted and thus never became part of the tale. Even the lives that had been lost fell into forgetfulness as those families touched by the tragedy also passed, leaving few to remember their losses. And, besides, the broken hearted find it easier not to speak of their losses, for to speak of them is to own what is often too heavy for a human heart to bear.

Jim Anthony has known for a long time the woman he irrevocably lost in the course of those events did not marry Jack; that after failed attempt after failed attempt to reestablish contact with the always traveling world adventurer, her love for Anthony had died of disappointment; that she had returned to care for the orphans on the farm where she had been raised. That he knows all this is to be expected; he is, after all, a super detective. And, of course, he has long since learned her true name.

That is not the one he speaks on those occasions when he finds it preferable to court the pain, for the hurt of loss is the only evidence that once, though ever so briefly, it was still true: he had possessed all that he could ever want of this world.

"Dana," he says.

The End

ABOUT OUR CREATORS

THE WRITERS

JOSHUA M. REYNOLDS is a freelance writer of moderate skill and exceptional confidence. He has written quite a bit, and some of it was even published. For money. By real people.

Other times, not so much.

Feel free to stop by his blog, Hunting Monsters [http://joshuamreynolds.blogspot.com/] and cast aspersions on his character.

+++

MICAH HARRIS, at about ten years of age, found himself alongside Carl Denham's crew, desperately trying to catch sight of King Kong and his captive, Ann Darrow. In young Micah's case, however, he wasn't peering through the fog of Skull Island's swamp land but the inclement static mist and morass that was television reception in the rotary antenna era of the early '70s.

As you may have guessed, Harris has since caught up with Kong, many times, and under much better conditions of observation. But it was this initial encounter that was the indelible beginning of Harris's love of 1930's style pulp / fantasy adventure.

While working a day job as a college instructor of literature and film, he finally made his breakthrough as a professional writer at the tender age of 42 with the publication of the Image Comics graphic novel *Heaven's War*. Illustrated by Marvel and DC artist Michael Gaydos, this historical fantasy pits real-life fantasists Charles Williams, C.S. Lewis, and J.R.R. Tolkien against occultist Aleister Crowley.

Harris's new Image comic book, due out in comic shops in the spring of 2010, is *Lorna, Relic Wrangler*, featuring a sort-of southern trailer park Lara Croft. Pulp adventure lovers are advised that Lorna's cast includes the

Mexican Doc Savage, brain-munching alien vampire beauties, and that Lovecraftian inter-dimensional entity "Jack Lord of Disorder." Expect lots of good-girl art from Loston Wallace, who has contributed to the *Flash Gordon* newspaper strip and rendered Bud Root's voluptuous *Cavewoman* for the popular one-shot *Klyde & Meriem*.

Those interested in the mysteries of Dana Sparrow's parentage and how her encounter with a certain island god was predestined before her conception need look no further than Harris's prose novel *The Eldritch New Adventures of Becky Sharp,* which Ron Fortier called "easily one of the best books" he read in 2008. It's available through Amazon.com or Harris's own web site, *www.booksofmicah.com*.

THE ARTISTS

INTERIOR ILLUSTRATIONS

PEDRO CRUZ is a Portuguese artist, architect and teacher with a background on animation at the Magic Toons studio. He won the first prize of the Amadora Cartoon contest in the year 2000. His comics, cartoons and illustrations have appeared in numerous publications including N*imbus, XL Magazine, DN Jovem* (the youth section of *Diario De Noticias*, one of Portugal's foremost daily newspapers), *Starscape* magazine, *Ronin Illustrated* and the *Kirby Martin Inquest*. He has also done the interior illustrations for Airship 27's *Jim Anthony Super-Detective Volume On*e.

You can see more of his art on his own blog at (*www.pedro-cruz.blogspot.com*)

+++

COVER PAINTING

CHRIS SEARS studied abroad in Japan, then later worked as an optical engineer on a missile defense program out in the Mohave desert. In his "spare time" he pursued his drawing and painting under the guidance of several movie poster illustrators and artists, including Mark Westmore, Mike Butkus and John Watkiss. Chris currently works as a freelance illustrator and concept artist in Los Angeles. You can contact Chris at his blog site (*http://ccsears.blogspot.com/*).

AFTERWORD

All of us have had brushes with coincidence. You will be talking about somebody and lo and behold they walk around the corner at the exact same time. Or you'll be thinking of what you would really like to have for dinner tonight and just like that your wife calls out from the kitchen that you are having that very dish. Spooky little touches of ESP that happen to all of us every now and then. But when those coincidences are just so filled with good natured whimsy and fun, as if the entire universe was lining up in a straight line just for you, well we give that an entirely different name. We call it serendipity.

Serendipity is how this particular book came about. We were in the process of putting the first volume of this series into final production. All of us were excited about getting Jim Anthony back in action and that enthusiasm seemed to affect many of our regular writers here at Airship 27 Productions; one of those being Josh Reynolds. Before volume one was even published, Josh approached me with an idea for a novella length adventure wherein the Super Detective would team up with the cinematic bad guy, Russian Count Zaroff.

In 1924, writer Richard Connell published a short story *The Hounds of Zaroff*. In the tale, a big game American hunter named Sanger Rainsford is stranded on an island while on the way to hunt jaguars in the Amazon. He learns the island is inhabited by a wealthy Cossack hunter, a General Zaroff. Zaroff is a twisted villain who, bored with hunting animals, has taken to hunting human beings such as shipwrecked sailors. He is excited at the idea of hunting another experienced hunter. Rainsford at first refuses to go along with this insane game, but Zaroff and his retinue threaten to murder him outright if he does not play along. Having no other choice, Rainsford accepts the challenge. He's given a knife, some food and a three hour head start. In the end, Rainsford proves to be the better hunter and manages to outwit Zaroff and triumph over him.

The tale became an instant classic and would later be adapted to film several times. The best and most remembered is the first shot in 1932 as *The Most Dangerous Game*. It starred Joel McCrea as Rainsford and Leslie Banks as Count Zaroff. This RKO production itself was unique as it was filmed at night on the same jungle sets used during the day for the Skull Island sequences of *King Kong*.

At the end of the Connell's story, and the film, Zaroff is killed off but Josh thought we could fudge this a little, as the actual death scene is never shown in either venue and the idea of playing with this classic villain was too great a temptation to pass up. Having always been a fan of the movie, I was only too happy to let Josh run with his idea and off he went to write *Death In Yellow*.

Jump ahead a few months in time. I had just reviewed a marvelous fantasy adventure called *The Eldritch New Adventures of Becky Sharp* by Micah Harris. Appreciative of my review, Micah started writing me in regards to our work here at Airship 27 Productions and hinted at possibly writing something for us. I sent along a list of those public domain characters we use which included Jim Anthony. By this time that first volume had come out and the book was selling briskly. So it was no great surprise when Micah came back to me saying he might consider doing a Jim Anthony story for us. What did shock me was the proposal he offered up. This is where that serendipity thing comes in. Micah's idea was to have Jim meet Count Zaroff and the two of them would end up on certain mysterious island in the South Pacific where eventually they would encounter a giant ape. Now all of this Micah was offered up innocently without the slightest knowledge of the story by Josh that I had sitting in our files. I was so blown away by this amazing, incredible, stupendous coincidence that immediately the idea of bringing the two of them together seemed the only natural thing to do.

I went on to tell Micah all about Josh's story and he asked to read it. I went to Josh, explained what had happened and Micah's his request to read *Death In Yellow*. What Micah now wanted to do was write his story as a continuation of the team-up between Jim and Zaroff. Then we would put them together as a novel in two parts. Josh liked the idea and gave us his blessing, allowing Micah to read his story. Once he had done that, Micah then went to work on his tale and ultimately submitted *The Periphery of Legend*.

Of course the fact that both *The Most Dangerous Game* and *King Kong* were both produced on the same lot by the same production team, director, etc.etc., never escaped me. For the very first time, thanks to these two talented writers, Zaroff was about to finally cross-over with the big gorilla. Somehow it all seemed most fitting and special.

To that end we recruited Pedro Cruz to do our interiors as he had done with volume one. All of us here at Airship 27 Productions think he's one of the finest illustrators working today. Then another of our writers pointed me to a fellow named Chris Sears who had done a gorgeous Doc Savage painting on display at his website. Upon seeing it, I immediately contacted Chris and all but begged him to do our cover for this book. As you've seen by now, he agreed and delivered this knock-down fantastically beautiful pulp cover. One of the best we've ever showcased.

There you have it, the story behind this truly unique book and the men who made it happen. We hope it will entertain you and if this is your first Airship 27 title, make you want to check out our other pulp adventure titles found at our on-line store - (*airship27hangar.com*) at a nice discount price. Or you can go to Amazon, Barnes &Noble and other reputable book distributors. In the months ahead we've got more great pulp heroes coming you way from the Black Bat to Secret Agent X to name only a few. Thanks your continued support of Airship 27 Productions; Pulp Fiction for a new generation!

Ron Fortier
8 Feb. 2010
Somersworth
(*www.Airship27.com*)
(*Airship27@comcast.net*)

JIM ANTHONY
SUPER-DETECTIVE

He's half Comanche, half Irish and ALL AMERICAN!! Jim Anthony the Super Detective returns in his fourth volume of brand new adventures from Airship 27 Productions.

Traveling the globe, Anthony battles all manner of twisted villainy in four new tales and his challenges are herculean. Writers Erwin K. Roberts, Joel Jenkins, Frank Byrns and Mark Justice have whipped up a quartet of high adventure stories that are the hallmark of the Super Detective. From Mexico, where he encounters a Nazi spy ring to the streets of Manhattan where he hunts down a brutal serial killer, Jim Anthony proves once again why he is one of the most exciting and fun heroes ever created in the golden age of American pulps.

This volume, the fourth in an on-going series, features interior illustrations by Michael Neno and a dazzling cover by Eric Meador, with book designs by Rob Davis. Airship 27 Productions is thrilled to continue the exploits of the one and only, Jim Anthony – Super Detective.

PULP FICTION FOR A NEW GENERATION!

BIRTH OF A LEGEND

In 1190, two years after wresting the crown from his father, Henry II, Richard the Lionhearted departed France for the Holy Lands and the Third Crusade. He left behind regents, Hugh, Bishop of Durham and his chancellor, William de Longchamp. But his younger brother, Prince John, lusted after the crown and saw Richard's absence as a golden opportunity to seize control. John began a program of heavy taxation that threatened to destroy the social-economic stability of England.

While the royals conspired against each other, it was the people of the land who suffered. Working under inhumane laws, they became no more than indentured slaves to the landed gentry. Amidst this age of turmoil and pain, there arose a man with the courage to challenge the aristocracy and fight for the weak and helpless. He was an outlaw named Robin of Loxley and how he became the champion of the people is a timeworn legend that has entertained readers young and old.

Now J.A. Watson brings his own vivid imagination to the saga, setting it against the backdrop of history but maintaining the iconic elements that have endeared the tale of Robin Hood to readers throughout the ages. With beautiful covers by fan-favorite artist Mike Manley and interior illustrations by Rob Davis, this is a fresh and rousing retelling of an old legend, imbuing it with a modern sensibility readers will applaud.

Airship 27 Productions is extremely proud to present –

Robin Hood

KING OF SHERWOOD · ARROW OF JUSTICE · FREEDOM'S OUTLAW · FORBIDDEN LEGEND

PULP FICTION FOR A NEW GENERATION

AVAILABILITY INFORMATION AT: WWW.AIRSHIP27HANGAR.COM